ALSO BY JOSEPHINE CAMERON

Maybe a Mermaid

A Dog-Friendly Town

Not All Heroes

THE DEPARTMENT OF LOST DOGS

JOSEPHINE CAMERON

FARRAR STRAUS GIROUX
NEW YORK

Farrar Straus Giroux Books for Young Readers
An imprint of Macmillan Publishing Group, LLC
120 Broadway, New York, NY 10271 • mackids.com

Our books may be purchased in bulk for promotional, educational,
or business use. Please contact your local bookseller or the Macmillan
Corporate and Premium Sales Department at (800) 221-7945 ext. 5442
or by email at MacmillanSpecialMarkets@macmillan.com.

Library of Congress Cataloging-in-Publication Data
Names: Cameron, Josephine, author.
Title: The department of lost dogs / Josephine Cameron.
Description: First edition. | New York : Farrar Straus Giroux
Books for Young Readers, [2023] | Audience: Ages 8–12. |
Audience: Grades 7–9. | Summary: When Carmelito's beloved
celebrity dog, Pico Boone, goes missing, eleven-year-old Rondo
must make friends with the new kid in town and keep his
siblings together in order to crack the case.
Identifiers: LCCN 2022035560 | ISBN 9780374389758 (hardcover)
Subjects: CYAC: Dogs—Fiction. | Lost and found possessions—
Fiction. | Siblings—Fiction. | Bed and breakfast accommodations—
Fiction. | Mystery and detective stories. | LCGFT: Detective
and mystery fiction. | Novels.
Classification: LCC PZ7.1.C327 De 2023 | DDC [Fic]—dc23
LC record available at https://lccn.loc.gov/2022035560

First edition, 2023
Book design by Aurora Parlagreco
Printed in the United States of America by Lakeside Book Company,
Harrisonburg, Virginia

1   3   5   7   9   10   8   6   4   2

For MJ, RJ, and KJ

(plus Andy and Simon, obviously) —J.C.

THE PROPRIETORS

Elly and Marc McDade (Mom and Dad)

Rondo McDade, age 11; Epic McDade, age 14;
Elvis McDade, age 9¾

THE GUESTS

Clive, Nicole, and Pico Boone

ROOM 1

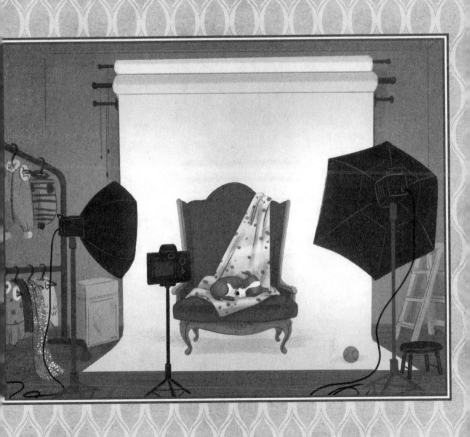

Social media staging

ROOM 2

Raúl Flores and Cheddar and Doughboy

ROOM 3

Hair and makeup

ROOM 4

Heaven Hsu and Roo

ROOM 5

Denver Delgado-Doyle and Bella

MOONDOGGIE INN

THE DEPARTMENT OF LOST D🐾GS

TUESDAY

9:22 P.M.

THE CRIME

The way Mrs. Boone was screaming—one panicky squawk after another, with heaving gasps of breath in between—you'd think aliens had invaded the Perro del Mar Bed and Breakfast and were pulling out her thick, glittery eyelashes, one by one. It was an overreaction to the lights going out, for sure, but Mrs. Boone has a way of convincing people to go along for the ride. Mr. Boone and my younger sister, Elvis, were right there with her, shrieking loud enough for the whole neighborhood to hear.

"Rondo, if you did this." Epic's big-brother voice was right in my ear. "Tell me now. I don't want to have another . . ."

I tuned him out, clipped a mini flashlight to my notebook, and scanned the shadows in the dark lobby. *I* had nothing to do with the power going out. Not that Epic—or anyone else in this house—believed me. Whenever something goes wrong at the Perro del Mar, our family's dog-friendly bed and breakfast, they all look at me first. Mom. Dad. The guests. Even their dogs. For real. There was a mini schnauzer in Room 5 who'd been giving me the evil eye all week. Whatever. It didn't matter what they thought. If they paid attention, they'd know the truth.

I focused on documenting the points of entry.

Front entrance—blocked: film equipment.

Back door—wide open.

"What are you writing? Are you even listening to me?" My brother was irritated. Which, unfortunately, had been kind of his thing lately. Mom and Dad called it the Eighth Grade Grumps. I called it a waste of energy.

"If you want to help," I said. "We need an inventory."

"Of what?"

"*People.*" It seemed obvious, but Epic stared at me like Mrs. Boone's eyelash-plucking aliens had slurped up my brains. "Never mind, I'll do it myself."

Mom had gone to check the circuit breaker. Dad was gathering every flashlight in the house. Most of the film crew was outside, where they'd been getting ready for the big rooftop scene in which an Italian greyhound (or Iggy, as the Boones liked to say) would jump out the second-floor window, walk along the roof's edge, leap to a lower ledge, and then attack an actor like the dog's best friend's life depended on it.

It was an impressive stunt, and it ought to be, because the dog trainer had rehearsed it approximately one bajillion times over the past two days. That guy was intense. He didn't allow anyone "nonessential" on the second floor during rehearsals, prep, or filming. Especially not kids. Even more especially: not Mr. and Mrs. Boone. It didn't matter that their Iggy, Pico, was the whole reason *Bentley Knows* was filming on location at the Perro del Mar. The dog trainer didn't care.

"The most important thing for canine actors is *focus*," he'd said. "How can they focus with excitables around?"

That's why, while Mrs. Boone and the rest of the "excitables" were downstairs in the lobby screaming, only the dog trainer, the actors, and a few handpicked, *un*excitable members of the crew were upstairs with the canine performers.

I'd barely completed the inventory when the lights flickered and turned back on. When the Boones and Elvis stopped screaming, the house got *extra* quiet. Which, weirdly, felt more stressful than the noise.

Mrs. Boone's eyelashes fluttered.

Mr. Boone sighed.

Elvis stood on her tiptoes to peek at my notebook, and I clicked off my flashlight. Epic flinched at the sound.

Then—predictably—a voice from outside shouted into a bullhorn. I'd already guessed what he was going to say.

"Attention! Attention! All hands! We're missing our canine actors!"

"I tried to tell you," I said.

But nobody listened because Mrs. Boone shrieked, "*Dognapped!*"

Members of the lighting crew raced upstairs.

People with clipboards raced down.

"Pico's been *dog*napped!" My sister's voice broke with a

suspiciously dramatic squeak. Sure, El had tears coming out of her eyes, but she was also bouncing on her toes with excitement, her blond curls looking even wilder than usual.

Epic, on the other hand, had gone ghost-white. He'd give up Robotics Club for Pico Boone, that's how much he likes that dog.

"Call the police!" he said.

Mr. Boone shook his head in a panic. "We know who can find him faster."

Exactly. Me. Why ask the police to start from scratch when I had on-the-ground, real-time information? I'd been watching everyone at the Perro for days. I knew who the suspects were, *and* I had experience exposing criminals. I glanced at my notebook. It was no coincidence that the most likely culprits were missing from my inventory. All I had to do was find them.

But Mr. Boone wasn't talking about me. Instead, he held a cell phone in his gigantic hand, his dark lips practically swallowing the speaker end of the device.

"Call the Department of Lost Dogs!" he barked.

It was a low blow. Here I was, ready to launch a full investigation, but the Boones trusted telepathic dog psychics more than they trusted me.

At least, they did until the cheerful operator on Mr. Boone's speakerphone explained that 9:00 P.M. was "after hours" and the Department of Lost Dogs only had one animal communicator on duty.

"Leif is on another call," the chipper voice said. "He'll be free in forty-five minutes. Would you like to leave a callback number, or would you prefer to hold?"

Mrs. Boone, tear-streaked and shaky, tugged at her husband's arm and pointed at me. Finally. Except, instead of asking me to investigate actual facts and clues, she went a different direction.

"*You* find him, Rondo," Mrs. Boone said. "You're as psychic as the BarkAngels. Ask Pico to show you where he is."

"And who he's with!" Elvis nodded like the request made perfect sense, and for whatever reason, Epic didn't call it out as nonsense.

I knew the Boones. They were *not* going to let this go.

If I could go back in time, maybe I would have listened to the kid magician and stayed away from the whole dog psychic thing. It had completely spiraled out of control. It had turned my brother and sister against me. It ruined my vacation week. And now Pico was missing and the Boones were going to let the trail go cold. Did they not realize what was at stake here? If I couldn't find that anxious, shivering dog soon, my favorite television show was going to get canceled.

Someone had to fix it.

"Fine," I said. "I'll talk to Pico. Then I'm going to look for clues."

It wasn't just about the show. I honestly thought if I did this *one* thing right, we'd all magically go back to getting along. I should have known better. Families don't work like that. And magic is just a bunch of tricks.

SUNDAY

(TWO DAYS EARLIER)

THE PERRO DEL MAR

"Rondo . . . Rondo . . . Rondo . . ."

My sister, Elvis, poked me a few times, then pushed aside one of Mom's custom-made dog benches so she could slide into the booth, across the table from me. Guest checkout for the Perro had already happened, so the dining room was nice and empty. All the cleaning and room turnover was done. And it was Sunday, the first official day of Restorative Week, which is our nonconformist elementary school's way of saying Spring Break.

It all added up to one thing. I was on vacation. Or trying to be.

The dining room was empty, but the nearby lobby was filling up with noisy people and their froofy dogs, and now my sister had invaded the corner booth. Elvis swung her feet under the table, kicking me every single time she said my name. I kept my eyes on my book, *A Magician Among the Spirits* by Harry Houdini, and estimated how long it would take for her to get bored and walk away.

The correct answer to that calculation?

Infinity minutes.

"Rondo . . . Rondo . . . Rondo . . . Rondo . . . Rondo . . . Rondo . . . Rondo . . ."

I turned the page to a chapter titled "Magicians as Detectors of Fraud" and pulled my feet up out of her reach. El's almost ten, only a year and a half younger than me, but she's so small, people who don't know her treat her like she's seven. My sister usually manages to work that to her advantage, but every once in a while, it works to mine. She tried a few more kicks, but her short-as-a-seven-year-old legs got nothing but air.

"*Ron*dooooo!" Elvis let her arms and head flop dramatically to the table. "Mom said you have to help me bring a whole bunch of packages upstairs."

"I cleaned up the dog poo in Room 2," I reminded her. "That was your room to clean, it was disgusting, and you owe me."

Instead of being annoyed at my answer, El grinned, satisfied that she'd gotten my attention.

"There's a crowd lined up outside waiting to see Heaven Hsu," she said. "Do you think she's as short as she looks on TV? I mean, on *Bentley Knows* she's standing next to a Saint Bernard all the time, so it's hard to tell. Did you see the film crew is here already?"

Of course I did. The whole reason I'd chosen the corner booth was so I could get some peace and quiet behind the tall booth walls—but also so I could sit on the edge and keep an eye on the lobby. I'd seen every episode of *Bentley Knows*, and even though I wasn't going to stand in line and fan all over her, I didn't *not* want to know what Heaven Hsu was like in real life.

"Mom and Dad need to step up their security if they're going to host Hollywood stuff here all the time," I said, sneaking another look.

"*Why?*" El leaned forward. "Do you see something? Can our detective agency solve it? I thought of a super-good name. The Mysterious McDade Mystery-Solvers Incorporated!"

"That's terrible," I said. "Besides—"

"We're *not* doing the detective thing anymore. You both promised." Epic had caught me peeking around the wall of the booth, and now he stood at the table holding a clipboard and an ancient toy walkie-talkie he'd rebuilt to have longer range and clearer sound. He held up the device. Announced, "I found them," then clipped the walkie-talkie to his belt.

"I promised not to solve *boring* mysteries," I said.

Epic rolled his eyes.

I nudged him. "Could you move? You're blocking my view."

"*What* are you looking at?" Elvis glared at me, then at Epic. "He sees something, but he won't tell me. He never tells me anything anymore!"

"It's nothing," I said. "Not yet. It *could* be something."

For the past twenty minutes, most of the people filling up the Perro's lobby had been members of the *Bentley Knows* film crew. They were hauling in crates, cords, lighting equipment, and what seemed like a thousand and one duffel bags. The rest were either *Bentley Knows* fans or the usual tourists collecting selfies in America's #1 Dog-Friendly Town. The selfie-grabbers never left Carmelito, California, without a pic at the B&B where a world-class jewel thief had gone viral two years ago. Mom and Dad kept saying it was all a fluke. Our fifteen minutes of fame. Things would quiet down and go back to normal. Any minute now.

Epic followed my gaze to the lobby. Elvis stood on her seat to look over the top of the booth.

"I really wanted to do a mystery this week." She sighed. "Don't you think that girl on the couch has a cute hairdo? I wonder if I could do mine like that."

Epic shook his head. Not about the hairdo. His eyes were on the Italian greyhound curled up in an armchair near the Perro's entrance. My brother is in charge of walking Pico as part of the Perro's Canine Comfort Guarantee. Iggys are strange, nervous dogs, but Epic always knows how to calm Pico down. They help each other out that way.

"I thought Pico was upstairs with the Boones," he said.

I ignored them both and focused on the dude with the gray-tipped mustache who'd come in exactly six minutes ago with the film crew. Nobody had seemed to notice the way he'd slunk in behind some big guys carrying crates and then quietly walked the perimeter of the lobby, scanning the ceiling and the front desk like he was checking for security cameras. He wore black jeans, a black T-shirt, and a black cap pulled over his eyes. He had dark sunglasses on and didn't take them off, even when he swiped a brochure off the desk and fake-examined it. If you're going to pretend to read something, you should at least tilt your chin down so it looks real.

When he'd entered the lobby, Mustache Guy had a cloth sling over his shoulder. It was the kind some people tote babies in, and there was definitely something infant-sized and lumpy inside. But El had distracted me, and now the guy and his sling were nowhere in sight. I had to scan the room twice before I found him again, hidden behind a plant near Pico and the armchair, acting like he was checking his phone. He wasn't. You could tell from the way he angled it, he was taking photos of the Perro's main entrance.

"Do you see that guy by the—"

I didn't finish my sentence, because suddenly, Mustache Guy looked up. He zeroed in on a high-heeled tourist with a fluffed-up poodle and an overeager smile, who was heading straight for a selfie with the up-and-coming canine co-star of the *Bentley Knows* reboot—Pico Boone.

A selfie she wasn't going to get.

If my siblings hadn't distracted me, I would have seen that Mustache Guy had set his bulky black sling down right next to Pico. I would have known what was coming. I would have stopped it.

Instead, I sat there and watched the man in black lean over the chair. Snatch up the Iggy. Put him in the sling.

And bolt out the front door.

MUSTACHE GUY

"Was that . . ." Epic gaped at the front entrance, trying to puzzle out what had just happened. It wasn't rocket science.

I launched myself out of the booth, but Elvis hopped off her seat and grabbed my sleeve.

"*What?* I missed it! Tell me!"

"That dude dognapped Pico!"

I didn't have to say it twice. Elvis sprinted toward the lobby, and I had to work to keep up with her. My sister is faster than she looks.

"Stop! Wait! Think a minute!" Epic isn't like me and El. He can't get on board the minute he hears something. He needs to take it apart and analyze it from every angle. Elvis, on the other hand? She gets a little *too* on board.

Instead of running directly outside, she paused in the center of the lobby and shouted her lungs out.

"Thief! Help! Thief!"

Instantly, tourists and members of the film crew surrounded us, half of them asking questions we didn't have time to answer and the other half filming on their phones while their dogs sniffed each other.

"*El!* How was that helpful?" I hissed as the small crowd followed us out onto Main Street.

Where we ran smack into Mom.

She took one look at me, Elvis, and our entourage and threw out her arms like a barricade.

"Hold up!" She placed a firm hand on my shoulder. "What's happening?"

"Pico got dognapped!" Elvis blurted. "By the celebrity dognapper! The same one who stole Trixie and Baby BombBomb! Rondo saw the thief and now he's getting away and we have to stop him! *Thief!*"

"I didn't say it was the celebrity dognapper . . ." I started, but it wasn't worth the breath. Elvis was way louder than me and everyone in the crowd was already murmuring about ransom money. The fact was, the chances of Pico getting nabbed by the same thief who'd stolen Trixie and Baby BombBomb were slim to none. Those dogs were massive canine celebrities. Multimillionaires at minimum. No offense to Pico, but he was the co-star of a TV reboot that hadn't even filmed yet. And before that? He did a couple ads for dog hats. It didn't add up.

The way I saw it, Mustache Guy was more likely to be a copycat, trying to cash in on someone else's multimillion-dollar idea. As I scanned the perimeter, it looked like he'd gotten away with it, too. With the crowd from the lobby, members of the film crew setting up a tent on the lawn, and *Bentley Knows* fans gathered on the sidewalk waiting for Heaven Hsu, the guy in the black cap had disappeared. I couldn't help being a little impressed. It was a smooth operation. Genius to come when everyone was distracted by the TV stuff.

I spotted Dad and his best friend, Luis, trying to organize the fans on the sidewalk. Luis wore his police uniform, which meant he was on duty. Perfect.

"Luis!" I shouted, and Elvis chimed right in. "Luis! We need you!"

"*Rondo!*" Mom's grip on my shoulder tightened, and she lowered her voice so only El and I could hear. "We talked about this. I can't have you playing your detective game this week."

That annoyed me. This wasn't a game. Pico had been *stolen*, but we were standing around like it was all part of the entertainment.

Epic pushed his way through the crowd and shot Mom an apologetic look.

"I tried to stop them," he said in his new older-and-wiser voice. All year, he'd been acting like the difference between eighth grade and sixth grade was some kind of time warp, but last I checked, it was still the same age difference we'd had all our lives. Besides, Pico was *his* pal, not mine. Shouldn't *he* be the one trying to save him?

I tried to wriggle out of Mom's grip, but surfing and

building furniture all the time had given her ridiculous arm strength. Dad was giving me his come-on-buddy-go-with-the-flow look, and Luis was trying to hide it, but the corners of his mouth twitched into a grin. None of this was funny. I turned my head to get their eyes off me.

Which is when I realized that the copycat dognapper was good, but he wasn't *that* good.

"Uh-oh," Dad said.

"He's smiling. Rondo, why are you smiling?"

On the far side of the lawn, by the alley, a group of workers unloaded a giant, boxy piece of equipment. One guy with a cloth sling over his shoulder wasn't helping. He was blending in, occasionally pretending to examine the box or check the controls, but in reality, he was using the whole operation as cover while he took more photos of our house. The way he leaned back, I could tell he was getting shots of the second floor.

"That's him!" I said. "Let's go!"

No one moved, and Mom held me firmly in place, but at least my family was looking in the right direction now. One of the workers opened a panel on the black box with a loud *snap!* and something flinched inside Mustache Guy's sling. A snout poked out. A long, pointed, Iggy-shaped snout.

"See?" I said. "Luis! That guy stole Pico!"

"*That's* your dognapper?" Mom asked. "The man by the generator?"

She let go of my shoulder. I probably should have taken

the opportunity to run after the criminal, but I was distracted because Mom pulled out her phone and tapped out a number. Who was she calling? We had the police right here.

Dad caught my eye and jutted his chin in the direction of Mustache Guy. Who answered his phone. Pico's snout was still sticking out of the sling, but now another, identical Iggy snout poked out next to it.

"Hi, Raúl?" Mom spoke quietly so the people around us wouldn't hear. "I know you said you're trying to avoid fans, but . . . as a favor . . . would you mind meeting my kids? They're really interested in Pico's stunt doubles."

"Wait. That's *Raúl Flores*? Trainer to the *STARS*?" Elvis asked so loudly that the high-heeled tourist with the froofy poodle perked up.

"It *is* him!" the woman said. "I knew it! Come on, Petals, let's go get you an audition!"

Before he knew what hit him, Raúl Flores—not a copycat dognapper, but a world-famous Hollywood trainer—was surrounded by a panting group of overly groomed dogs and their humans. My own siblings were right there with them, grinning their faces off like they were about to meet the first astronaut to land on the moon. They didn't even notice they'd ditched me.

Across the lawn, Raúl lowered his sunglasses and glared at Mom like she'd done it on purpose. Mom turned the same look in my direction. I couldn't decide which was worse. That

I'd gotten it wrong? Or that I'd gotten it wrong in front of my family.

"How was *I* supposed to know?" I asked. "That dog is identical to Pico."

Dad tried to shrug it off. "Cheddar's the stuntdog," he said cheerfully. "Doughboy's the understudy. Cute, right?"

Mom watched Raúl sign an autograph and sighed. "He *is* dressed like a burglar," she said. "And the way he was sneaking around to dodge fans was ridiculous. If he didn't want to see them, why didn't he hide in his room until they left?"

"Exactly!" I said, but before I could feel too vindicated, some fan with a golden retriever paused mid-selfie and turned his camera on me.

"Hey! You're the Houdini kid. Show us a magic trick!"

Dad locked eyes with me. I shook my head. No way. But more people chimed in.

"What tricks can you do?"

"Can you make my dog disappear?"

"I read that you can escape from handcuffs, like Houdini."

Two years ago, some reporter wrote an article that claimed I knew how to pick locks with bobby pins, just because I'd tried it once. And then, because they'd seen my collection of Houdini books on my shelf, they'd announced—in print—that I was a "promising kid magician."

What people don't realize about Houdini is that "magician" is the least interesting thing about him. Sure, he pulled off some okay magic tricks, and he was a master of escape. But what I like to read about is how he used his skills to expose the tricks of criminals and frauds. Does anyone ever ask me, *Hey, you're into Houdini. Want to help out with an investigation?* Nope. Instead, I've been asked to do a thousand and one card tricks since I was nine.

"Do the coin trick," Dad whispered. "Fast and easy."

Mom glanced toward the generator where Elvis was doing windmill arms, singing, "You Ain't Nothin' but a Hound Dog," like she'd done in the Sharon Henderson video that went viral, and Epic showed the tourists the walkie-talkies he'd rebuilt. I bet no one even asked them to.

I'd heard the lecture dozens of times. *It doesn't hurt to walk the Path of Least Resistance. Be nice, give people something they want, make them feel good, then walk away. Most important: Keep your comments to yourself. Everyone wins.*

Except me.

I set my chin and made my voice extra loud.

"If you want a show," I said to the crowd, "go to the circus!"

Luis couldn't help it. His laugh burst out. "That's my Rondo." He gave me a jokey punch in the arm and grinned at Mom and Dad. "Keep him busy this week, or he'll find trouble. All kinds."

TRANSCRIPT: DAILY DOG DISH PODCAST
Sunday: Hollywood Hounds News Roundup

(Daily Dog Dish intro music.)

Del: Hey, everybody! Thanks for tuning in to the *Daily Dog Dish*—your five-minute furbaby fix! I'm your host, canine reporter Delphi Jones, and as always, I'm joined by my pawsome partner in all things doggo, soon-to-be *Doctor* Melissa Dubois, animal behavioral scientist in training. Say hello, Melissa.

Mel: Hello, Melissa.

(Sound effect of groans and laughter.)

Del: Okay, the clock is ticking! It's our Sunday news roundup, and our dog dish overfloweth. Before we dig in, we need to tell you that today's episode is sponsored by . . .

(Star Wars music fades in.)

Del: . . . Lucasfilms Canine Division, presenting a new movie in their blockbuster *Star Wars: The Pendleton Trilogy*! Last year, *Puppisode One* was a smash hit, so you don't want to miss *The Puppies Strike Back*. In theaters this weekend!

(Music fades out.)

Del: Mel, do you remember the first time we saw *Puppisode One* in the theater?

Mel: Labradoodles with lightsabers! Aw, Del, I sobbed my eyes out when Penelope's paw got eaten by that rathtar, and don't say you didn't!

Del: *(Sniffs.)* It wasn't my fault. That dog's eyes could melt an icicle's heart. Anyway, in other damaged-paw news, we have an update on this rash of celebrity dognappings, right?

Mel: Yes, multiplatinum recording artist Sharon Henderson posted that her Pomeranian, Newt, was dognapped this weekend! Don't worry, he made it home safe and sound. After a full physical, his doctors reported a bruised paw, but otherwise good health. We hope your paw feels better soon, Newt!

Del: Oof! I hope Sharon's wallet feels better. I heard she shelled out a $750,000 ransom!

Mel: That's unconfirmed.

Del: We'll dig up the truth. Remember, you heard it here first when Chippy Chihuahua was napped for a cool million.

Mel: Napped? Is that a word?

Del: It's making me sleepy, that's for sure. We'd better hurry into a Lightning Round before I curl up in Morrissey's dog bed.

Mel: Okay. Let's do this! Ready, set . . .

(Lightning Round bell rings.)

Del and Mel: DISH!

(Sound of a clock ticking.)

Mel: In fashion news, Dog Elegance launched the first outfit in their LuxLux Luxury line. The limited edition Sparkle Suit is already sold out at a purebred price tag of $1,000. Last week, I said the glitter trend was over, but this glitzy outfit begs to differ.

Del: *(Whistles.)* If you can't afford that price tag, Houndstooth Haberdashery released their new line of doggy pirate gear, and arrrrgh-you-kidding-me? It's to die for. Seriously. I'd walk the plank. I liked it better when that adorable Iggy, Pico Boone, was their spokesdog, though. This year's model is a sassy shih tzu who needs to work on her camera appeal.

Mel: Speaking of Pico, he's co-starring in the reboot of *Bentley Knows*. What can you tell us?

Del: From what I hear, getting the series off the ground has been dicey, but the studio's filming the season premiere on location at the Perro del Mar—the same inn where Sir Bentley's jeweled dog collar got stolen two years ago. I hope they've got better security this time!

Mel: Or at least insurance.

Del: I also heard Sir Bentley only plans to be on set for one full day of the shoot.

Mel: For real?

Del: Yep! America's favorite Saint Bernard has a daily rate that's too expensive for the studio to afford, so they've saved all Bentley-related scenes for one twenty-four-hour period. In the meantime, everyone else will be working like dogs—literally—while Bentley's on a luxury cruise around Norway. It must be nice to be top dog!

Mel: I can't even—

(Sound of clock ticking is interrupted by a loud alarm.)

Del: Thanks for listening, furever friends! Tune in tomorrow for the *Daily Dog Dish*, and in the meantime . . .

Mel and Del: Hug ALL the dogs!

(Daily Dog Dish outro music.)

CANINE SWAG

"I don't see why *we* have to get banished," Elvis said. Meaning her and Epic. Not me.

"I don't know." I shrugged. "Maybe because you're the one who screamed your head off and made a huge deal out of the whole thing?"

"I wouldn't have if I knew you were talking about *Raúl!*"

"How was I supposed to know what the dog trainer looks like?"

"That's what *I'm* here for!" Elvis exploded. "If you don't tell me stuff, I can't help!"

"Can we do this in quiet?" Epic asked. "It'll go faster."

We all stared at the mound of packages that had arrived for Pico. It had taken us six trips up the stairs to bring them all to Room 2. Our job was to unpack them and spread everything out on display. The Boones had their own house in Los Angeles, but they paid my parents an annual fee to come to the Perro whenever they wanted. They'd basically lived in Room 1 for three years straight, and after Pico got the *Bentley*

Knows gig, they'd taken over Room 2 for "social media staging." Which, so far, meant storage for all Pico's stuff.

I sliced open package after package and handed the canine swag to Epic, who silently sorted it into perfectly categorized piles on the bed: food and treats, toys, clothes, and a stack of who-knows-what miscellaneous business.

Elvis bounced on the bed.

It was typical. El was doing absolutely nothing to help, but Epic kept giving *me* the eye. As if opening boxes and then breaking them down so we could fit them in the recycling bin was a task I could barely manage without his expert supervision. I swear, the way he'd kept apologizing to Mom and Dad, he thought it was *his* fault that I'd accused Raúl Flores of dognapping and then exposed him to his fans.

Which, honestly, didn't seem like that big of a deal. The guy clearly fake-hated signing all those autographs, because when he'd finished with the fans on the lawn, he came over to the sidewalk and offered to sign a bunch of stuff for the people who *hadn't* chased after him.

Mom and Dad were more upset that I'd been rude to the guy who wanted a magic trick. I'd had to promise that next time, I would get on board. Be kind. Walk the Path of Least Resistance. No questions asked.

Fine. All I had to do was make sure there *wasn't* a next time. Avoiding people should be easy enough. My vacation plans involved a) reading and b) investigating frauds, Houdini-style. I didn't need to be around tourists for that.

Elvis was ignoring Epic's silence rule and chattering while she bounced. "I wouldn't be *surprised* if Pico got dognapped. He's at least as cute as Newt. Remember how Newt sat on Sharon Henderson's guitar when I got to go up on stage—"

"We know you sang with a famous person, Elvis," Epic said. "It's old news. Really old."

"Jeez, Epic, you're super cranky today." Elvis slid off the bed and came over to look inside the box I'd opened. "Is it because Miyon's not coming to visit? You know that stinks for all of us, not just yooo . . . Oooh, Pico's going to love this!"

Elvis held up a shiny, red, pup-sized hat with a wide, flat brim and the letters *DE* outlined in sparkling pink rhinestones. She balanced it on her head and squinted at the mirror before holding up a matching silk dog jacket, a set of four red silk booties, and a bright red collar, each emblazoned with pink glitter and jewels in the shape of the Dog Elegance logo.

Mrs. Boone thinks that glitter convinces people to treat you like a star. But that's another one of her bunk theories. Like how she swears that eating chia seeds helps her complete the *New York Times* crossword puzzle in record time. Or that putting butter in her coffee gives her brown skin a deep, ruby glow. It's next-level stuff.

"I heard about this on the *Dog Dish*!" Elvis said. "The LuxLux Luxury Sparkle Suit! It costs a thousand dollars."

A panicked look crossed my brother's face, and he grabbed the outfit from El's hands, checking it for damage.

"It's not fair that Mom lets you listen to that podcast on her phone," I said. "She doesn't let me do anything on her phone."

Both my siblings ignored me. They obviously didn't care about justice.

Epic placed the Sparkle Suit carefully on the bed and scowled. "Why are the Boones spending money on this junk?"

"Because they want Pico to be an influencer," Elvis answered patiently, like it was a real question. "He has to promote brands so he can get more fans. Mrs. Boone says he needs at least a million followers to count as a 'mega-influencer.'"

"That is so . . . *idiotic!*"

For once, Elvis held still. My brother never says negative words. For him, *idiotic* is as harsh as it gets.

Epic saw our shocked faces and let out a long sigh. He stared at all the stuff on the bed. After five calming breaths, he apologized.

"Sorry. I'm being a jerk."

It was true. He *was* being a jerk. Still, I felt kind of bad for him. My brother gets overly stressed out about stuff, and I could tell he was worried about more than canine swag. I knew he was bummed that his friends Declan and Carlos were at soccer camp, but it had to be more than that. Maybe El was on to something with the Miyon angle. We were all sad that our friend Miyon Kim wasn't coming for Restorative Week. She and her dad were supposed to bring their houseboat up to Carmelito, and Epic had planned all kinds of stuff for them to do. Robots to build, games to play. He'd even saved up to buy a new dry suit for spring surfing, not because *he* loves to do it, but because Miyon does.

The coolest thing about Miyon is that even though she's a year older than Epic, she hangs out with all of us. Last summer, she taught me how to ollie even though it took forever to learn and when I crashed, I cut myself and puked from seeing the blood. Miyon didn't mind. She spent hours listening to Elvis read the entire stack of postcards from her "best friends"—the Saint Bernard from *Bentley Knows* and her trainer, Madeleine Devine. Those postcards are mind-numbing, but Miyon listened to every single one and then asked to hear them again. She's that nice.

But even missing Miyon didn't explain Epic's mood.

"Weird dog stuff is awesome." I reached back into the box and tried to get my brother to smile. "Look: canine caviar! Yummy!"

I held up the can and pretended like I was going to open it and lick it all out, sniffing at the label like a hound dog. Epic didn't smile. Instead, he snatched the caviar from my hands. Like he actually thought I was going to eat it.

"Why can't the Boones unpack all this?" my sister complained. "If I miss Heaven Hsu . . ."

"They're too busy talking to the BarkAngels." Epic rolled his eyes.

"The BarkAngels?" I asked. "Now? Like, *right* now?"

I looked at the pile of packages still left to unpack. We were only half done.

"I'll be right back," I said.

BARKANGEL

"Pico, honey, do you hear what Mom and Dad are saying? They're worried about you. How come you're not eating your food?"

The woman on the computer screen had curls almost as messy as El's, but her hair was rusty-red and her face was dotted with hundreds of brown freckles. She leaned forward and squinted into the camera like she was trying to use her mind to teleport through her laptop, into Room 1, and straight into Pico's soul.

Of all the fads Mr. and Mrs. Boone had gotten into, the BarkAngel obsession was my favorite. I took a small notebook out of my pocket and, careful to stay off-screen, slid into my usual spot on the carpet in front of the couch, hoping I hadn't missed much.

"Do you have to breathe so hard?" Mrs. Boone leaned out of view of the laptop's camera to shush me before focusing back on the woman whose screen name read *Mandee Skye, Certified BarkAngel.*

I grinned and clicked on my pen. The Boones worked with a few BarkAngels, but Mandee Skye was the most convincing.

"He says he's nervous about his performance this week." Mandee shot the miniature greyhound a sympathetic look, and he shivered in Mr. Boone's lap, as if to confirm.

"Of *course!*" Mrs. Boone slapped her forehead so hard, her tight black curls bounced around like springs. Mr. Boone's worry lines relaxed, and they both started talking.

"He's about to film his first TV show!"

"Who could eat at a time like that?"

"Donchu worry, baby. You've got so much *doggone* talent. You're going to be a superstar! An *influencer!*"

"I bet you'll get a Pawscar!" Mr. Boone rubbed Pico's ear.

Mandee Skye smiled, but she looked concerned. "Here's something I'd love us to work on," she said. "Instead of *adding* pressure, let's practice helping Pico feel supported no matter *how* the show does. How can we support you, Pico? Can you tell me some specific things you're worried about?"

I shifted my position on the carpet, and the three of us watched Pico tilt his head to the side. One of his pointed ears flopped inside out as he matched the curly-haired woman's posture. I'd seen Pico do that side-tilt thing with the BarkAngels before. I wrote down *copycat head tilt*, and Mr. Boone nodded at me like he was glad someone was documenting the moment.

That was one good thing about the Boones. As long as I didn't talk a mile a minute like Elvis, or, apparently, breathe too hard, they didn't care if I hung around in the suite. They even let me watch their TV when they weren't there. Which was especially nice because Mom and Dad don't allow screens or devices on our side of the house. I've tried to argue that *they* have laptops, tablets, and smart phones, but Mom and Dad claim those are "for business purposes" and that when I'm an adult, I can make my own choices. Fine, I will.

"He says he wants food that doesn't smell funny," Mandee said. "Does it smell funny?"

Mr. Boone tapped my shoulder and motioned toward a bag of Chowzee dog food on the counter of the suite's tiny kitchen. I hopped up to grab the bag, and when I tossed it to him, Mr. Boone stuck his face in to get a good whiff. Pico flinched in his lap.

"*Chowzee*?" The BarkAngel made a face. "Poor Pico."

Mr. Boone tossed the bag of dog food back to me, like he wanted to get the offending brand off-screen as fast as possible. I pushed my hair out of my face, peered inside at the star-shaped kibble, and sniffed.

"It does smell funny," I said, fanning the air in front of my nose. "Like . . . rotten fish?" I took another whiff. "Guh. Fish, for sure."

"Um, hello? Is someone else here with us?" Mandee asked.

I blew air out of my nostrils a few times. "I can't stop smelling it!"

"It's only Rondo," Mrs. Boone said. "He's practically part of the f—"

Most people who've been literally living in your house for three years straight would say *family*, but that's not Mrs. Boone's style.

"—furniture." She crinkled her nose at the Chowzee dog food and waved for me to put it away in the kitchen.

"Pico also says it would help if he could play with his *happy toy*," the BarkAngel said. "Do you know what he's talking about? He says he doesn't have it anymore."

Mr. and Mrs. Boone looked at each other, and Pico leaned his head back to rub against Mr. Boone's shirt.

"I'm seeing something soft . . . and maybe green or blue . . . no . . . bluish-purple," Mandee said.

"It's probably his octopus," Mr. Boone said.

Mrs. Boone nodded enthusiastically. "Octo's purple, and we accidentally left him in LA."

At the word "Octo," Pico's ears perked up, his muscles tensed, and he wiggled with excitement, looking around like he expected his toy to show up any second now. It was the same response he had whenever someone said "Epic" or "walk."

"Octo!" Mandee gave an embarrassed laugh. "Pico told me it had lots of legs and swam in the water, but that seemed silly, so I thought I got it wrong!"

I started another entry in the Fill-in-the-Blanks Technique section of my investigation notebook. Houdini used to sit in on sessions with mediums who claimed to read minds and talk to the dead, but the whole time, he was taking notes and learning their tricks so he could expose the psychics as frauds.

Most of the time, the tricks Houdini documented weren't that elaborate. Some of them were the exact same methods Mandee Skye was using, one hundred years later. For instance: Hint at a detail that could be true for anyone, then wait for people to fill in the blanks and give their own explanations. I added *soft toy (three possible colors)* to my running list of things the BarkAngels had "seen." It was genius. Every dog that had ever stayed at the Perro had some kind of soft toy. If Mrs. Boone had said Pico had a flamingo, the BarkAngel would have claimed that the Iggy told her his toy had one leg instead of eight.

"Psst! Rondo!"

My brother stood behind me in the doorway of Room 1 holding a cardboard box. "What are you doing?"

I stuffed my notebook in my pocket and motioned to the Chowzee bag. I made a big show out of closing it up. As slowly as humanly possible.

They asked me to put this away, I mouthed, nodding toward the Boones, who were getting stressed out again.

Mrs. Boone's voice got shrill.

"The *boy*? *What* boy is making him nervous? *Why*?"

CALMING TECHNIQUES

"Which boy are you talking about, Pico?" the BarkAngel asked. "How's he upsetting you? Can you tell us more?"

Even Epic was sucked in now. He took a few steps into Room 1 and locked eyes with the Iggy, who wagged his tail, then looked back at the computer screen and tilted his head at Mandee Skye. If any human could *actually* communicate with that dog, it was my brother. I swear the two of them had some kind of secret code.

"He says it's the boy who's always around," the BarkAngel said. "'The boy is not what he seems.' Do you think he's talking about that Rando?"

A laugh almost bursts out of my mouth. Was she doing what I thought she was doing? If she'd seen me writing in my notebook, maybe she'd guessed I was on to her. If so, it'd be smart for her to get me out of the picture. Make the Boones suspicious of me before I could convince them to stop paying her two hundred fifty dollars an hour to pretend she could talk to their dog. There was a medium named Margery who did the exact same thing to Houdini. Only he won in the end. Sort of.

"*Rondo*, not Rando," Mr. Boone corrected her. "Short for *Elrond*. Like the elf."

"The *elf*?" Mandee asked. "What elf?"

I groaned. Thankfully, Mrs. Boone snapped everyone back to focus.

"Maybe 'the boy' is Epic?" she suggested. "He and Pico spend a lot of time together."

My brother took another step forward. I could tell even the *thought* of making Pico nervous was stressing him out.

"Maybe . . ." the BarkAngel said. She sounded confused, like she was working extra hard to understand what the dog was trying to say.

I had to hand it to her. She was good at making it look real.

"I'm getting conflicting images," she said. "Dogs communicate in pictures, so it's hard to tell if he's talking about something that's happening now or if it already happened in the past. The other tricky thing is that dogs are clairvoyant, so he *could* be telling me about something that's going to happen tomorrow. Or next week."

I tried to catch Epic's eye. It was hard enough to believe the Boones bought into this stuff. But my brother was staring at Pico like he was trying to figure it out, too.

"Pico, honey," Mandee Skye said, "I want you to practice your calming techniques, okay? If you feel nervous around this boy, I want you to use your tools. Lick your lips, yawn, blink your eyes. It'll help you feel better. Okay? And listen *very* carefully to your trainer this week. He's there to help you be the best actor you can be. I believe in you. We all do and . . . um . . . Hold on, my sister's texting me some social media posts . . . about *Pico* . . . ?"

Pico tilted his head the other way, flopping the opposite ear inside out, as if he was as surprised as the rest of us. I'd never seen Mandee Skye distracted during a BarkAngel call. Especially not right in the middle of one of her pep talks.

Suddenly, a second video popped up on the screen. It was Leif Skye, another one of the regular BarkAngels. I'd taken notes on him before, but today, his screen name read *Department of Lost Dogs*. He had the same shade of red-brown hair as Mandee, and it was pulled back into a ponytail as long as his rust-red beard. The BarkAngels all used the same mystical space-themed background, and right now, Leif's hand kept pixelating and disappearing into the Milky Way as he looked off-screen, apparently writing something on an invisible board.

"I saw Tara's text about the dognapping and logged on as fast as I could," he said in a rush. "Poor Pico! Have you been able to locate him telepathically? How can I help . . . ?" Leif's voice drifted off as he turned toward the camera and took in the image of all three confused Boones. "Whoa, you found him already! Is he okay? Good work, Mandee!"

"*Dognapping?*" Mr. Boone asked.

It took me a second to remember that the Boones didn't

know anything about the whole Raúl Flores debacle. They'd been here in Room 1. They didn't have a clue that an entire crowd of people had videoed my sister yelling her head off about Pico's dognapping. And, apparently, posted it online.

Which led to an interesting point: the BarkAngels didn't know about Raúl, either. If they could talk to animals, shouldn't they know the facts by now? Pico would have told them he'd been in Room 1 the whole time, and they could have tuned in to Cheddar and Doughboy for their side of the story. I scribbled in my notebook. It was a key moment in my investigation.

But Mandee Skye was smart. Instead of looking caught, she tilted her head at the Iggy, waited, then said, "Pico says it's a silly mistake. He thinks it must have something to do with . . . I don't know . . . I'm seeing another dog that looks exactly like him. Jumping off a roof? Does that make any sense?"

"Yes!" Elvis burst from the hallway into the kitchenette. "He has a stunt double and an understudy, and they're going to practice jumping off a roof today!" She pushed past me and Epic, whispering, "*Thanks for ditching me.*"

El joined the Boones at the couch and launched into a play-by-play, hamming up the part where she'd tried to save the day by screaming her head off in front of the cameras.

Mrs. Boone checked her phone and squeaked like someone had poked her with a pin. "Pico has five hundred new followers!"

Mr. Boone perked up. "*Why?* Because people thought he went missing? That's amazing!"

"Let's focus on the fact that he's safe." Leif laughed. "I'll text Tara so she won't worry."

"*Thank you* for coming so quickly." Mrs. Boone hugged Pico close. Like she'd forgotten that he hadn't been lost at all.

"No prob. It's all part of our service," Leif said. "We're here to help Pico live his best life."

Mandee nodded, visibly relieved. "Let's hope that's the *only* time Pico needs the Department of Lost Dogs! Keep an eye on him, okay?"

After the BarkAngels signed off, the Boones did what they always did. They started listing off all the amazing ways the animal communicator had been able to read Pico's mind. My sister joined right in, kneeling in front of the couch to rub noses with the Iggy.

"Pico, you *guessed* about the body double, you're so smart you wittle sweetie, aren't you, smartie wartie?" She turned toward the Boones and added in a quieter nonbaby voice, "No offense to Pico, but five hundred followers isn't that many. He needs a way bigger boost."

Pico yawned, hopped off Mr. Boone's lap, and trotted toward Epic. My brother knelt down to pick him up, and I started laughing.

"What?" Epic asked.

They made it *look* good, but the BarkAngels' techniques were so basic. So obvious. And yet the Boones believed every word. It's not like they weren't smart people. Mr. Boone was a retired psychiatrist, and Mrs. Boone had done something in finance that made them boatloads of cash. Smart wasn't the issue.

Back in Houdini's day, it was the same. *Scientific American* magazine—a *science* magazine—claimed that the mediums were real. Famous, smart people like the author of the Sherlock Holmes stories wanted to talk to their dead friends and family so badly that they bought into all of it. Literally. The mediums made a ton of cash. It wasn't until Houdini showed how the tricks were done that *Scientific American* admitted they'd been wrong. But the guy who created Sherlock? He never stopped believing. And he *never* forgave Houdini.

Watching the BarkAngels was like a real-life reenactment of everything I'd been reading about in *A Magician Among the Spirits*. I opened my notebook one more time and reviewed Pico's "calming techniques."

Blinking, yawning, licking lips.

"What's so funny?" Epic asked again.

"The minute you picked him up." I nodded toward Pico. "He started blinking."

"*What?*" Mrs. Boone raced toward her miniature greyhound. "Clive!" she said, plucking the dog out of my brother's arms. "Rondo says Pico blinked. Wait! Look! He licked his lips. It's Epic! *Epic's* the boy who's making our baby nervous."

"Epic? Maybe . . ." Mr. Boone let out a long breath. "We should pause your morning walks."

"No!" Epic said.

"Sorry, Epic. It's an important week for Pico."

Epic froze. The Boones had done this to him before. Freaked out about Pico's safety and yanked his dog-walking privileges. Most people would have taken the chance to sleep in and enjoy a week off, but not my brother. Epic looked miserable. Lucky for him, I could help.

"That's not what I meant." I held up my notebook, gripping my evidence. "Pico blinks his eyes, yawns, and licks his lips all the time. All dogs do, right? The fact that he even does it near Epic, who's obviously his favorite human, is solid proof that the BarkAngels are frauds!"

But Mrs. Boone was peppering my brother with questions, Epic was trying to get his job back, Mr. Boone was soothing Pico, and Elvis was complaining that she'd "missed *every*thing" and didn't know what was going on.

No one had listened to a word I'd said.

Epic frowned at me. "I'll be in Room 2," he said, grabbing his messenger bag and flinging it over his shoulder. "Unpacking the boxes, like *you* were supposed to do."

"Me too!" Elvis shot me dagger eyes and scooted next to Epic.

"Wait. You're mad at *me*?" It made no sense. I didn't do anything wrong. And honestly, who cared if the Boones thought Epic was "the boy" the BarkAngel had made up? It wasn't real. I flung my hands out in a what-did-I-ever-do-to-you gesture, but Mr. Boone was standing closer than

I thought, and I accidentally clocked Pico in the nose. The Iggy yelped, and Mr. Boone lowered his massive eyebrows in my direction.

"Sorry, I'll leave, too," I said.

People didn't listen to Houdini the first time he tried to debunk the mind readers, either. In fact, they got mad. Super mad. I shouldn't have expected it would be any different for me.

MAGIC TRICKS

I *should* have gone straight to our room in the family wing of the house, flopped down on my beanbag chair, and read my book. In fact, I should have stayed there, camped out, until the entire *Bentley Knows* entourage finished filming and left town at the end of the week.

Instead, I followed my siblings to Room 2 to finish unpacking boxes. Partly because I felt bad for ditching them with the chore in the first place and for putting Epic in an awkward spot with the Boones. But partly because they clearly didn't *want* me to follow them, which meant of course I was going to.

And when Mom called up to Epic's walkie-talkie to tell us she had a surprise for me—something to keep me "busy" for Restorative Week—I should probably have climbed out the window and run away. But I didn't have time.

The sound of a crowd was already drifting up from the lobby below us.

"Heaven Hsu!" Elvis dropped an armful of Bubble Wrap

and bolted out of the room, leaving me and Epic with the canine swag.

I groaned. "We should have finished moving this stuff earlier."

"Oh, yeah?" Epic didn't bother to point out whose fault that was. He didn't have to. He knew as well as I did that I'd set my own trap. From the guest wing, there was no way to get to the family side of the house without walking down the wide, bright staircase and cutting straight through the fan-filled lobby.

I used to think having celebrities at the Perro was interesting, but that was before I knew how predictable and fake they all were. At least Heaven Hsu was an improvement on your typical celebrity guest. Halfway down the stairs with Epic, I spotted her right away. She was standing near Mom and Elvis at the front desk signing autographs for a line of people, a black-and-white mini schnauzer at her side. She looked exactly like she does on *Bentley Knows*. Jean jacket, shaggy black bangs, hair pulled into a ponytail.

What I liked about her character on the show is they never tried to make her look perfect. A lot of detective shows mess that up. How many times does someone stay up all night risking their life chasing down a bad guy, and in the middle of it all, they look like they just got a makeover? It really ruins the effect.

In the early episodes of *Bentley Knows*, Heaven Hsu looked like a regular kid, pimples and all. In this latest season, she was almost eighteen, but they didn't polish her up like most of the teenagers you see on TV. She still looked like a human. Messy hair. Bags under her eyes. I respect that. It makes it feel real. Or as real as it gets on a show about a dog detective. I've seen all of the *Bentley Knows* episodes on the Boones' TV, and they're good. Really good. So even though I was planning to sneak as quickly and invisibly through the crowded lobby as I could, I kind of wanted to meet her.

"Hey, look!" someone shouted. "It's the kid magician! Come on, kid, show us some magic!"

Heads swiveled toward the guest staircase. Even Heaven Hsu looked up at us. I stopped moving and let my hair fall in front of my face.

"I hate this," I muttered.

"Be nice." Epic handed me a quarter. "You promised. Do the coin thing."

The coin thing was a trick for toddlers.

Dad came through the kitchen door and smiled at me. I could practically feel him telepathing *Path of Least Resistance* into my brain. I could feel Mom's eyes on me, too. I shoved my hands in my pockets and squeezed the quarter until the edges dug into my palm.

"Do you want *me* to do it?" Epic whispered.

Which made me grind my teeth. Everyone loved Elvis because she was adorable and fun and could stand around being the center of attention all day. Everyone loved Epic because he was responsible and smart and did everything the grown-ups wanted him to do. Including pull a coin from behind someone's ear for no reason except to perpetuate a lie that some reporter started out of nowhere. What was the point? I stood by what I'd said before: We weren't circus performers.

"I don't do magic," I said quietly through my teeth. "I don't get why I have to pretend to."

"Rondo . . . give me the quarter."

I was weighing whether to hand over the coin, or stomp off, or shout at everyone to go away and get their own lives when a short boy with perfectly trimmed brown curls, a book under his arm, and a red cape around his shoulders climbed the stairs to meet us. Close behind him was a border collie with a matching red cape. Several people in the lobby pointed and said, "Awww!"

"You've got to be kidding me," I said.

Epic grinned. "I didn't know your Mini-Me was in town!"

"He's *not* my Mini-Me," I hissed. Instinctively, I looked toward Mom. I hoped this wasn't her idea of a surprise.

Denver Delgado-Doyle, our neighbor's nine-year-old nephew, who thankfully lived most of the year in San Diego, reached out and grabbed my hand to shake it. As if we'd never met before. Or we were about to engage in a duel. He gave a solemn head nod, then appeared to pull a magic wand out of the spine of his book, *Escape! The Story of the Great Houdini*, before setting the book slowly and dramatically on the stair in front of the collie. The dog barked at the picture of Houdini and put his black paw on the cover, earning more *Awwws*.

Denver raised his wand, shot me a grin that was more of a smirk, and turned to the crowd.

"What you are about to see is a magic trick beyond your *wildest* dreams!"

The border collie barked again, and people who'd been milling around, even the ones in line to get autographs from Heaven Hsu, moved toward the bottom of the stairs to see what was going on.

Denver tucked the wand under his armpit and held up a silver foil ball. He made a big deal out of closing one small brown fist around the foil. Then, with the other hand, he grabbed the magic wand, tapped it on his closed fist, and—*poof!*—the ball disappeared. The crowd *oooh*ed and clapped. Epic elbowed me and grinned. It wasn't *that* amazing, but whatever. I was fine with it if it meant I was off the hook.

Which I wasn't.

"Your turn," the kid whispered, shooting me a grin, like we were both in on a super-fun secret.

Which we weren't.

"Rondo McDade," he said loudly, flourishing his magic wand with dramatic flair, "I am Denver Delgado-Doyle, and I challenge YOU to a Magic Duel!"

Mom was grinning. Like she actually thought I would love this. Being ambushed by some kid magician in front of a crowd in my own house?

Next to Mom, Heaven Hsu had paused signing autographs. The mini schnauzer stood on the autograph table, tilted his head, and I swear, locked eyes with me. The fur on the dog's face was black except for a white patch around the muzzle, which was groomed into the shape of a bushy, black-tipped mustache that made the schnauzer look permanently angry. That furious dog stared at me. Then he blinked his eyes and licked his lips.

I don't know if it was the schnauzer using Mandee Skye's "calming techniques," the annoying red cape, or Mom's victory smile, but suddenly I could see the Path of Least Resistance stretched out in front of me. And for once, I was ready to walk it.

"Okay." I raised my voice loud enough so that people could hear, but I didn't smile or move my stringy hair out of my face. If they wanted a show, I'd give them a show, but it wasn't going to be all cheesy. I was going to talk in my regular voice, and if my sister started to sing, I was walking. "What I can do is better than magic."

"Better than *magic*?" Denver Delgado-Doyle gasped dramatically and did an overacted double take complete with jazz hands, like we'd rehearsed this. Pure cheese. The crowd ate it up. Maybe the caped magician was my *sister's* secret twin. I didn't know anyone else who loved to ham it up as much as Elvis.

"Yeah," I said flatly from behind my hair. "I'm psychic. I can read dogs' minds."

"*Nice!*" Denver looked so happy that I was playing along that I almost decided to quit right then. "Do you want to start with Bella? She's exceptionally intuitive."

He pointed toward the border collie. Exceptionally intuitive? Did I use words like that when I was nine? Probably. That didn't mean he was a Mini-Me. *Or* that we needed to be friends.

I shook my head. "I'll start with that one over there."

There was a murmur from the crowd as they followed my finger, pointing to Heaven Hsu's mini toy schnauzer.

"*Rondo,*" Epic whispered. "This is a terrible idea."

He was probably right. If I hadn't stopped to watch the BarkAngels, I'd be on my beanbag right now reading my book. With no interruptions. No pressure. No drama.

Instead, I was standing on the guest stairs, under the spotlight of Mom's handmade upcycled-champagne-bottle chandelier, getting ready to read the mind of a cranky celebrity schnauzer in front of a whole bunch of people with camera phones.

What I *wanted* to say to my brother was "Get me out of this, bro."

Or maybe better: "Run!"

But the deed was done. I'd opened my mouth, and I couldn't reverse time. Besides, it bugged me that my brother assumed I was going to mess it all up.

"Relax," I said to Epic. "I know how to do it."

THE FRENCH DROP

The crowd parted to make way for Heaven Hsu to approach the stairs with her fluffy dog in her arms. She didn't smile. In fact, up close, it looked like she might hate crowds as much as I did. Her shoulders were tensed up, and even though a chunk of hair had come loose from her ponytail, she let it hang in front of her eye and didn't try to push it away. If I hadn't been so busy wishing I was somewhere else, I might have found it funny. The way we were standing there, staring at each other through our hair.

"Okay," Heaven said. Her voice was gruff, and her eyes were the same deep brown as the schnauzer's. She narrowed them straight at me. "Read his mind. I'm curious."

The schnauzer lifted his chin and made a barely audible snarfing sound, almost like he was taunting me.

"I'll need to know your dog's name," I said, testing out my voice. It wasn't too shaky. Maybe I could pull this off. "And what you want me to ask him."

"His name's Roo." Heaven looked at the dog, then back at

me. They both smirked, like they were testing me. "Everyone says he looks mad. Maybe ask him if he's angry?"

Roo's ears had pricked up at the sound of his name, and he made a move with his mouth that looked like a full-on scowl.

"Sure," I said, and tested out a Mandee Skye move. I leaned forward, focused in on the schnauzer, and scrunched my eyebrows together, pretending to look straight into the dog's soul. "Hey, Roo," I said. "Did you hear what she said? Are you annoyed about something?"

I tilted my head to the side, BarkAngel-style, and waited for everyone to think I was listening. Roo gave his chin a slight tilt.

"All right," I said finally. "He says he's mad about lots of things."

"Oh yeah? Like what?" Heaven asked, though she didn't look surprised. Or even that interested, really. For a second, I wondered if maybe she'd only walked over here as an excuse to stop signing autographs. Made sense. I'd rather talk to a fake dog psychic than hang out with a bunch of starry-eyed lemmings, too.

I locked eyes with the dog again and seriously tried to think about it. If I were Roo, what would I be mad about?

"His name, for one," I said. "He doesn't like being named after a cartoon baby kangaroo." That was an easy one. I knew a thing or two about getting a name you didn't ask for. Mom had named me Elrond after an elf in her favorite novel.

Which was fun for *her*, but did she ever think about what it would be like to walk around with an elf name? I doubt it.

"Oh," Heaven said. Unimpressed? Bored? Disappointed?

I didn't get the idea that Heaven was buying it, but everyone else seemed to be. Elvis had elbowed her way to the bottom of the stairs and was watching me with her mouth wide open, like I'd grown rainbow wings.

"What else?" El blurted. It's one of the things I've never understood about my sister. She's smart, maybe even genius-level, but sometimes I think Elvis loves drama more than logic.

I did the soul-search look in Roo's direction again, but I was paying attention to Heaven. She had Roo tucked tightly under one arm, and she hadn't smiled once. Anyone could see she wasn't happy to be here. Her free hand kept fidgeting with the strap of a worn-out messenger bag that had pens and pencils stuffed into the front pocket. The flap of the bag was closed, but in the gap at the corner, I could see the hint of a spiral-bound notebook. And the jagged-edged plastic wrapper of what could only be a meat stick.

"He wants something in your bag," I said. "Something he says is 'yummy in his tummy.' Weird. I wonder what that is?"

"Ha. Ha." Heaven rolled her eyes and pulled out the meat stick, holding it up for everyone to see. A few people in the crowd giggled, and a couple gasped. Epic, on the other hand, gave me a knock-it-off nudge. But I'd just gotten started.

"I also see . . ." I channeled my inner BarkAngel, looking

straight into the dog's mean-looking eyes, "A notebook? He says there's something you're writing down, or . . . something you're reading, maybe, that he doesn't like. Do you know what that could be?"

Heaven didn't answer. She didn't move. She looked spaced-out, like she wasn't even listening. Epic nudged me again, harder this time, but it didn't matter. It wasn't like he was going to do anything about it. My brother hates making a scene. Besides, I was on a roll. This whole animal communicator thing was kind of fun.

"I see it now," I said. "He's mad about some decision you're making. I think it's about your . . . career? He thinks it's a super-bad idea."

It was the most general thing I could think of. Every celebrity who'd ever walked through the door of the Perro del Mar had been obsessed with career decisions. But something about the question snapped Heaven to attention. She jerked her head toward Roo.

"Seriously?" She spat out the word, and it kind of seemed like the question was aimed at the dog, but Heaven looked back to me for the answer.

"Well . . ." I stumbled a little. I hadn't expected such a strong reaction. Heaven Hsu's scowl was almost as scary as her dog's. I decided to steal another line from Mandee Skye.

"Animals, uh, communicate in pictures," I said. "Plus they're clairvoyant."

My voice had gotten shaky again, and I heard Epic stifle a

groan. Elvis, on the other hand, nodded like everything I'd said was common knowledge. A dude standing next to her nodded, too, so I took a breath and kept going.

"You can't always know if dogs are talking about the past, present, or future, so . . . Roo could be telling me about a decision you already made or something you don't even know you're going to do yet. It's hard to say."

Heaven Hsu's scowl got deeper. "Go on," she said, only it sounded more like a dare.

The brief moment of fun had worn off fast. I could feel all the eyeballs in the room boring into me. I let my hair fall farther over my face. Whatever zone I'd been in, I'd definitely lost it. I needed to wrap this thing up. But how?

I glanced at my brother. He was always good at getting us out of messes. I could see right away that he knew I was in trouble, but he shook his head with his worst I-told-you-so look. I'd seen that face so many times, and I knew it meant two things. One: He'd known I was going to mess things up from the very beginning and now I had. Two: He didn't have any ideas, either.

Denver Delgado-Doyle had been standing next to me with his mouth open for most of the mind-reading session. I'd barely even remembered he was there, but now he stood on his tiptoes and leaned in close, aiming a stage whisper at my ear.

"I know what you're doing."

He grinned at me in this overly excited way that made me

clench my teeth. I wouldn't have opened my mouth at all if it wasn't for the kid in the cape. And if Mom thought I was going to spend my entire Restorative Week playing babysitter to Denver? I didn't have a choice. This had to end now.

I gave the schnauzer one last look.

"Roo says he's also mad about this 'magician,'" I said, putting the word in air quotes.

"What?" Denver's voice came out all squeaky.

I turned to look at him and shrugged. "He says you lied. He says you didn't make the ball disappear, and liars make him mad."

The crowd *oooh*ed. Like they were watching an actual magicians' duel.

"I did so! I made it disappear. Look!"

Denver waved his left hand at the crowd to prove that he didn't have the ball.

"I'll ask the dog," I said.

I stared Roo in the face, and who knows why, but that little dog decided to choose that moment to make a low, growling sound in the back of his throat.

I nodded. "Yep, thanks, Roo. He says you're still holding it in your other hand."

Denver pulled himself together and, all showman-like, waved his right fist in the air.

"Impossible!" he said. "I'm only holding my magic wand."

He waved the wand around like it was proof, but he had his fingers spread a little too far apart, and a few people gasped at the glimpse of aluminum foil peeking through the spaces.

It was a rookie move. Just because I don't do magic tricks doesn't mean I don't understand how they're done. I've practiced a French Drop a thousand times. You hold an object between the thumb and index finger of your right hand, then pretend to take the object away with your left. In reality, you've only let the thing drop down into your right palm. Then you distract everyone by making a big deal out of the fact that you now have the object in your left fist. Which is only holding air.

Meanwhile, you grab the magic wand with your right hand—the one that's still holding the object—but people never guess it's there because now that hand's holding a wand. Like you can only hold one thing in your hand at a time? People *want* it to be real, so they forget about common sense. For the big finale, you tap your empty left fist with the magic wand, and poof! When you open your fist and wiggle your fingers around, the object is gone. But it hasn't disappeared. Because it was never there in the first place.

In fairness to Denver Delgado-Doyle, it's not as easy as it seems. He'd actually done it decently well. Way better than me. I'd never been able to hide the ball. The way his face fell when his trick got exposed, I felt kind of bad for throwing him under the bus.

On the other hand, if the worst thing that was likely to happen here was that I wouldn't have to spend my vacation week with a show-off kid magician two years younger than me? I could live with that.

"Sorry, dude," I said, matching his loud stage whisper. "That dog shouldn't have told everyone. I don't know why he did that."

DENVER
DELGADO-DOYLE

Everyone knows that magicians are hyper protective about their secrets. Revealing the trick behind Denver's French Drop should have made him mad. So mad that he'd go back to his uncle Brody's and never want to see me again. In fact, next vacation week, he might even decide to stay in San Diego.

But I'd underestimated the endless cheerfulness of Denver Delgado-Doyle.

"We should put on a show together. The crowd loved it, don't you think?" He tugged Bella's leash and hurried to keep up with me as I sped through the farmers' market.

"Martinez Antiques," I said, pointing as I rushed past the booths. "Flo's Floral Essences."

"You don't have to give me the tour," Denver said. "I visit my uncle all the time."

He was wrong, though. I *did* have to give him the tour. Like

Denver, Mom seemed to think the performance on the stairs had been a blast for everyone. And the next step in solidifying our BFF-dom and my parents' plan to Keep Rondo Out of Trouble was apparently a grand tour of America's #1 Dog-Friendly Town.

"Show him all the fun stuff," Mom said. "Take Bella to the new pupcake shop and the leash-free beach! When you get back, you can do whatever you want."

"For real?" I asked. "Whatever I want?"

"Sure," she said. "But take your time. I bet you want a break from all this hoopla."

She wasn't wrong about that. Heaven Hsu had disappeared to her room, so the fan action had calmed down, but the *Bentley Knows* film crew had blocked off the main entrance to the Perro del Mar so they could build scaffolding up the front side of the building. Inside, the lobby was filled with mounds of extension cords, duffel bags, crates full of duct tape, and long extension poles. The selfie-grabbers were still around, eating it up.

My plan was to give the fastest tour known to humankind. We'd already gone up Main Street past Dogma Cafe, Fat Puppy Natural Foods, and Nails 'n' Tails doggy salon. In Paradiso Park, I swerved around two dudes in Animal Universe movie studio hats and hooked a right toward the junior high school and Dog Run. At this rate, we'd get to Carmelito Beach and the Moondoggie Inn in about four minutes flat. Denver's uncle owned the Moondoggie, so I could drop him off there and be free. To do whatever I wanted. As promised.

"Uncle Brody said I could do some magic for the guests at his hotel," Denver said. "Have you ever been to Yips and Sips? It's a party every Thursday for people and dogs, and my uncle gets—"

"I know what it is," I said. "It's a rip-off of the Perro's Monday Night Yappy Hour."

I knew I wasn't being very friendly, but I could see exactly how this was going to play out. If I gave Denver one ounce of encouragement, it was a guarantee that my entire Restorative Week would become a series of "playdates" with a nine-year-old. Who wanted to do performances together. It was a no go. There were lots of kids in Carmelito. If I was the most boring one, he'd move on.

The problem was, Denver Delgado-Doyle didn't seem capable of being bored. By the time we got to the Moondoggie, not only was he *not* canceling our playdates, he was doubling down.

"I'll make a matching cape for you," he said. "What color do you want? My uncle said I can come over every day this week because he's so busy, plus I'll be back for the whole summer, so we could do a trial run of the show now and perform it all summer long! It's cool to hang out with a fellow magician. Right?"

A "fellow magician." Me. He'd already talked my ear off

about all the articles his uncle had sent him about me and my siblings. Then he'd rattled off a long list of magic tricks he'd learned. I almost felt bad for the kid. His whole copycat identity was based on a lie.

"This is your stop." I nodded toward the Moondoggie's patio.

Bella stopped to drink from the canine water fountain, but Denver shook his head.

"I left some stuff at your place," he said. "Plus, I don't have to be back until dinner. Want to stop at the taco truck? Uncle Brody gave me money for snacks. I'll buy you one!"

"I'm not hungry for tacos." It was a gigantic lie. I could eat a six-course meal, and there'd still be room in my stomach for tacos. But Denver was planning our whole *summer*, not just Restorative Week. He wanted to make me a *cape*. I couldn't use his taco money. That would make it look like I wanted to be friends, and I'm not a fake.

Denver shrugged and pulled Bella toward the truck anyway. "I'll get one for myself, then."

It was torture, watching him stuff his face with that juicy mouth-magic. Even Bella got to snack on a Bow-Wow Burrito. She flopped right down on the sidewalk to slobber all over it, and we had to sit on a bench to wait for her to finish. Which felt way too much like an actual hangout. It was time to remind Denver why *he* should be ditching *me*.

"Must have been a bummer that your French Drop got revealed," I said.

"Not really. I know a magician's never *ever* supposed to reveal someone else's tricks, but busting me for the French Drop made the psychic stuff look extra real. That was smart. I get why you did it. But . . ."

Denver took a giant bite, and taco juice dripped down his chin.

"But *what*?" I asked. Not because I wanted to know. Because I needed the conversation to cover up the sound of my growling stomach.

"I don't think we should do the mind-reading thing for Yips and Sips," Denver said. As if I'd already agreed to be part of his third-grade magic show. "My mom won't like it. She doesn't believe in magic. I mean, she's okay with magic *tricks*, but she doesn't like me messing around with occult stuff."

I held back a laugh. What I'd done at the Perro was the furthest thing from occult. But Denver looked nervous. As if Bella could tell, she looked up and licked Denver's hand. Or maybe she only wanted a taste of the taco he'd been holding.

"You know Houdini said pretending to read minds was basically criminal," Denver said. "Right?"

There was no arguing that the kid knew his stuff. It was why Houdini had quit using mind reading and séances as part of his act. He hated cheating people out of their money. He figured with a magic trick, everyone knew it was a trick. The audience understood they were paying for the fun of getting fooled and for the puzzle of trying to figure out how he pulled it off. But the mediums told people they were *actually* talking to dead people, and the customers believed it. They paid a lot of money to get messages—fake messages that they thought were real—from their dead friends and family.

That, Houdini said, was just plain stealing.

"Houdini was right, don't you think?" Denver asked.

I stared at the kid. What I *thought* was a) of course Houdini was right, b) I wasn't taking money from anyone, c) I wasn't planning to read any other dog minds, d) especially not in his magic show, and e) if I *did* do it, it would be to prove the BarkAngels were frauds. That was the opposite of criminal.

"Bella's done. We should get back," I said.

Bella looked up from her project of licking every last Bow-Wow crumb off the sidewalk, but Denver didn't move.

"Think about it, Rondo. Even when Houdini was doing the mind-reading tricks to *expose* the psychics, all kinds of bad things happened. You can get in a lot of trouble if you mess with that stuff."

He leaned closer and lowered his voice, glancing at Bella like he didn't want the collie to overhear what he was about to say.

"Some people say . . ." He dropped his greasy chin and looked up at me with eyes wide, like someone about to tell the scariest part of a ghost story. "That Houdini made the mediums so mad . . ."

I *might* have accidentally leaned forward like I wanted to hear what he had to say next.

". . . they murdered him."

I laughed so loudly that Bella scrambled to her feet and rushed to Denver's side. Was that a threat? Or did Denver Delgado-Doyle actually think something terrible could happen if I pretended to communicate with dogs?

The truth was, for a nine-year-old, he wasn't completely uninteresting. But that didn't change anything. The kid magician had to go.

ROOF STUNT

By the time we got back to the Perro, the scaffolding had been built all the way to the roof and more tents, tables, and rolling carts full of equipment had been set up on the front lawn. Someone had parked a gigantic truck with a crane right on the sidewalk, and Luis Sánchez pulled his police car up to it while his partner set out orange cones. To remind people not to accidentally walk into the gigantic piece of machinery, I guess.

"You guys!" Elvis raced toward us. "Pico and Cheddar are up on the roof, and one of them's going to jump off! I mean, not all the way off. Yet. They're rehearsing, so they're only learning a little piece at a time. Raúl is *ah*-mazing! Wait'll you see what he does with the dogs. Rondo, I think he can talk to them—like you!"

Pico stood in the second-floor window, looking out at the street from Room 4 while my whole family plus Denver, the Boones, several members of the film crew, and a few curious passersby stood on the sidewalk staring back up at him. At least I *thought* it was Pico. Raúl's Italian greyhounds, Cheddar and Doughboy, were also taking part in the roof-jump rehearsal, which, so far, was nothing but standing around. Elvis had really oversold the event.

According to El, *Bentley Knows* filming wouldn't start until Tuesday, but the dogs were practicing a "midnight window escape." They had to run through it in the daytime until the Iggys were comfortable enough to "hit their marks" in the dark. My sister said all three pups had to learn how to do the tricks so Raúl could decide who to feature in each shot of the scene.

I couldn't tell any of the Iggys apart, and I honestly didn't understand how anyone else could, either. All three of them had the exact same narrow face and pointed ears. Even their tails had identical white tips.

"Cheddar's Pico's stunt double," Elvis said. "She's been in over fifty commercials and three movies with super-famous actors. Doughboy is only an understudy. I don't think I'd choose him for much."

"How do you know this stuff?" I asked, and Elvis handed me a small, glossy business card that said *Raúl Flores, Trainer to the Stars*. The word *Stars* was studded with yellow glitter. Mrs. Boone must love this guy.

"I got his card," El said. "When I get my dog, we'll probably decide to be in films together."

"What kind of dog are you getting?" Denver asked. This whole time, he was still wearing his magician's cape.

"She's not getting a dog," I said at the same time that Elvis said, "A rescue like my old one, Yoda."

Yoda had died so long ago that I'm surprised El even remembers him, but she'd asked for a new dog almost daily ever since. So far, Mom and Dad hadn't budged. They said our family was too busy taking care of other people's dogs to manage one of our own. Personally, I thought their argument was flawed. There were already so many dogs around, one more wasn't going to make or break anything.

"Bella's a rescue, too!" Denver grinned. "We think she's a border-collie–Alaskan-husky mix, and that's why she has those blue eyes."

Elvis had already dropped to her knees to snuggle and coo at Bella. "You'll be besties with my brand-new Baby Yoda, wonchu, sweetie cutie Bella-Bella?"

My sister gave Bella an extra-energetic head rub, and the collie lowered her nose and took a small step closer to Denver.

"Be gentler, El," I said. "She doesn't like that."

Elvis hopped to her feet like I'd reminded her of something important. She pointed her finger in my face. "How come you didn't tell me you could do that?"

"Do what?"

"Talk to dogs."

"Seriously?" I asked. "You think I can talk to *dogs*?"

"Show me how you do it."

"No."

"Teach me!"

"Nope."

"*Please?* Pleasepleasepleasepleaseplease?"

"El, it's not going to happen," I said.

Before I could tell Elvis that believing I could talk to dogs was one of the silliest things she'd ever fallen for, my parents and Epic showed up, and Denver made a big flourish with his cape.

"Rondo and I are going to do a magic show together!" he announced. "At the Moondoggie Inn!"

The minute he said the words *magic show*, my parents lit up. This kid was good.

"Oh my gosh, that's a great idea!" Mom said.

Dad reached out one hand to me and the other to Denver for a double high five. Denver gave Dad an enthusiastic slap, but I left him hanging.

"*Rondo* agreed to be in a magic show?" Epic asked.

El examined my face like she didn't recognize me anymore. Like aliens had come down from space and replaced her brother with some kind of extraterrestrial being.

"I didn't . . ." I started, but Denver flipped his magician's cape again with a perfectly coordinated wave and a wink. He'd clearly been practicing that move.

My parents beamed. I know them well enough to know they were smiling full-on *relief* smiles. A magic show would keep me busy. Like Luis said, so I couldn't find trouble. Or it couldn't find me.

Before I could burst their bubble and explain that Denver's fictional magic show was never going to happen, a tall, thin man suddenly climbed out the window of Room 4 on all fours. We craned our necks to watch as he perched precariously on the shingles of the roof and beckoned for Pico to follow him. The crew had lined the entire front of the house with netting and giant foam pads, but it still looked dangerous.

"That's Raúl! He's *very* intense," Elvis said. As if I hadn't recognized the guy we'd chased out of the Perro. His hat and sunglasses were gone. He obviously didn't care about dodging fans anymore.

Pico (or one of the Pico look-alikes) had barely lifted a paw over the windowsill when Mrs. Boone sucked in her breath and gasped, "*My baby!*" several times in a loud, terrified whisper while Dad explained to us that Raúl was using a clicker and special treats to motivate the dogs.

"Raúl says homemade treats are more effective than store-bought," Dad said. "He whipped up a batch in our kitchen this morning, but he won't share his recipe."

Mom pulled a hand out of her bulging skirt pocket and winked.

"I *might* have stolen some for you. For research."

"*What?*" Elvis stared at the handful of nuggets like Mom had confessed to a jewel heist, and Mom laughed loudly as Dad kissed her cheek.

Mrs. Boone hadn't stopped chanting. *"Baby baby baby baby . . ."*

Abruptly, Raúl held up his hand. He said something to someone inside Room 4 who whisked the Iggy safely inside and closed the window. Raúl, still on the roof, stood up to his full height and waved his arms at us.

"Too excitable! Too much talking!" he announced. "Clear this area. No one but crew for sixty minutes."

"Pico *needs* us for moral support—" Mrs. Boone began.

"*Sixty. Minutes,*" Raúl bellowed. "No one upstairs. No one within eyesight. Complete. Silence."

"See?" Elvis said. "Intense."

On our way through the backyard, Bella went berserk when she saw our chickens, and someone from the film crew had to come hurry us all up before Denver's dog got us permanently banned from the set.

"Banned? But our Pico . . ." Mrs. Boone's whisper was barely audible, she was so afraid to make a sound.

Mr. Boone patted her arm. "It's for safety," he whispered back. "Remember what the BarkAngel said. Raúl *always* gets good results."

"*Pico* gets good results. *He's* the one who does the work." Mrs. Boone pouted. "You tell Raúl, when Pico's a mega-influencer, *we're* going to call the shots."

DISAPPEARING ACT

We were all basically prisoners inside the Perro for the next hour. We couldn't even go upstairs to our rooms. The Boones sat in the lobby as close to the front window as they dared. Not that they could see anything. All the action was happening up on the roof. Mom and Dad went to the kitchen to work on the Monday Night Yappy Hour menu. Which left me, Epic, Elvis, Denver, and Bella on our own. We headed for the guest dining room to figure out something to do.

The corner booth has always been our favorite spot in the house because the tall U-shaped walls are built out of old headboards that Mom salvaged from antique wooden beds. The effect was more like a secret fort or a clubhouse than a table to eat at.

"I wish they'd let us have a TV," I said, sliding into the booth without looking.

My shoulder bumped right into Heaven Hsu, who ripped an earbud out of her ear with one hand and flipped over a notebook she'd been writing in with the other. Her laptop was open on the table in front of her, and she lowered the lid with a slap.

"Oh, crud! Sorry!" I said.

"We didn't mean to interrupt you," Epic added in a more guest-friendly tone.

Heaven and Roo both stared us down like we'd come to kick them out of our spot and they were willing to fight for it. Actually, I take that back. Heaven looked at all of us that way, but Roo wasn't staring at anyone but me. Less than twelve inches away, he lifted his lip and bared his tiny yellow teeth in a sneer.

I started to back away, but Elvis slid right into the seat across from Heaven Hsu like she'd been invited.

"Elvis. Don't bother her," Epic scolded, which only made El scootch in farther. She patted the seat next to her and waved at Denver, who shrugged and joined her. Bella shook her ears and hung back, sizing up the schnauzer before making a move. Probably wise.

"Are you here early because you have to rehearse, too?" Elvis asked Heaven. "Madeleine Devine says the biggest stars, like Sir Bentley, don't *have* to rehearse. That's why she's not coming until Wednesday night. Did you know Sir Bentley's a girl but she plays a boy on TV? She stayed here once. Probably you know that already, 'cause you've been on the show so long. That's why I thought *you* would have been one of the biggest stars but I guess not if you're here and Bentley's on a luxury cruise with—"

"El!" Epic said.

Heaven's mouth had fallen open a little. My sister was *not* getting the message that we needed to find someplace else to be.

"Virginia Woolf!" she said, pointing to a thin paperback next to Heaven's notebook. "She was born Adeline Virginia Stephen, and her siblings called her the Goat. I didn't know she wrote about dogs."

"She memorizes trivia so she can beat us at games," Epic explained before Heaven got too impressed.

Denver picked up the book and examined the snooty springer spaniel on the cover. "*Flush*? Never heard of it. My dad loves Virginia Woolf because her stuff is kind of gender-bending, but my mom says she's elitist. What do you think?" he asked.

Denver Delgado-Doyle was surprising, you had to give him that.

Heaven looked surprised, too, but she put her earbud back in her ear, opened her messenger bag, and started dumping her stuff into it.

"I think," she said, "I need to find somewhere to focus."

Elvis shook her head. "We're on lockdown."

For some reason, Heaven looked at *me* for confirmation.

I nodded. "Raúl said—"

"Got it." Heaven held up her hand and rolled her eyes like she knew all about Raúl.

"You don't have to move," Epic said. "We're leaving. *Aren't we, Elvis?*"

"*Fine.*" El gave Denver a small push. The two of them reluctantly scooted out of the booth.

I scooted out of my side, too, but I kept my eye on Roo. The schnauzer had been staring at me from the moment I sat down. The eye-lock made it hard to turn my back on him.

"Got anything you want to ask my dog before you go?"

I couldn't tell if Heaven Hsu was joking. I shook my head even though I'd glimpsed enough of her notebook, laptop, and the Post-it notes sticking out of her paperback to have pulled off a few good animal communicator tricks. For instance, I'd seen the phrase *Step 1: Total darkness is key* written in her notebook. I could have used that. But I held back.

Instead, we retreated to the other side of the dining room. Bella flopped down at Denver's feet, and Elvis and Epic peppered us with questions about my least favorite topic: the Yips & Sips magic show.

"What kind of tricks are you going to do?" Epic asked.

"I could be your assistant," Elvis said. "Or I could sing. Do you need music? Tell me everything you've got planned!"

"There's nothing to tell," I said, and my sister blew out her breath in an exasperated sigh.

"Why are you always like this?" she moaned.

"Like what?"

"Secretive!"

"Why do you have to *know* everything?"

Denver interrupted our bickering with a suggestion that made Epic grin.

"We could do a disappearing act," he said. "Something big, like how Houdini vanished Jennie at the Hippodrome Theatre."

"Yeah, *that* should be easy," I said. "Good luck."

"Rondo, be nice," Epic said.

"I could be Jennie!" Elvis said. "Vanish *me!*"

"You have no idea what you're talking about," I said. "Jennie was an elephant. And I'm not doing a magic show."

"I bet Houdini used mirrors for that trick," Denver said. "All we'd need—"

"It wasn't mirrors," I said, and Epic gave me a look that clearly meant correcting people wasn't in the "nice" category. I ignored him. I wasn't trying to shoot Denver down. It's just that he had his facts wrong. "It was probably a double wall in the elephant's crate."

"Sure, or a trapdoor in the bottom of the stage? For an elephant?" Denver hooted. "No way. Jennie was huge! It had to be mirrors."

"Nope. Houdini wasn't that great of a magician. He would have used the simplest method."

Denver gasped like I'd insulted his mother, which was overplaying it for sure. I didn't say Houdini wasn't a genius. Just that his magic tricks weren't all that amazing. It was fact.

"If he wasn't a great magician," Denver said, "how come

no one's figured out how he made the elephant disappear? *I* think he's underrated."

Epic tried to play peacemaker.

"Mirrors could be worth trying, Rondo," he said. "You don't have to be negative about everything all the time."

"Yeah, at least Denver's trying to do something *fun*," Elvis said. "You never want to do anything fun anymore."

"Like what?"

"Like be in our detective agency!"

I laughed, which made her even more furious.

Sure, we used to dream about raking in the big bucks, solving crimes and kicking baddies to the curb. But that was before we knew any better. No one wants to hire a group of little kids to solve mysteries, and if they do, it's only because they think you're being cute. Or because they want to see you prove how smart you are. Neither of those things are interesting.

Besides, it's not like mysteries are hanging around everywhere, waiting to be solved. Even when you see a sketchy dude steal a dog in front of your eyes, it turns out to be nothing. Last summer, my sister got so desperate she asked Mom to pay us to solve the Mystery of the Missing Sock, and that was when I quit.

"You had a detective agency?" Denver asked. "That sounds awesome!"

"*See?*" Elvis stuck her tongue out at me. "Denver gets it."

"Maybe we could make *Denver* disappear."

The whole table went silent. Epic looked apologetic. Like he was sorry he had to have such a jerk for a brother.

"Denver didn't do anything but be *ah*-mazing," Elvis said. "Unlike you."

There it was. My siblings barely knew this kid, but they already liked him better than me. Denver was nicer, more extroverted, more fun. Fine. They could have him.

"You want to see a good disappearing act?" We were all so absorbed in our argument that none of us had seen Heaven Hsu approach our table with Roo in her arms. "Keep watching. I just figured out how to pull off one of my own."

I lowered my voice as we watched her disappear into the lobby. "What do you think she meant by *that*?"

"That we're loud and obnoxious, so she had to leave," Epic said.

"I don't think so." Heaven hadn't looked annoyed. She'd looked satisfied, like she'd put the pieces of a puzzle together.

Denver was scratching Bella's neck, where her matching red dog-magician's cape was tied. He looked defeated and lonely, and I honestly felt bad about what I'd said. Sure, he was a show-off and he thought he knew everything, but I shouldn't have wished he would disappear. At least not out loud.

"What about dog tricks?" I tried to make my voice sound as nice as Epic's would be. "Bella was a good part of your French Drop act, barking on cue like that. Can she do anything else?"

My siblings each shot me a surprised, grateful look. Like I'd done the right thing for once and made the family proud.

It was a strange, unfamiliar feeling.

And it was totally short-lived.

BANNED

"How was I supposed to know Bella had so many barking tricks?" I asked.

"Sure thing, Rondo," Epic said with absolute zero confidence.

"I bet you *asked* Bella to do that," Elvis said ridiculously, "in your *mind*. That was low."

It turned out that Denver's border collie, Bella, could do a ton of tricks. Really good ones. Sure, she could shake hands, roll over, and play dead, but she could also jump over Denver's outstretched arm, dance on her hind legs, and bark out the exact rhythm and cadence of "Happy Birthday" on cue. Elvis made her do it twice so she could sing along.

Asking about the dog tricks was the best thing I'd done all day. Within minutes, all four of us were laughing and cheering. And I'm not going to lie, when the first round of "Happy Birthday" started up, I knew all the noise wasn't going to earn us any points. I thought about shutting it down. For real. But then I didn't. Maybe *partly* because I knew what would happen if we kept it up. But mostly because Bella was a dog genius and my siblings weren't mad at me anymore.

Until they were again.

Elvis wasn't even all the way through her second rendition of the birthday song—her voice completely drowned out by Bella's—before Mom and Dad were flying out of the kitchen with warning looks on their faces.

And *they* hadn't even started to scold us before Raúl Flores himself entered the dining room and flung a long, skinny finger in Bella's direction.

"Whose collie?" he asked, eyes blazing.

Denver Delgado-Doyle raised his hand, and Raúl's finger immediately swiveled to point at him. We all held our breath as the word we knew was coming exploded into the air.

"BANNED!"

MONDAY

TRANSCRIPT: DAILY DOG DISH PODCAST
Monday Fit & Friendly Call-In Show

(Daily Dog Dish intro music.)

Del: Welcome back to the *Daily Dog Dish* with Del and Mel!
Say hello, Mel!

Mel: Hello, Mel.

(Sound effect of sad trombone: WAH-wah.)

Del: It's Monday morning, and you know what that
means . . .

Mel: Yay! Our Fit and Friendly Call-In Show!

Del: Brought to you by FETCHi, makers of Fit and Friendly
Protein Pops, designed to bring a pep to your step and a
wag to your tail. Our bulldog, Morrissey, loves the pumpkin
pops, doesn't he, Mel?

Mel: He sure does, Del! Pumpkin is a superfood for
dogs. It's low in calories, high in fiber, and a source of
beta-carotene, potassium, *and* vitamin C!

Del: Wow, folks! If *you* have a Fit and Friendly question for
Smarty-Pants Dubois, call 1-800-555-DISH, and Melissa
will tell you everything she knows.

Mel: We only have five minutes, Del.

Del: Okay, she'll tell you a tiny fraction of what she knows. Talk fast, everybody!

(Fit & Friendly Call-In jingle.)

Del: Caller #1 from San Luis Obispo, you're on the air!

Caller #1: Hi, my name is Damien. I've tried to switch my basset hounds to the healthier dog food you've recommended, but they won't eat it. Why not?

Mel: Damien, you have a problem with excessive soluble carbohydrates adding too much to your hounds' glycemic load.

Del: Come on, Mel. Say it so we understand it.

Mel: Sugar! Some of the most popular dog food brands are packed with sugar—or starches that turn *into* sugar. That stuff is addicting, and it tastes good, so it's hard to make a change. Try adding a bit of the healthy food to your old brand, and gradually cut out the sugary stuff. Soon, your basset beauties will love their new Fit and Friendly lifestyle!

Del: Great advice, Mel!

(Sound effect of a correct-answer bell.)

Del: Our second caller is from Culver City. Go ahead, caller!

Caller #2: Hi, I'm Brit. I have the cutest rescue dog, Shonda! I think she should be a famous pet star, but she's

shy. What if it's too much pressure? Should we go to a pet therapist? And how do I get her discovered?

Mel: First off, Shonda needs training, not therapy. With behavioral science, most dogs can learn canine acting skills: fetching, tricks, facial expressions—

Del: The ability to sit still under hot lights with stressed-out people and moving equipment all around?

Mel: Exactly! Del, Hollywood's *your* wheelhouse. Do you have advice for Brit?

Del: Get an agent! Never pay for an audition! For training, you've got two options: life-consuming hard work *or* . . . a legendary trainer like FiFi Khan or Raúl Flores. If you've got the cash, *that's* the fastest way to break into the biz.

Mel: Like Pico Boone!

Del: If Pico makes it as an actor, it'll be because his people shelled out serious dough for a top-notch trainer. Raúl Flores has a magic touch. Rumor has it that he will go to *unusual* lengths to make sure his pups are successful in their careers.

Mel: Money can't buy happiness, but it *can* buy a canine celebrity career?

Del: You said it, Mel!

Mel: But honestly, Brit? Just because Shonda's adorable doesn't mean she has to be in the spotlight. Think about if it's something you want more for *you* than for her.

Del: Wise words from a Fit and Friendly woman.

Mel: Look, Del! Our third caller is Anonymous from Carmelito—America's #1 Dog-Friendly Town! How can we help?

Caller #3: What should I do if my dog gets dognapped? Pay the ransom? Or call the police?

Del: I'd be so mad, I'd go *straight* to the police!

Mel: Would you, though? What if the thieves threatened your dog's safety if you didn't pay up?

Del: Eek, poor Morrissey! I'd pony up the dough. You know, Mel . . . Carmelito isn't a bad guess for where the celebrity dognappers might show up next. Think we should go on location and sniff around?

Mel: Maybe!

Caller #3: *(Coughs.)* No offense, but the last time you came to Carmelito, you caused a lot of trouble. Maybe you should stay home.

(Sound of a dial tone.)

(Silence.)

Del: Not fit. Not friendly.

Mel: Let's end on a happier note. We've got a great show lined up tomorrow. Del got us an extra-exclusive interview with Sharon Henderson and her recently rescued superstar pup, Newt. We'll get all our dognapping questions answered! Until then . . .

Mel and Del: Hug ALL the dogs!

(Daily Dog Dish outro music.*)*

BEACH DAY

My brother's alarm goes off at dawn every Monday. Next to his bed, he's got this giant mechanical monster that we call the Beast. He started building it when he was younger than Elvis, and he adds to it every time he thinks of an interesting component. Flashing eyes, a spinning tail, and most recently, a super-annoying surf song that—only on Mondays at 4:45 A.M.—blares out of a speaker hidden in the Beast's armpit.

"Epic!" Elvis complained from her bed in the bunk below me. "Turn it off! You *know* Mom and Dad aren't surfing today. The water's freezing."

I heard the soft *plop!* of something, probably a bear or a dog from her mountain of stuffed animals, that El must have thrown across the room at Epic's bed.

I turned over in the top bunk and pulled my pillow over my head.

Dawn Patrol is something we used to do every Monday— early morning surfing while the waves were good and almost no one else was awake. When I was younger, it was non-negotiable. Rain or shine, as long as conditions were safe. Mom and Dad said it was the best way to clear their heads and get centered for the week. I don't remember exactly when it stopped, but the busier the Perro got, the more tired everyone was, and gradually, it disappeared. We hadn't surfed Dawn Patrol in almost a full year, though every single Monday, Epic tried to rally everyone.

In fact, Mom and Dad were so busy with the Perro, they hardly surfed at all anymore. We weren't allowed to take our boards out without an adult, so unless Luis took us, or Epic's best friend, Declan, could convince his mom to go, we were pretty much stuck on land. Whenever Miyon visited, though, we went out every day. Her dad used to be a pro surfer, and Miyon was so good, she was practically a pro herself. The fact that her dad had decided to surf Malibu instead of Carmelito this week was so depressing, I'd almost be willing to get up at dawn.

I woke up the second time to the warm, wet smell of dog breath in my face. Pico's mini greyhound nails dug into my arm, and his rough tongue scraped my cheek. I jerked my head and tried to move out of the way, but Elvis was sitting on my legs.

"I hate it when you do this," I said, fending Pico off with my arms until Epic, who was standing on the bunk bed ladder, finally called him off.

"We wouldn't have to do anything to you if you'd wake up like a normal person," Elvis said. "I opened your eyelids with my fingers six times."

"Gross."

Both Epic and Elvis were already dressed, and El had her hair pulled up into two high pigtails with ribbons. Her "fancy day" hairdo. They didn't look happy.

"What time is it?" I groaned. "I don't want to help you walk Pico."

"I already walked him," Epic said. "But thanks to you, I had to beg, and they made me bring Mr. Boone's phone and stay on FaceTime with Mrs. Boone the entire walk."

"Why?"

"In case I did anything suspicious." Epic glared at me. Apparently, the Boones hadn't let go of the whole boy-making-Pico-nervous thing.

"*Did* you?" I asked, which was a mistake, because Epic sicced Pico on me again. I squirmed to get away from the dog breath, but Elvis has an iron grip.

"I was *planning* to watch Heaven Hsu get her hair and makeup done, but *you* got Denver banned from the movie set, and now Mom says *we* have to leave and take him to the beach." She shook her pigtails in a rage. "You should see what they did to Room 4. The whole thing is filled with lights and mirrors, and it looks like a beauty salon. It's a *beauty salon in our house*, Rondo, and I can't stay because of you. Did you know after Heaven's done, they're doing makeup for the dogs?"

"Fine." I threw my covers off. If there was one thing I did *not* want to do, it was watch dogs get their makeup done in Room 4. "Let's get out of here."

The Perro was already mobbed with people. The film crew was set up in the lobby taking "establishing shots." In the backyard, someone had backed up a small trailer where two guys were loading all of our chickens into crates.

"What are you doing with Dominique?" Elvis scowled at a man holding her favorite fluff-footed hen.

"Raúl says the hens are breaking Cheddar's concentration," the guy said. "We're moving them for a few days."

"Ra-*úl*." Elvis said his name in the kind of growly whisper you hear when a cartoon nemesis shakes their fist at the sky.

Around the other side of the house, crew members had set up lights and big white screens. All of Main Street had been blocked off from traffic, and tourists and people from town gathered around to watch as a movie set took shape around our house.

"Cool stuff, huh?" Luis waved at us. His cop car was parked diagonally in the middle of the street in front of Dogma Cafe. He and a policewoman were setting up more orange traffic cones around a bunch of trailers.

"I guess," I said. "If you like getting kicked out of your house all day."

"Jeez, I wonder who's fault *that* is," Elvis seethed.

Fair.

My siblings gave me the silent treatment the whole walk to the Moondoggie Inn. I tried not to care. Elvis went inside to get Denver, and Epic pretended to look at flyers on the window so he didn't have to talk to me. Fine. If he wanted to be mad at me for accidentally getting some kid we barely knew banned from the *Bentley Knows* film set (which was boring anyway), there wasn't anything *I* could do about it. He'd get over it.

I let my hair fall in front of my face and tried to focus on my book, but the way Epic was sighing, I couldn't concentrate.

"Are you okay?" I asked.

He crumpled a piece of paper and studied my face.

"What if Pico got dognapped?" he asked. "What would you do?"

"*That's* what you're worried about?" I laughed. My brother is so weird sometimes. "That little dude is *not* getting dognapped."

"Be serious, Rondo. I want to know what you would do."

"Brody gave us taco money!" El burst out of the inn with Denver and Bella, took one look at Epic's stressed-out face, and glared at me. "What'd you do to him?"

"*Nothing,*" I said, but I gave Epic's question a shot. "If Pico got dognapped, I'd start by figuring out who was around at the scene of the crime, then—"

El shook her head. "The Department of Lost Dogs would find him before Rondo. Guaranteed!"

"Are you kidding me?" I asked.

"Telepathy is *science*, Rondo. Quantum physics. I looked it up."

"*Where?* Bunk.com?"

"Forget it." Epic shoved the crumpled paper in his pocket and hurried to the crosswalk toward Carmelito Beach. His face was red, and he didn't even bother to say hi to Denver. Even *I* was polite enough to do that. Not that it won me any awards. Denver looked skeptical, like he was worried my friendly wave might be a trick.

"You don't have to talk to him, D-cubed," she said, pulling him across the street after Epic. "*We're* not."

"What did you call him?" I sped up my pace to stay close as we crossed over the parking lot for the beach.

"D^3," she said with a massive eye roll. "Like D to the third power? I'm not talking to you, remember?"

"You're talking to me right now," I said, even though I knew it was only going to make her madder.

"That was only to explain why I was calling Denver by his new nickname."

"You're talking to me *now*, too." I grinned.

We kicked off our sandals when we hit the beach, and El used one of hers to draw a long line in the sand.

"Stay on that side," she said to me. "We want to have fun today, don't we, D-cubed?"

Denver didn't look like he loved the new nickname. In fact, he seemed like he was second-guessing whether he wanted to hang out with us McDade kids after all. Epic was down at the edge of the water, walking all slow and looking broody. El and I were fighting like six-year-olds. If I was him, I'd rather hang out at the Moondoggie by myself. But Denver rallied, threw a Frisbee for Bella, and he and El chased after the collie without looking back.

I found a place on my side of El's sand line where I could lay down my towel and pretend my siblings and "D-cubed" didn't exist. At least the fog was burning off and the sun was starting to shine through. I'd brought two books to read and my *own* taco money.

I didn't need them.

They obviously didn't need me.

CANINE COACHING

"Pico tells me he feels fine—are you sure he's still not eating?"

Tara Skye adjusted her giant gold-rimmed glasses and typed something on her keyboard. Unlike her siblings, Tara always dressed up for a BarkAngel call. Her bubblegum-pink blazer matched the pink streaks in her virtual Milky Way background so perfectly that you had to wonder if she'd planned it.

"He's not eating anything *we're* giving him," Mrs. Boone said. "His dog bowl has been full for two days!"

"Is he mad at us, do you think?" Mr. Boone said. "Raúl says we can't give Pico *any* treats or he won't be motivated during filming. No treats! Don't you think that seems—"

"Controlling," Mrs. Boone said. "The man's on a power trip. He won't let us be on set. It's criminal. We need to be close! What if Pico's the next celebrity dognap—" She shot a guilty look in Pico's direction and slowly whispered, "*V-i-c-t-i-m!*"

"Let's pause." Tara put her hands in a prayer position. "There's a lot to unpack there."

She breathed deeply and waited for the Boones to do the same. While they were exhaling, Tara grinned like she'd heard something adorable.

"Awww," the BarkAngel said. "Pico told me he likes it when Mom wears her 'fancy hair.' That's a sweet doggo you've got there."

It was Tara Skye's go-to move: Distract and Change the Subject. I didn't even have to write it in my notebook. I flipped to the Diversion Tactics page and put another check next to *Tara talks about Mrs. Boone's hair.*

Of all the Skye siblings, Tara was the worst at "communicating" with Pico, but her distractions always worked. Already, Mrs. Boone's worried pucker had turned into a smile, and Mr. Boone patted Pico proudly.

"That's so nice, Pico," Mr. Boone said, relaxing a little. "She does look pretty today, doesn't she?"

Mrs. Boone's dark, silver-tinged hair was piled up into a pouf tied with a glittery red hair ribbon that matched Mr. Boone's glittery red bow tie and Pico's thousand-dollar LuxLux Luxury Sparkle Suit. They were dressed like they were ready for the Oscars, not the *Bentley Knows* kickoff party at Yappy Hour.

The Boones never missed the Perro's weekly Yappy Hour, and they never minded if I hid out in front of their television while it was happening. Nothing against Yappy Hour. Dad makes good snacks, and it's sometimes entertaining to watch dressed-up dogs and guests wander around the backyard for an hour. But you have to be in the mood, and it's more fun when Epic and El people watch with you. Since they were still cold-shouldering me, I'd come straight to Room 1 after the beach. Mrs. Boone had eyed my damp shorts and set a towel down on the carpet. Far enough away so I wouldn't get sand on her fancy shoes while I watched the BarkAngel call.

"Why don't we move on to Pico's emotional forecast?" Tara said. "I see lots of areas of energetic intensity coming up this week."

I was pretty sure the "emotional forecast" was a thing Tara did to kill time. Every Monday, she went over the Boones' plans for the week ahead and pointed out times when Pico might feel tired, anxious, overstimulated, hot or cold, and then gave the Iggy "tools" he could use in each of those moments to calm, cool, or energize himself. Mostly the "tools" were ripped-off versions of Mandee's advice: yawn, lick your lips, blink your eyes. But if the Boones noticed the recycled, nonpsychic material, they didn't seem to care. They were happy that someone was looking out for Pico and helping him prepare for the week.

Tara had barely started forecasts for Monday and Tuesday before Mandee Skye appeared on the screen. Mrs. Boone was in the middle of reading from Pico's film schedule, and I was so bored I was drawing mazes in my notebook.

"Tomorrow night we're filming the roof scene," Mrs. Boone said. "Pico needs to be on set at . . . Oh! Hi, Mandee!"

Tara kept right on going like she didn't notice her sister on the screen. "Will the Saint Bernard be in that scene?"

"No, Bentley doesn't arrive until Wednesday."

Tara made a note. "Pico might feel unsafe around a dog that big, so I think we should map out every time Sir Bentley—"

"I read the script!" Mandee jumped in, too excited to wait any longer. "Sorry, Tara, but this is huge. I think you're right, Nicole—the roof stunt is his Pawscar moment!"

Mr. Boone shook his head. "Raúl gave Cheddar that stunt. All Pico has to do is stand at the window and walk onto the roof for a couple close-ups."

"He gives Cheddar all the glory!" Mrs. Boone complained.

Mandee shook her head. "The stunts aren't what I'm talking about. Pico's the star because he's got the *emotional* range. Can I take over the rest of your time, Tara? Please? I love this script!"

"Do I have a choice?" Tara laughed, but she also looked like she wanted to stick her tongue out at her sister, Elvis-style. "Mandee's on a campaign to turn the BarkAngels into a canine acting agency," she said to the Boones. "Watch out, Pico, she's got ambitions! She's going to make you famous!"

This made the Boones extra happy, but Mandee sucked in her breath and tilted her head at the Iggy. "Oh! I don't mean we *expect* awards, Pico. All we want is for you to feel confident and do your best." She paused, then plowed forward. "And I think if we focus on page forty-nine . . ."

Tara disappeared from the screen, and I reached over and grabbed the highlighted copy of the script off the Boones' coffee table. I'd read it already, but I flipped to the roof scene. The original *Bentley Knows* series is about a crime-solving Saint Bernard named Bentley, who does heroic things like saving babies from burning buildings. To me, the reboot looked like more of the same. In the first episode, Bentley's partner, Lulu, played by Heaven Hsu, recruits a promising young Italian greyhound sleuth to be Bentley's sidekick after she sees the Iggy jump off a roof in the middle of the night to save a little boy's life. Based on the script, it was going to be a pretty exciting episode.

"Pico, honey, I want you to imagine yourself on that roof, okay?" Mandee pushed her hair behind her ears and leaned forward to make sure Pico was paying close attention. "When you're up there, it's going to be very high and probably scary. That's okay, because we're going to *use* that fear to create a good performance, aren't we?"

Pico scratched his ear with his front paw in a convincing display of hearing her but not quite getting it. Mandee plowed forward, her cheeks pink. No offense to her sister, Tara, but this was way more interesting than an emotional forecast.

"Here's what I want you to do, Pico. Go ahead and be scared at first. Embrace that. But then, I want you to set your jaw. You know that feeling when you clamp your teeth right down on a bone?"

Since I was sitting next to a box of Pico's chew toys, I figured I might as well be useful and see where the BarkAngel was going with this. I handed Pico a piece of rawhide. Not a bone, but close enough, and he immediately clamped his teeth down on it. Mandee shot me a surprised smile.

"Was that Rando? That was . . . super helpful. Thanks!" I was surprised she remembered my name. Sort of. "Like *that*, Pico," she said. "Remember that feeling, nice and strong. Then, when you hop out onto the roof, it says here that your trainer is going to ask you to lift your head to the sky."

I stood up, took the rawhide out of Pico's mouth, and held it above his head. He lifted his nose and sniffed at it.

"Yes!" Mandee beamed. "Exactly!"

According to the script, this was the moment where Pico was supposed to look up at the star that he and the kidnapped boy had wished on, hold for a beat, and then leap heroically off the roof to save his friend. Which Cheddar was going to do.

Actually, Cheddar was going to walk along the edge of the roof, jump about a foot onto a piece of foam, then take a small leap onto some special scaffolding and land on a larger block of safety foam. The "bad guy," who was secretly covered in padding, would catch her on her next jump but look like he was fighting her. Dad said they rehearsed it a thousand times while we were banned at the beach, and if Elvis could actually shoot daggers with her eyes, she would have murdered me for sure.

"When you look up at the sky, Pico, I want you to think of your octopus, Octo," Mandee coached. "The one we talked about yesterday. Remember how you felt when Octo was left behind?"

At the word *Octo*, Pico's whole body went tense and alert. He whined a little, wagging his tail.

"See that?" Mandee clapped her hands, satisfied. "Now imagine it's dark, and the stars are shining. He'll look so determined and heroic, won't he?"

We were all grinning now. I got so caught up that I forgot to write any of it down. Mrs. Boone got so caught up that she didn't even care that I got sand on the carpet, dangerously close to her red shoes.

Mr. Boone couldn't stop talking in exclamations. "That was fabulous! You're a natural! You should come visit the set!"

"Are you serious?" Mandee asked. "Do you think I could meet Raúl Flores?"

Mrs. Boone shrugged. "Why not?"

Mandee ran through the whole roof scene three more times, telling Pico to visualize himself at his various "marks," feel the emotions, and let himself shake, clamp his jaw, and look heroically up to the sky.

It was kind of fun. The Boones had forgotten their worries about Pico's career and their frustration with Raúl shutting them out. Maybe I could understand why people liked working with the BarkAngels. I bet it felt good having a team of people helping out your pup. Their tricks were fun to watch. Some of them *did* seem amazing.

Which reminded me. That was the thing. They were tricks. As nice as the BarkAngels were, and as good as they made the Boones feel, they were still charging money for a lie. At two hundred fifty dollars an hour, I calculated that it was costing ten dollars every time Mandee repeated the scene. I switched back to investigation mode.

"What were you going to do?" I asked. Mandee, Pico, and the Boones looked surprised that I'd interrupted their flow. "Yesterday. If Pico really was stolen, how were you going to find him?"

I'd been thinking about Epic's question. The logical answer? Call the local police, animal shelters, and interview all the Perro guests, neighbors, and tourists to gather clues and information. For a start.

The BarkAngels had a different approach.

"We'd connect telepathically and ask Pico to show us clues about his surroundings and the people near him," Mandee said. "Sometimes that doesn't give us enough information, but luckily, Leif is skilled at dowsing. That's a method for—"

"I know what it is," I said. Back in Houdini's day, mediums would swing a crystal pendulum over a map until the tip mysteriously hovered over the correct location of something or someone they were looking for. "How much does it cost?"

"*Rondo*," Mrs. Boone scolded. "That's rude!"

Mandee looked legitimately sad about the question. Like I'd hurt her feelings. "Lost dog location is a free service for our clients. We wouldn't charge for something like that," she said. "Don't you think that would be wrong? To capitalize on someone else's suffering?"

"Oh. Yeah." I didn't know what else to say. It wasn't the response I'd expected.

I was saved from the awkward silence by a knock on the door. I hopped up to answer it. Which I immediately regretted.

"Mom says you have to get ready for Yappy Hour." Elvis pushed past me and waltzed into the suite in a brand-new bright red dress. I wondered if she'd gotten it specifically to match the Sparkle Suit.

"Go away," I said. "I'm not coming."

"You have to," she said. "I told Mom and Dad you'll do your pet psychic thing for the whole crowd. Raúl's interested to see it."

"Why would you do *that*?"

Elvis shot me one of her widest smiles. The kind she uses when everything is going exactly according to her plans.

"Punishment," she said.

REVENGE-ELVIS

Elvis knelt down next to the couch so she could smother Pico with affection. He tried to wiggle away from her intense kisses, but that was a battle the Iggy was not going to win.

"Was that the BarkAngels?" El asked as the Boones closed their laptop. "I'd ask Rondo, but he thinks he's soooooo smart and secretive. Did they say anything new about Epic? He's been soooooo bossy lately. Hasn't he, Rondo? See? He won't even answer *that*!"

I didn't respond for two reasons.

One: The answer was obvious. Epic *had* been extra crabby. He'd practically sprinted ahead of us after we'd dropped Denver off at the Moondoggie Inn, and by the time we caught up to him at the Perro, he pretended to be too deep in conversation with Luis and his police buddies to even notice we existed.

Two: Epic had shown up at Room 1 ten seconds after my sister. Neither El nor the Boones seemed to notice him in the doorway, scowling like a bossy crab. Before I could warn her, Elvis made it worse.

"Don't you think Mandee was talking about Epic?" Elvis asked Mrs. Boone. "The boy who's not who he seems? He's *bothering* Pico, isn't he?"

"*Elvis*." I jutted my chin in Epic's direction. But El's mouth curved into an evil grin. She knew perfectly well our brother was standing right behind her. Weirdly, he didn't look mad, he looked nervous. I didn't blame him. Elvis had gone to the trouble to get Mom and Dad on board with her Yappy Hour punishment plan, and now she was throwing Epic under the bus with the Boones. Somehow we'd unleashed Revenge-Elvis. And she is not a person you want to mess with.

"Why doesn't *Rondo* ask Pico about the boy?" She fluffed Pico's short fur the wrong way and turned to Mr. Boone. "Rondo can talk to animals like the BarkAngels do, and he's going to show everyone his *ah*-mazing skills at Yappy Hour tonight. Un-*less* . . ."

El formed her mouth into a wide O like an *ah*-mazing idea had popped into her brain.

"What do you want, El?" I knew what this was. Blackmail. My sister is an evil genius.

"If you showed us your skills now and *taught* me a little—and I mean something real, not an easy thing anyone could do—I could convince Mom and Dad not to make you do it at Yappy Hour. In front of *all* those people."

I glared at her. The Boones looked intrigued.

"I heard he communicated with Heaven Hsu's schnauzer," Mrs. Boone said. "You know, Rondo, you might have a gift worth exploring."

"If you're good at it, you could make a lot of money," Mr. Boone said. "It's a lucrative career."

Epic stepped closer to Pico and Mrs. Boone immediately scooped up the Iggy, studying him for signs of distress. Mr. Boone examined my brother. Who fidgeted and shot a guilty look at the dog.

"I only came over to see if Pico's okay," he mumbled. "I'm not bothering him . . . I don't *think*."

Even *Epic* was worried that he was responsible for making his pal jumpy. All because a dog psychic made up some random story about "the boy." It was ridiculous.

"Why don't you try, Rondo?" Mrs. Boone asked. "It wouldn't hurt to know the truth."

I looked at my notebook and thought about all the money the BarkAngels had basically stolen from the Boones. I'd gathered plenty of evidence, and Mrs. Boone was right, a dose of the truth would be good for everyone. It would get Epic off the hook for his bizarre rap as "the boy," it would get me out of performing at Yappy Hour, it would help the Boones not get fleeced, and it might even snap Elvis out of . . . whatever was going on with her. I felt a burst of confidence. I could do this. I could fix it all in one fell swoop.

"Okay, El," I said. "It's a deal. I'll show you how it's done."

My sister flopped down on the floor, pulling Epic along with her. They both eyed me as I pretended to flip through my notebook. Really, I was taking an inventory of the Boones' messy suite. They'd been so busy dressing up for Yappy Hour, they hadn't even cleaned up from breakfast. There was an omelet pan still on the stove, completely coated in leftover eggs and bits of bacon. It was gross.

"I'm not actually going to talk to the dog," I explained. "I'm not tapping into any energy fields. I'm going to prove that I can do exactly what the BarkAngels do. It's a trick."

I shoved the notebook back in my pocket and sat up on my knees in front of Pico and the Boones. I put my hands together in a prayer, closed my eyes, and took three deep breaths. Then I blinked three slow-motion blinks and locked eyes with the dog.

As much as I hated to make it cheesy, I knew my sister and the Boones weren't going to believe me about the BarkAngels unless my performance was as close to theirs as possible. Each of the animal communicators had some kind of starting ritual to make it look like they were creating a telepathic connection. Houdini used to say that showmanship was more important than the trick itself. If you make it *look* good, people will believe it.

"Hey, Pico." I changed my voice to sound more like a BarkAngel. Low-key and super friendly. "How's it going, buddy?"

The calm voice was doing *something*. Or maybe it was only

that Pico wasn't used to me paying so much attention to him. He sat on Mr. Boone's lap, stared at me like I had three heads, and sniffed.

"Is he talking to you?" Elvis asked seriously enough that Epic groaned.

"Shhhh!" Mrs. Boone leaned forward. I pretended to be so in-the-zone that I didn't notice them.

"Oh, really? That's a bummer," I said to the dog.

"What? What's a bummer?" Mrs. Boone asked.

Mr. Boone was eating it up, too. I was a little disappointed that it was so easy. I wasn't even trying very hard.

"He says he wanted something but someone wouldn't give it to him, and it hurt his feelings. I'm seeing an image of a stove . . . and a hand . . . with a spoon? Or a spatula? Do you know what he's talking about?"

A guilty look flashed over Mr. Boone's face. Mrs. Boone shoved his arm.

"What did he want? When?" she asked. "Why didn't you give it to him?"

"It's hard to tell about the timing . . . ," I said, drawing it out. "Because dogs only talk in pictures, right? But I'm getting a breakfast vibe?"

Mr. Boone nodded. "That's right. I put bacon in the omelet today, and he begged for it. Did it honestly hurt his feelings? I could tell he was upset, but Raúl won't allow it. It's too fatty, Pico!"

"Did you hear that, buddy?" I asked, all slow and relaxed.

"It's not part of your performance plan. You wanna stay alert for the show, right?" To the Boones, I added in my normal voice, "You probably shouldn't eat bacon in front of him if he can't have it. It's rude."

"Rondo." Epic frowned at me. "You're not helping."

He was right. I was getting offtrack. There were so many ways you could go with the whole animal communicator thing, it was hard not to get carried away. I rejected ten different telepathy ideas and tried to focus on the task at hand: clearing my brother's name and proving that the BarkAngels were frauds.

My plan was to give the Boones a couple convincing examples of me "reading" Pico's mind, and then explain how I did it. I'd seen the bacon in the omelet pan, and since every dog on the planet wants to eat bacon? No-brainer.

I needed one more example to prove the bacon wasn't a fluke, and then . . . the big reveal! I was going to save the Boones so much money on BarkAngel sessions, they would probably buy me my own TV out of gratitude. Or at least a couple donuts from Dogma Cafe.

"Ask him about the boy, like Elvis said." Mrs. Boone scooted up in her seat a little. "Ask him if it's Epic. Then we'll know."

"Don't do that," my brother said. He looked pained.

"I've got this," I told him.

I closed my eyes again, did the breathing thing, and blinked at Pico.

"Buddy, we want to know about this boy who was bumming you out. Is that still bugging you?"

Pico shivered a little, which was nothing new. It happened all the time. He was tiny, and he barely had any hair. I'd be cold, too. But the Boones and Elvis gasped like the shiver was a sign.

"He says the boy is hiding something," I said. Which was a rip-off of what Mandee Skye had said yesterday, but nobody seemed to notice that was an obvious red flag.

"That's what Mandee said!" Mrs. Boone squealed. "He 'isn't who he seems.' What else?"

"He says the answer is inside . . . I'm seeing something made of cloth . . . with a long strap . . . I think it's . . . a bag?"

Everyone's head swiveled toward Epic, his messenger bag slung over his shoulder. His eyes got wide in a what-are-you-doing-to-me-bro kind of way. I grinned. Epic always had his messenger bag, and it was always packed with stuff. Electronics, notebooks, components he was building. I didn't know what all was in there, but it didn't matter.

Out of the dozens of things in Epic's bag, the Boones would find some way for Pico's message to make sense, and then I could show them I *hadn't* talked to the dog. I'd led them in a direction and let them draw their own conclusions from a bunch of random junk my brother was lugging around. Once they understood the techniques, they'd see the BarkAngels weren't mind readers any more than I was.

"Okay if we take a look?" Mr. Boone looked apologetic and a little embarrassed. Like even though he totally believed my brother was a fraud who was freaking out his dog, he was still kind of sorry about it.

Mrs. Boone had barely opened the bag when she yelped, startling Pico, who yelped, too, and shrunk closer to Mr. Boone's chest.

"Why do you have our Peek-a-Boo-Peek-at-You?" Mrs. Boone demanded.

Elvis gaped at Epic. It was obvious that, unlike Mr. Boone, she'd never thought Epic was hiding anything. She'd only wanted to put us both in the hot seat. For whatever revenge she was trying to extract. Mission accomplished.

It didn't make sense to me, either, and the last thing I wanted to do was make the situation worse, but the words were out of my mouth before I could stop them.

"You *stole* their pet camera?"

PEEK-a-BOO

"It, um, wasn't working," Epic said, his eyes suddenly fixed on his fingernails.

Mr. Boone took the Peek-a-Boo and put it back on the shelf where it usually sat, aimed at the living room. It's not like the Boones left Pico alone much, so the pet cam was sort of a waste of space, but it was weird that Epic had taken it without asking. My brother has an overdeveloped sense of responsibility. He always does the right thing. It's one of his most annoying superpowers.

We all waited for him to explain.

"I just, I think it's the wiring on the, maybe, on the battery pack. I didn't mean to *steal* it, I was going to, you know, fix it. And. Put it back."

It was a logical excuse, because Epic loves to tinker and he's always fixing things around the house, but we all knew it wasn't true. In addition to being a rule follower, my brother is a terrible liar.

Mr. Boone looked like he *wanted* to believe Epic, but he

pressed the power button on the Peek-a-Boo anyway. The green RECORD light turned right on.

"Seems to be okay now," Mr. Boone said.

Mrs. Boone wasn't having any of it. "Rondo, you were right. Pico jumped the minute I touched the Peek-a-Boo! It *has* to be what he was telling you about. The clue in the bag! Epic *was* hiding something!"

"I wasn't hiding—"

Mrs. Boone held up her hand to shush my brother. "*The boy is not who he seems*," she said, supposedly quoting Pico. "I'll say! He *seems* like such a responsible young man, but clearly not! Epic, what's going on? Is this teenage boy stuff? You know . . ." She lowered her voice to a whisper. "*Hormones?*"

My brother froze and his face got so red it was almost purple.

This was getting out of hand. Whatever was going on with Epic, he looked miserable, and it didn't matter how bossy or crabby he'd been. It was time to end it.

"It's *not* what Pico was telling me about," I said. "Pico wasn't telling me anything. The BarkAngels aren't psychic. They're not talking to dogs, and neither was I."

"Rondo," Mr. Boone said quietly. "You don't have to cover for your brother. I'm sure there's a reasonable explanation."

"I'm not!" I said. "There *is* a reasonable explanation. That's my whole point."

But Mrs. Boone was looking at me funny. Everyone was.

"Can you talk to all animals? Or just Pico?" Elvis looked proud and like I'd stabbed her in the heart at the same time.

"I can't talk to animals, El."

"He's messing with us," my brother grumbled. "As usual."

It felt like a low blow. I'd been trying to help him. And it had been working. It had all been going in the right direction. How was I supposed to know he was hiding a guest's pet camera in his messenger bag? It's not like I was a mind reader. In fact, that was the point I was trying to prove.

"I've seen him studying those BarkAngels," Mr. Boone said, talking about me like I wasn't in the room. "Writing things down. He's a smart cookie."

"Smart?" Mrs. Boone shook her head. "The boy has a *gift*."

"I was only using the same techniques that Houdini and the mediums . . ."

But I stopped explaining when I noticed Epic's dagger-eyes.

"I'm going to go help Dad with Yappy Hour pupsicles," he said. "Come on, El."

"In a minute," Elvis said. "Rondo has to teach me how to talk to Pico. He promised."

How many times did I have to say it? "I'll teach you how to *fake* it, but I can't teach you how to do it. I. Can't. Talk. To. Dogs."

Elvis made a growling noise in the back of her throat and scooted next to Epic. "Fine, the deal's off," she said. "Have fun performing at Yappy Hour. I heard there are going to be *lots* of people there tonight. Lots and lots and *lots* of people. All. Watching. You."

Elvis picked up my brother's messenger bag from the floor at Mrs. Boone's feet. My brother had been staring at it, too nervous to ask for it back.

"Let's go!" El shoved the bag at Epic, a little too aggressively, because several batteries and a few small barrel-shaped nuggets fell out. Pico lunged for them, but Mr. Boone held him tight.

He furrowed his bushy eyebrows in Epic's direction. He looked even more worried than he had when they'd found the Peek-a-Boo. "Where did you get those treats? You're not . . . feeding them to Pico, are you?"

"Of course not!" Epic said. "I took them from . . . I was *trying* to . . ." He sighed. "Never mind."

Elvis picked up a nugget, licked it, then pretended to gag, but her comedy routine didn't get the reaction she was looking for. Mrs. Boone was practically hyperventilating.

"I think we'd better take a break," Mr. Boone said. "We need to get ready for the party. We'll talk about this later, Epic. Thank you, Rondo. This was very enlightening."

"Yeah," my brother said under his breath. He bumped me with his shoulder as he moved toward the door. "Thanks a lot."

YAPPY HOUR

I found Mom and Elvis in the kitchen slicing strawberries for Dad's signature Yappy Hour margaritas.

"Wow, look at you!" Mom smiled. "You look nice."

I tried to smile back, but I'm pretty sure it came out as a grimace. I'd washed off all the beach sand, put on a pair of shorts without holes, and even combed my hair, which was a real project. Not because I wanted to. It was a bargaining chip.

"I *really* don't want to perform tonight," I said. "Seriously. Please don't make me put on a show."

"Oh, honey. Why would I do that?" Mom set down her knife and gave me a concerned look.

I glared at my sister. "I don't know. Elvis, why *would* she do that?" I didn't know whether to feel relieved or angry, but El was laser-focused on her strawberries. She kept her head down, carefully slicing off the tops like she was performing brain surgery.

"This week is going to be hard enough to get through."

Mom lifted a strawberry-stained hand and pushed her bangs out of her eyes with the back of her wrist. She looked exhausted. "Find a quiet spot and read your book. When Denver gets here, I'll send him to find you. Maybe later we'll do something fun."

Elvis perked up. "Can we play board games?" she asked. "Family Night?"

"We haven't done that in a *while*, have we?" Mom looked kind of stunned, like she'd forgotten Family Night was a thing. We used to put a TUCKED IN FOR THE NIGHT sign on the kitchen door so no one would bother us, and then we'd make dessert and listen to records. Elvis always beat the pants off me at Trivial Pursuit, and I didn't even mind because it was fun.

"Can we?" I asked.

"Not tonight." Dad pushed through the swinging door carrying a tray full of empty glasses. "We promised the Boones we'd move the furniture around in Room 2 so they can do glamor shots for Pico's feed. They want that dog bed you made out of the vintage TV. Is that in storage?"

Mom let out an actual whimper. "That's tonight? Do we have to?"

"Yep. Nicole says this week is 'pivotal' for Pico's 'brand elevation.'"

Mom pouted. "The Moondoggie still has a few rooms available. Can't they elevate his brand over there? Or . . ." She rubbed her forehead. "What would it take to move the whole film crew? Blackmail? We could threaten to sell Raúl's recipe on the black market. Now, *there's* a million-dollar idea!"

"Ha. Ha. We don't want to get in the way of doggo success, do we?" Dad gave Mom a kiss on the cheek and turned to me. "Whoa, Rondo, you look sharp. What's going on? I thought for sure you'd stay upstairs for this one."

I stared down my sister, but she was the Michelangelo of strawberry cutting.

"Hey, as long as you're here, I could use an extra hand with the Pooch Platters," Dad said. "You don't have to talk to anybody, just walk around and give people food to stuff in their faces. It'll be fun."

"Only until Denver comes." Mom said it like she was doing me a favor. "Then you're off duty and you can do . . . whatever you two peas in a pod like to do."

I let the "peas in a pod" comment pass, but bored my eyes into my sister's skull as I picked up a Pooch Platter. She'd straight-up lied about talking to Mom, Dad, and Raúl. They weren't expecting me to do the pet psychic thing. No one was.

Dad had lied, too. Walking around our backyard with the Pooch Platter was not "fun." But it was better than being on the spot doing magic tricks or fake telepathy for the entire cast and crew of a national television show plus all Mom and Dad's friends and half the business owners from town. I kept my head down and avoided eye contact while the Chew

Toys—Dad's latest bone-shaped meat-and-cheese snack invention—disappeared from the platter in my hands.

Most people didn't even notice me. They were so caught up in their boring conversations that the Pooch Platter could have been delivered by a Chihuahua in a glowing hovercraft and they would have reached over, piled more Chew Toys onto their napkins, and kept talking. In a way, the Pooch Platter served as a cloak of invisibility, which I liked.

"I'm surprised Pico hasn't been nabbed yet." Mrs. Boone, as usual, was talking about the dognappings to anyone who would listen. In this case, it was Doug from Dogma Cafe and two youngish *Bentley Knows* crew members. "I mean, of course we're taking every precaution. You can't be too careful. I'm sure it's only a matter of time."

"Aren't those dognappings über-high-profile dogs, though?" one of the crew members asked as she chose a Chew Toy from the platter. "They're all world-famous, right? Pico's . . . not." If she hadn't been so busy weighing her cheese options, she would have seen the look of horror on Mrs. Boone's face.

"Pico's a *top* canine influencer," Mrs. Boone said. "He's getting more popular every day!"

"Don't worry," Doug said. "All Pico needs is one big media boost, and he'll blow up. International."

"That's *exactly* what we're working on!" Mrs. Boone relaxed and grabbed a Chew Toy of her own.

"His acting coach is incredible," Mr. Boone said, trying to

change the subject. "Talk about talented! Pricey, no doubt, but worth every *single* penny!"

I looked around for another hungry group of chatters and caught Raúl Flores eavesdropping with a satisfied smile on his face. His sunglasses and cap were nowhere in sight. He took a few steps closer, using the Pooch Platter in my hand as an excuse to listen to Mrs. Boone brag about him. Raúl combed his perfect mustache with his fingers and fake-gazed at the Chew Toys.

"The emotion Pico can show—that he *never* could have before!" Mrs. Boone said. "We owe it all to the dedication of our amazing . . ."

Raúl picked up a pecorino-prosciutto Chew Toy but then let it drop back on the platter as Mrs. Boone finished her sentence.

"BarkAngel."

I swallowed a laugh. It wasn't at all funny to see Raúl look disappointed or to watch the way he sighed and shuffled off toward the tiki bar, but it was *so* Mrs. Boone. Here was a guy who'd been working with Pico for more than a year, training and teaching that nervous, wiggly dog how to be calm and do tricks in front of a camera, and she was giving all the credit to a woman who meditated with him over the computer. That had to hurt.

When the final five Chew Toys left on the Pooch Platter happened to be cheddar-salami, which is my favorite, I decided to take that as a sign or, really, a random statistical coincidence that it was time to take a break. I'd already stashed my book in one of my favorite Yappy Hour reading spots—the tree stump that butts up against the far side of the chicken coop. It's a good place to go because you can lean against the wall of the coop, and the angle is set just right so you're mostly hidden, but you still have a view of the backyard if you want to watch the crowd and take notes on people's strange behavior.

Except when I rounded the corner of the coop, someone in a black hoodie was already sitting on the tree stump. In my spot. Reading my book.

The spot stealer looked up, pushed the hood back, and gave a nod to the dog digging furiously at the ground next to the stump.

"Look, Roo. Snacks!"

Roo stopped digging, sniffed the air, and bared his tiny teeth at me. His bushy, old-man eyebrows furrowed in a scowl. Heaven Hsu didn't exactly smile, but she held up *A Magician Among the Spirits* and looked mildly amused.

"Your book?" Heaven asked.

I nodded. The schnauzer took an aggressive step forward and chomped his teeth in my direction. They looked sharp and mean, like mini daggers.

"In case you didn't already read his mind," she said, "Roo really wants you to share those."

ROO

I only got one of the cheddar-salami Chew Toys because Heaven Hsu ate the other four.

"Roo can't have cheese," she said, fishing a pig ear out of her messenger bag. The second it hit the ground, the mini schnauzer attacked it with a serious vengeance.

"Is he always so intense?" I asked.

"Relentless," she said. "Schnauzers were bred to kill. Rodents, not humans. But don't worry, he likes you. Sit."

I sat down awkwardly, trying to find a spot close enough not to be rude, but far enough away that I'd be safe if Roo decided to mistake my foot for the pig ear he was ravaging. I couldn't help thinking it was lucky the film crew had whisked away our chickens.

"You have to do this every week?" Heaven asked, nodding toward all the people and dogs mingling in the backyard.

I shrugged. "It's not always this crowded. And I usually skip it."

"Smart kid."

We watched the Boones set up a photo op of Pico eating out of one of the jars from the doggo swag in Room 2. The rhinestones on Pico's LuxLux Luxury Sparkle Suit glittered in the sun, and his ears were perked up, the red hat balanced perfectly between them. He licked at the jar so intensely that he kept knocking it out of the shot. So much for their worries about Pico's appetite.

"That's canine caviar," I said. "They're doing a product placement."

"Of *course* they are." Heaven Hsu wrinkled her nose, then pulled her hood down closer over her forehead and thumbed through my Houdini book. She must have been out here a while, because she'd already read half of it. Roo rolled over on his side to get a better chewing angle on the pig ear. More like kill angle. He let out a low growl, and I scooted another inch away.

"Don't *you* need to go . . . I don't know, do selfies and stuff?" I asked. I kind of wanted my book back.

Heaven shrugged. "They don't care what I do."

"You're the star of the show."

"Sir Bentley's the star." She didn't say it like it bothered her. More like it was a fact. "And I guess *that* guy now?" She nodded toward Pico and his rhinestones. "*If* we make it."

"Make what?"

"The show."

"I think . . . that's already happening?"

Heaven shrugged. "We'll see. I don't think the studio's

very invested. Look at the small crew they sent up here. And barely any equipment."

Our backyard was filled with *Bentley Knows* people and gear. Crates with the studio logo were stacked up all along the fence. How much stuff did they *usually* use?

"We've only got one crane and one generator that looks like it came from the 1990s." She said it like a massive *crane* in the front yard was nothing. "I think they already know the whole thing's going to be a train wreck and get canceled."

"Could that happen?"

"Sure. If the execs don't like the first episode. Or we do something awful like get a bad American Humane violation. I could get sick or go missing . . . well," Heaven tilted her head, reconsidering. "Someone *actually* important would have to be taken out. They'd keep going without me, I'm sure. But yeah, shows get shut down all the time. Not every-one would be sad, either."

She winked and went back to reading my book. Roo gnashed away at his treat, and my gaze drifted over to my sister chumming it up with the *Bentley Knows* showrunner. Even at a distance, I could see her pouring on the charm. I bet she thought if she was adorable enough, they'd give her a part in the show.

Elvis was doing her usual head-tilting, curl-twisting, and eyelash-batting moves, but her smile wasn't right. She looked tired. Sad, even. Which didn't make sense because Yappy Hour is El's favorite time of the week. Make it a Yappy

Hour full of filmmakers and movie stars? It was pretty much her idea of paradise.

I glanced back at Heaven. "Do you ever get sick of acting?"

I'd been curious about it since she'd checked in to the Perro del Mar. On TV, she was so good, you assumed acting was her dream or something, but in real life it didn't seem like she wanted any part of it.

Heaven put her thumb on the spot she was reading and looked up from the page.

"Never had a choice. I mean. Obviously." The blank look on my face made her add, "My contract? My family? My sister?"

I shook my head. "Who's your sister?"

Heaven raised her eyebrows at me like she thought maybe I was joking. Spoiler alert: I wasn't.

"Kendra?" And when I still didn't respond, "Kendra Kwong?"

"Seriously?"

Kendra Kwong is one of the biggest movie stars on the planet. I swear, if you scroll through superhero movies on the Boones' TV, practically every other one would have Kendra Kwong's face on the promo. She didn't look that much like Heaven, though. Or at least she was a lot more glamorous.

"You have different last names," I said. Which felt like an overly obvious thing to say. Lots of people have different last names from their siblings. But Heaven shook her head.

"Only in Hollywood."

Again, I had no clue what she was talking about. This whole conversation was El's specialty, not mine.

"You honestly think my real name is *Heaven*?" She stuck her tongue out like even saying the name made her gag. "Some marketing executive named me Heaven Hsu when I was little. Said it sounded 'more exotic' than my actual name."

"Gross."

"Yep. Still can't believe my parents agreed to that. They said I'd need all the help I could get to catch up to Kendra. Nice, right?"

"What's your real name, then?"

"I'm contractually obligated not to tell you."

"Very funny." I rolled my eyes.

"No, for real. And I'm stuck in that contract. The whole thing is a load of garbage."

Her gaze shifted back to Pico. Raúl had caught wind of the photo shoot and was racing over to confiscate the caviar while Mrs. Boone followed behind him, talking and waving her hands. I couldn't hear what they were saying, but I was pretty sure I knew what they were arguing about. Raúl was upset about Pico getting contraband snacks, and Mrs. Boone only cared about boosting Pico's subscriber numbers.

"That guy cares a *lot* about the show," I said.

Heaven sniffed. "Doubtful. Everyone in Hollywood's got an ulterior motive."

That was interesting. "Like what?"

"Who knows. You need the cash because some deal went wrong. You want your nephew to get hired. The studio promises if you do this one job, they'll give you something next-level." Heaven nodded toward Mrs. Boone. "Whatever it is, it must be huge, because she's his worst nightmare. You can't have *two* divas on a project."

Heaven looked thoughtful for a moment. You could almost see a cartoon light bulb hovering over her head.

"What is it?" I asked.

"I think I just had an epiphany." She looked sort of gleeful about it. "Sometimes when you feel stuck, you have to blow up the whole thing. You know?"

I didn't, really.

Heaven Hsu straightened up, pushed her hood off her head, and looked around at the Perro, the chicken coop, and the backyard, like she was studying it—or making up her mind about something.

"I like this place," she said, giving the Perro an approving nod. "It's inspiring. Probably the criminal history makes it good for coming up with schemes, don't you think?"

I had to ignore the comment about the Perro's "criminal history" because Roo's assault on the pig ear had finally calmed down, and now he was baring his teeth at me. He shook his fierce doggy mustache in my direction, and I froze as the teeth came closer and closer. I tried to pull my shorts down to protect my knee-skin, but Roo sniffed, shoved my hand out of the way with his head, flopped his slobbery chin down on my thigh, and blinked his angry eyes at me.

"What's he doing?"

The words sounded a lot more scared than I meant them to, and I must have looked silly, inching away from that tiny dog, because Heaven Hsu grinned a full-on ear-to-ear grin, which I hadn't seen her do once since she'd arrived at the Perro.

"I told you," she said. "He likes you."

Heaven nodded at me, so I carefully patted his head. Roo climbed right up on my lap and snuggled in. He shifted his head in my palm, and I got the distinct feeling he wanted me to rub his ear.

Heaven Hsu laughed out loud at my shocked expression. The sound of Heaven's laugh surprised me almost as much as how soft and cuddly Roo was. Since her light-bulb moment, Heaven seemed different. Like there was a weight off her shoulders.

"When I was a kid, my sister and I used to practice reading each other's minds." Heaven held up my Houdini book, still grinning. "I'm going to give you some tips, okay?"

Roo made a snuffling sound and shifted to get more comfortable. I obviously wasn't going anywhere.

"Don't assume stuff based on appearance and forget to look at body language," Heaven said, pointing at the schnauzer. "Look how sweet he is."

Fair point. Roo's massive eyebrows were furrowed in an old-man frown, and his bushy mustache wiggled at me. He looked furious, sneering at me with his piranha-teeth, but he was cuddling against my belly like a kitten.

"Also: Don't settle for the easy answer."

"I never do that," I said. Maybe a little defensively.

"You sure? Roo is short for Karou, one of my favorite fantasy characters."

I felt my face get warm, and I laughed. Okay, maybe I wasn't as good a fake psychic as I'd thought. "So . . . not Piglet's pal."

"Right. Ready for the master class? I'm going to look into your soul and tell you everything I see."

My smile disappeared as Heaven leaned forward and rubbed her hands together like she was getting ready for some devious plan.

"I'll need you to be totally silent. And trust me. Completely. Okay?"

A MAGICIAN AMONG
THE SPIRITS

"I'm warning you," Heaven said. "I'm extra good at mind reading. Not everything I tell you is going to be stuff you want to hear."

It was a weird thing to say, but I nodded.

"Got it," I said. Like a nervous twitch hadn't jolted through my spine.

Heaven leaned forward, rested her elbows on her knees, and closed her eyes for a long time. Roo's eyes closed, too. His body was warm and cozy, and I rubbed his ear to the rhythm of his breath until even the Yappy Hour party noise felt like it was fading into the background.

"Interesting!"

I'd been so lulled into silence that I flinched. Which made Roo reach out in his sleep and scrape my thigh with one of his razor-sharp nails. I sucked in my breath.

"I see . . ."

She moved one hand slowly through the air like she was trying to push away a veil or a cloud of smoke.

". . . that you definitely don't like . . ."

Heaven was a genius at drawing out the suspense. My mind raced, trying to remember if I'd already told her about something I hated that she could use. I knew it wasn't scientifically possible, but she'd said she was good at this, so I scanned my brain for any tingling or prodding sensations. On the .05 percent chance that she actually *could* read minds, it'd at least be interesting to know what it felt like.

Heaven made another quick swipe at the air with her hand and nodded, like the answer had finally become clear.

". . . you don't like being named after an elf!"

I groaned. "*Who* told you my name is Elrond?"

Heaven pretended to lock her mouth shut and throw away the key.

"That's too easy," I said.

"Fine," she said. "Let's go deeper. I see . . . a younger boy who pushes your buttons . . . He wears something flowing . . . maybe a cape?"

I laughed again. She wasn't any better at this than I was. Denver had been standing next to me the whole time I'd done the animal communicator trick on Roo, and before that, everyone in the room had seen the kid in the cape show off his whole overblown, cheesy magic trick. It couldn't take much to get to the pushes-your-buttons conclusion.

"Why do you feel threatened by this boy, Elrond?"

I frowned.

"*Rondo*," I said.

Besides, Denver was annoying, not threatening. That should be obvious.

Heaven closed her eyes tighter now and held the book to her chest. Her voice got husky and low, spooky even. "I see . . . a family . . . a *close* family . . . but one person is standing farther from the others. Maybe too far for the rest to reach him? I see him looking . . . at the open space where he used to stand. It's like he's wondering where his place is. He's about to make some decisions . . . about how far away to drift?"

It was probably only because she was such a good actress, but I leaned in, curious.

"This other boy . . . the one with the cape . . . he seems to fit right in. He's the right shape for that empty space. But *he's* lonely. And I can see that first boy . . . the one who's drifting . . . could fix it. If he wanted to. If he decided to be more . . . generous."

I mean. I knew she was riffing off stuff she'd seen when Denver had done his French Drop. I guess it wasn't that hard to tell that I'd sabotaged him when "Roo" revealed his trick. And even though I knew Heaven was making it all up as she went along, I didn't like where it was going. I didn't need to be more generous. Other people needed to be less annoying. Roo whimpered in his sleep and pressed his head into my hand. I'd forgotten to keep rubbing his ear.

"I'm getting one more thing." Heaven opened her eyes and looked at me from beneath her hood. "Do you want to hear it?"

I didn't. But for some reason, I said, "Why not."

"There's someone else in that family who's having a hard time." She was looking into my eyes now, and I would have squirmed or maybe even gotten up and left if I didn't think it would wake up Roo. I let my hair fall in front of my face instead.

Heaven glanced toward my sister, who stood alone by the tiki bar, searching the crowd. I felt a small pang of guilt, knowing how jealous she'd be if she knew I was hanging out with Heaven Hsu without her. It wouldn't have been that hard to get her attention and call her over. I knew I could make her day. But I didn't.

"I haven't talked to my sister in a year. Texts, but that doesn't count." Heaven dropped the spooky séance voice, and I couldn't tell if she was still trying to read my mind. It didn't seem like it. It seemed like she'd moved on to a totally different topic. That was fine with me.

She pushed the hood off her head and leaned back against the henhouse. "It's fine," she said. Like I'd asked. "She's been filming in Australia, and I've been busy . . . trying to figure out my life. She's nothing like me, but we used to be good friends. We had so much stuff we liked to do together, and now . . ."

I couldn't help thinking of Epic and Elvis and the stuff we

liked to do. Surfing. Eating donuts at Dogma Cafe. Taking Pico to the farmers' market and looking at the cool junk at the Martinez Antiques booth. Laughing until someone snarfed. We hadn't done a single one of those things in months. In fact, ever since the Perro del Mar got famous, we'd barely done any of it at all.

It took me a second to realize Heaven was still talking.

". . . and everything always came so easy for her. Anyway. There were a thousand little choices we made. Sometimes I think if we'd chosen differently, we'd still be friends, but time doesn't move backward." She nodded toward the party in the backyard. "If I could get out of this circus, maybe she and I could do a project together. Collaborate. Fix it. You know?"

"Are you still mind reading?" I asked. I was starting to feel uncomfortable.

"No. Yes. Kind of?" Heaven chuckled. "I guess I'm giving advice. The choices we make. They matter."

Advice? What, did she think my siblings and I were going to drift apart and never be friends again? Unless I made different choices? That seemed overly dramatic. Luckily, Heaven's hoodie pocket buzzed. She pulled out a phone, swiped at it, and moaned.

"My publicist is on the hunt. She says she doesn't see me in any of the trending Yappy Hour photos."

She stuck her tongue out at her phone like Elvis does when you do something she doesn't like.

"Should I . . . ." I hesitated and glanced down at Roo,

wondering how to wake him up without startling him into attack mode.

"Watch this." Heaven reached back into her pocket and pulled out a barrel-shaped nugget. Exactly like the ones Epic had in his bag.

"What *are* those?" I asked. The Boones had freaked out when they'd seen them.

"Don't tell Raúl," she said. "He already thinks I have a habit of taking things that don't belong to me."

"Do you?" I asked.

"I usually give them back." She winked. "Except for these. Roo goes wild for them. Watch."

She waved the treat in front of Roo's face, and at first, only his nose twitched. Then his mustache started to wiggle, and one of his ears perked up. Suddenly, his tongue flicked out and he lunged for the treat with so much force that he shoved me flat on my back.

"I told you," Heaven said. "He goes wild."

We both stood up and brushed ourselves off. Her smile disappeared as she looked over at the tiki bar.

"Maybe the show will get shut down. Like you said," I offered. Not that I wanted it to happen. The last season had ended on a real cliffhanger, and I needed to see how it turned out.

Heaven did a weird thing with her thumb, touching it to her lips, her chin, then her forehead. When she saw the look on my face, she blushed a little.

"My sister made it up," she said. "For when you need things to go the right way. It's silly, but I still do it. In case it works."

As if on cue, Raúl threw his hands up in the air and said something loud that was probably a curse in Spanish. People around him shushed enough that Heaven and I could hear the rest.

"I have never been so *undermined* in my entire career!" he fumed, pointing his finger in Mrs. Boone's face with every emphasized word. "Don't *think* I can't shut down this show. *One* phone call. That's *all* it would take."

Mr. Boone took a step forward, but Raúl swiped the jar of caviar out of Mrs. Boone's hands and stomped away. Heaven started to giggle.

"I think I made that happen with my mind," she said. "Told you I was a good telepath. Catch you later, Elrond."

I reclaimed my stump and had barely gotten comfortable when I realized that Heaven Hsu had snaked my book and was using it as a writing surface to autograph cocktail napkins. Since I couldn't read, I took my notebook out of my pocket and started a page on Heaven Hsu's suspense-building techniques. *Long pauses. Low voice. Dreamy, far-off gaze.* I got so absorbed that I'd finished my entire list before I noticed that Denver Delgado-Doyle was sitting on the ground next to me, writing in his own notebook.

"The actress told me you were here," he said. "What have you observed? I'm collecting data, too."

He nodded toward the party, which was, thankfully, winding down.

When I didn't answer, Denver reviewed his own notes out loud. "The prosciutto Chew Toys were twice as popular as the salami. Pico's owner checks her phone approximately six times a minute. Your brother said he was going to the bathroom and then I saw him walking down Main Street with the policeman instead. There's a black dog with a spot on its—"

"Why are you writing that stuff?" I asked. I also wanted to know what Epic had been up to with Luis.

Denver shrugged. "Elvis said *you* like to do it. She told me you keep notes on strange behavior. I borrowed a notebook so we could do it together."

That explained all the hearts and sketches of Sir Bentley on the cover of his notebook.

"But what for? *Why* are you collecting the data?"

Denver grinned. "For . . . the same reason you are?"

I understood that everyone wanted me to be nice to Denver. Even Heaven, with her whole mind-reading thing. I could decide to help him out and include him. There was one problem.

I really didn't feel like it.

"Looks like everybody's going home," I said, getting up from the stump. "I should help clean up."

Denver didn't look surprised that I was ditching him. I didn't exactly regret it, but I felt bad enough that I decided to throw him a bone.

"You can sit on my stump," I said, and the kid actually smiled. Like I was being generous. Which, a nagging thought in my brain reminded me, I wasn't. I shut the thought down, on the off chance that it was Heaven telepathing into my mind, and told myself it was fine. He was happy. I was happy.

My sister, on the other hand, was standing alone by the back door, looking extra unhappy. When I waved at her, she turned around and went inside.

ELVIS

I couldn't fall asleep because Elvis wouldn't stop tossing and turning in the bunk below me. It was almost like she was doing it on purpose, throwing her body around to make the bedsprings squeak as loudly as possible.

"Knock it off, El. Go to sleep," I hissed.

Which worked great, because she stopped tossing and instead started kicking the bottom of my mattress. I knew her legs weren't long enough to reach, so she had to be putting some serious effort into making contact.

"What is your *problem*?" I asked.

My sister's feet pounded into my mattress in a slow one-two rhythm, testing out a new spot with each pair of kicks, aiming for my butt. I scooted toward the wall to get out of the impact range, and when she didn't stop, I grabbed my pillow and leaned my body over the railing to swat her with it. Elvis grabbed the corner of the pillowcase and pulled it right off.

"Hey, give it back!" I hung upside down and lunged for it.

Epic turned on the light next to his bed, which at least

made Elvis loosen her grip long enough for me to snag the pillowcase and sit back up on my bunk. My brother sat up, too, his hair poking in all directions.

"Are you three years old?"

"She started it," I said.

"*You* were trying to finish it." That was usually Mom's line, but Epic used it as he rubbed his eye and padded across the room. He looked extra worn out, and he dragged my beanbag chair next to my sister's bunk before flopping onto it with a heavy Dad-sigh. "What's going on, El?"

I lay on my stomach and let my head hang over my bed so I could see them both. El's hair was even wilder than my brother's, probably from all the flailing around during her temper tantrum.

"I'm. So. *So*. Mad." Obviously. El could barely get the words out.

"Why?" Epic held in an eye roll and used his extra-patient-older-brother voice. "What did Rondo do?"

Me?

"I'm mad at both of you," Elvis said.

This time, Epic did roll his eyes.

"See? You're so . . . *mean* now." Elvis hopped out of the bottom bunk so she could stand in the middle of the room and glare at both of us. She wore fluffy fleece T. rex pajamas, and tiny blond strands of staticky hair floated all around her head. On top of it all, her eyes were red from crying or rubbing or both.

I couldn't help it. I laughed.

"What?" she asked.

"You look ridiculous," I said. I was just being honest.

"YOU look ridiculous," El said. She put her hands on her hips and practically shook with rage. "You *used* to be nice. You used to *like* me. Now Epic's being all bossy and stealing things, and *you* leave me out of *everything*!"

"Whatever." I sat up and focused on putting my pillow back in the pillowcase. Which is way harder than it should be. "Go back to bed, Epic," I said. "She's being a diva."

"A DIVA?" Elvis exploded. "Denver told me! You hung out with Heaven Hsu at Yappy Hour. Heaven Hsu! Why would you do that without me?"

Epic looked surprised. "You hung out with the actress?"

"I was trying to get *away* from people," I said. I gave up on the pillowcase and threw it at my sister. "Is that why you gave Denver your notebook and sicced him on me?"

"Take a breath," Epic said.

He started to do his I-can-fix-this routine, but Elvis was seriously mad. Like, beyond-her-usual-dramatics kind of mad.

"From now on," Elvis said, "Denver's the only one on my team."

"*Denver?*" I blurted. "Why? The only reason he hangs out with you is because he wants to hang out with *me*."

El bared her teeth and let out a frustrated T. rex growl before running full speed for her bed and throwing herself onto it so hard that it shook our whole bunk.

"Elvis." Epic tried his nicey-nice voice again, but El had crossed over from mad to sad, crying so hard that I was worried she was going to wake up the whole house.

Epic gave me a helpless look, and I climbed down from my bunk. He scooted over to make room for me on the beanbag, and we sat there watching El sob into a stuffed bunny.

"I'm sorry, El," Epic said. "Don't cry."

I nudged him. El had bad meltdowns sometimes—even now, when she was almost ten years old—and telling her not to cry didn't help. But I couldn't think of anything better. Besides, I had to concentrate on blocking the Heaven Hsu thoughts that kept popping into my brain. *The choices we make. They matter.* I was 99.9 percent certain those were my own thoughts. Memories of what Heaven had said. But I tried to think of other things. Just in case she was tapping into my brain waves.

Elvis wasn't completely wrong. About any of it. Epic had been bossy, and he *had* been doing his own thing a lot more. But part of that was like Mrs. Boone had said. Teenager stuff. It probably made sense that he'd rather hang out with his friends than with his kid brother and sister. Still, El had a point. I missed the old days, when we used to build projects together, and spend Yappy Hour stuffing our faces with pizza. I hadn't seen my brother all night.

The stuff she'd said about me was true, too. I wasn't sneaking around, but of *course* I knew she would want to hang out with Heaven Hsu. A couple years ago, it was the first thing I would have done—get El's attention so she could come talk to Heaven, too. I could picture the way El's face would have burst into pure-joy mode and how she'd skip over and immediately start talking Heaven's ear off. It made me smile a little thinking about it. I didn't know why I didn't do it this time.

One thing I did know? The three of us used to be a team.

"I wish the Perro never got famous."

I only mumbled it, but Epic heard me clearly enough that he sighed and added, "Me too." And from the dark back corner of her bunk, in a weepy, quiet voice muffled by her stuffed bunny, Elvis said, "Me three."

If Heaven Hsu *was* in the guest wing trying to telepath messages to me, it was working, because her voice was still in my head. I couldn't imagine not talking to one of my siblings for a whole year. I didn't want that to happen to us. I elbowed Epic, and we climbed into El's bunk. Epic pulled a giraffe out of her massive stuffed animal pile and held it on his lap. I chose an elephant and did the same. We sat on each side of her with our animals, not saying a word. Eventually, El's sobs settled down.

"We'll hang out more, El," I said. "I promise."

"Like when?"

"Tomorrow," Epic said. "We'll go to the farmers' market. And the beach."

"But for *real*," El said. "Don't talk to your friends and read and leave me alone on the sand."

"We won't. We'll do whatever you want," Epic said.

"Yeah, you choose," I said.

"Can we do our detective agency?" Elvis tilted her head to look at each of us, one at a time. She was testing us, and we knew it. "Wasn't that the best? Solving a crime no one else could figure out?"

It *was* the best. And we were really good at it. It made sense that El couldn't let it go, but the Raúl fake-dognapping fiasco had confirmed what Epic and I had already figured out: It was a once-in-a-lifetime kind of thing. Elvis was in denial.

"If a *real* mystery ever comes up," Epic said, choosing his words carefully, "we'll do it. I promise. But not until then. We'll do something else fun tomorrow."

"What about the celebrity dognappings?" She waggled her eyebrows at us like she thought she could tempt us.

"*El!*" Epic looked pained, but I laughed.

"Yeah, right. All those dogs went missing from different towns," I said. "There's no evidence to show they're linked, and every owner paid the ransom, so the criminals got away without a trace before the cops could even *start* an investigation. That'll be an easy one to solve."

El stuck out her tongue at me, but she giggled. "It was worth a try."

"And don't go the other way, either," I warned. "Not like someone's missing sandal on the beach. *Although* . . ."

Maybe it was because we were talking about the detective agency, or maybe my brain randomly chose that moment to put the pieces together. The more I thought about it, the more it made perfect sense. It wasn't exactly a mystery, or even a crime, but—

"What is it? Look at his face!"

"Oh no. Rondo. What now?"

I snapped myself back to reality. "I think Heaven Hsu is planning to sabotage *Bentley Knows*."

"What?"

"She would never do that," Elvis said, though she looked a tiny bit wistful, like she wanted us to be detectives so badly that she *wished* it was true.

"Yes, she would," I said. "She wants to get out of her contract, but she can't. She hates acting. I think she's desperate. She might even have some plan to get Raúl involved—"

"You don't have to do this, Rondo," Epic said.

El squeezed her stuffed animal and smiled at me. "Thanks, though." She hopped her bunny over onto my lap and made it hug my elephant. "It's nice that you'd make up a mystery for me, but I'll wait for a *real* one, like Epic said."

"I'm not making it up."

But Elvis looked happy again. She even bounced on the bed.

"I can do whatever I want tomorrow?"

Epic nodded, but I braced myself. I hoped she didn't want to spend the day at Nails 'n' Tails watching dogs get their hair done.

"Let's have a normal day," she said. "Like before. When we had Carmelito all to ourselves."

"A normal day," I repeated. It did sound pretty good.

"Want to have donuts?" Epic asked. Even he was perking up. "And look at the T-shirts at Furever Friends?"

"Yes! And I want to do Denver's magic show," Elvis said, throwing it in like it was on the same scale as donuts and window-shopping. "I want us *all* to do that. A group project. Like we used to do."

Epic and I exchanged a look.

"Come on!" Elvis bopped us both with her bunny. "Who else is he supposed to hang out with? It's the nice thing to do, *and* it'll be fun!"

"I could make some special effects," Epic said. "And props."

Elvis could see she was losing me. "You don't have to perform, Rondo. I'll do that part, and you stay behind the scenes. Give us some tips, tell us how to make it better. You can pick all the tricks if you want!"

She was up on her knees now, getting excited. She even had a glimmer of the old pure-joy mode in her eyes. I had to admit, she was good at selling it. Working on a project with Epic and El like old times, building stuff, and making plans. I hugged the stuffed elephant in my lap and tried to focus on making generous choices.

"All right, Elvis," I said. "Let's make some magic."

TUESDAY

TRANSCRIPT: DAILY DOG DISH PODCAST
Teatime Tuesday with Special Guests: Newt & Sharon Henderson

(Daily Dog Dish intro music.)

Del: It's Teatime Tuesday at the *Daily Dog Dish*, when we spill the tea with a special guest. Today, we're joined by Newt, everyone's favorite pop-star Pomeranian, and his special superstar someone, Sharon Henderson!

Newt: Yip yip!

(Sound effect of a crowd going wild.)

Del: We're your hosts, Delphi Jones and Melissa Dubois! Say hi to our guests, Melissa!

Mel: Hi to our guests, Melissa.

Sharon: *(Laughing.)* Do you two do that joke every single day?

Del: Maybe.

Mel: Pretty much.

Del: So, Newt, before we spill some serious tea into the dog dish, we want to tell you how glad we are that you're home safe and sound.

Mel: Dognapped! That must have been super scary.

Newt: Yip! Yip!

Sharon: It sure was! Those dognappers were *explicit* when they described how they'd hurt Newt if I didn't pay the ransom. I'm talking horror movie descriptions.

Mel: What happened exactly?

Sharon: *(Sighs.)* I usually carry Newt in my bag, but we were trying out this adorable Dog Elegance Rainbow Light Leash—

Del: Aw, the one that projects a hologram rainbow?

Sharon: Yes! It's to die for. A little rainbow was following Newt around, and I got this perfect idea for a song—I only took my attention away for twenty seconds. Thirty, tops.

Mel: Someone swiped him?

Sharon: Clipped Newt's leash! It was *(sob)* . . . hanging there . . . Sorry, it's still raw.

Del: *Then* what?

Sharon: I got a phone call. Unknown number. I was so frazzled, I couldn't even remember my own address! Thank goodness I had the Department of Lost Dogs on speed dial. They are literally angels. Without their help, I would have melted down into a puddle. I *know* I would have lost Newt!

Del: That's high praise!

Mel: I'm so glad you felt supported.

Del: Did you ever think about *not* paying the ransom?

Sharon: Are you kidding me? I knew from my friends in the industry that Chippy, Baby BombBomb, and Trixie all got returned immediately after their ransoms were paid. Of course I wired the money. I couldn't risk it.

Del: I know Newt's only been home for a hot minute, but what's next for you two? I heard you canceled your tour?

Sharon: We're heading into the studio to see if we can pour some of these emotions into a new album.

Mel: Wow! I have two things to say. Number one, I can't *wait* for a new Sharon Henderson album, and number two—

Del: Wait! Did you say "number two"?

(Sound effect of kids saying "Ew!")

Del: Sorry, everyone, but that was the perfect lead-in to today's sponsor, Doggy Do! Doggy Do is a revolutionary new brand of poop scoopers guaranteed to seal in even the strongest smells. *Don't* hold your nose, use a Doggy *Do!*

(Doggy Do jingle plays.)

Mel: I don't know if that was sensitive timing, Del.

Sharon: It's fine because I want one of those. Badly.

Mel: *Any*-way. Before Del put her foot in it, I was about to suggest that we spill some Tuesday Tea. Do you feel up for it?

Newt: Yip!

Sharon: Let's do this.

(Tuesday Teatime jingle plays.)

Mel: Round one! Lucasfilms Canine Division announced they've signed the Pendleton Triplets to a new six-movie contract. Newt and Sharon, what do you know?

Sharon: I know FiFi Khan uses an average of twenty-five stuntpuppies per film. She's going to have to outsource some labradoodles to keep up with that pace. Puppies are tough on filmmakers because they grow so fast!

Newt: Yip! Yip! Yip!

(Tuesday Teatime bell rings.)

Del: Round two! Misty LaVa's Lhasa apso, Pipsqueak, was spotted in the Big Apple sporting a bouffant bow made of hair extensions. Newt and Sharon, doggie extensions? Hot or not?

Newt: Yip!

Sharon: Hot! Misty LaVa's fashion sense is *never* wrong. Besides, Pipsqueak is a mega-influencer with more than

six million followers! Hot or not, every dog who's any dog will have extensions by the end of the week.

(Tuesday Teatime bell rings again.)

Del: Final round!

Mel: Filming for *Bentley Knows* starts up today! Rumors of the reboot started at least two years ago. Why did it take so long to start filming?

Sharon: I definitely have some inside scoop on this one. I'm BFFs with Sir Bentley's human.

Mel: Madeleine Devine!

Sharon: Poor Madeleine! It's been one thing after another. Contracts, divas, rewrites. There were so many problems with the story line, they fired five different screenwriters. If things don't go perfectly this week, I bet the studio will cancel the show.

Del: You mentioned divas. Let me guess: "Sir" Bentley had to negotiate maximum cash for minimum effort?

Sharon: Hey, Bentley *is* that show. She's the highest-paid canine actor in Hollywood because she deserves it! The real diva holdup was that lawsuit with Heaven Hsu.

Del: I heard about that. When she started the whole child-actress thing, her manager locked her into a contract that's

got her on a short leash. She's basically married to *Bentley Knows* as long as it's on the air. She can't get a raise, and Bentley makes six times her salary!

Mel: She can't renegotiate?

Del: Not yet. She's only seventeen.

Sharon: Honestly, I'd be grateful if I were her. If wasn't for *Bentley Knows*, Heaven Hsu wouldn't have a career.

Mel: Still. It's not fun to feel locked in.

Sharon: It is if you're an actor. That's called job security. The truth is, *Bentley Knows* will succeed if Raúl Flores wants it to succeed. The rest of it doesn't matter.

Mel: The dog trainer? *Really?*

Del: You and Newt worked with Raúl on the video for "Let Sleeping Dogs Lie," right?

Sharon: Unfortunately.

Del: But that song went multiplatinum!

Sharon: Yeah, it did. It made a bajillion dollars because Raúl Flores is an evil genius.

Mel: Wait . . . wasn't Newt *bald* in that video?

Del: That was a major scandal!

153

Sharon: Exactly what he wanted. Raúl knew I'd throw a publicity-worthy tantrum about it. That's why he shaved Newt behind my back. The photos on social media caught people's attention, but the controversy about consent kept that song top-of-mind for almost a full year!

Mel: Evil.

Del: Genius.

Newt: Yipyipyipyip!

Sharon: I *still* can't believe he named his dogs Cheddar and Doughboy. That man loves cash more than anyone I've ever met.

Del: Are you thinking what I'm thinking, Mel?

Mel: I'm not a mind reader.

Del: We *need* to visit that film set.

Sharon: In Carmelito? You're not going to . . . cause any trouble, right?

Mel: Oof, our reputation! We're *changed* women! Older and wiser . . .

Del: And *way* over our time limit! We'll talk later, Mel. I've got a new idea for tomorrow's episode. Sharon and Newt gave me a brain spark!

Mel: *(Giggles.)* Don't start any fires! Thanks for joining us, everyone!

Mel and Del: Hug ALL the dogs!

(Daily Dog Dish outro music.)

DOGMA CAFE

"Five bucks." Epic pronounced the *f* so strongly that a puff of donut sugar exploded around him.

"I'll take that bet," I said. "There's no way you can tell those three dogs apart."

"Pico has white on the tip of his tail." Epic wiped powdered sugar off his cheek. "His back leg has a stripe of white down the side. His nose isn't as pointy, and those other dogs have sadder eyes. Do you want more?"

It was an impressive list, but not impressive enough.

"First of all, the body doubles have white on their tails," I said. "*And* a stripe on the back leg."

I took a satisfied bite of my donut. I was already mentally spending my five bucks on whatever cool old junk Mr. Martinez had in his farmers' market dollar bin, but my siblings smirked at me.

"You sure about that?" Epic asked.

Elvis wiggled her eyebrows at the back table where we'd spotted Heaven Hsu and Raúl Flores having a cup of coffee together. I'd tried to point out that this played right into my theory about Heaven, but Epic and Elvis both shut me down. Since we were having fun for once, I didn't push it.

On the floor next to Heaven, Roo and the two Italian greyhound stand-ins lounged on Dogma Cafe dog beds. I squinted at the Iggys.

"They did yesterday," I said. "All three of them had white tips and a stripe on the leg."

Elvis bounced in her seat with glee. "That was makeup!"

Epic reached out to give her a high five, but she shook her head and withheld her hand.

"I'm in on the bet," she said. "You only told us about *Pico*. First one to say three differences between Cheddar and Doughboy wins the money! Rondo, you say when."

I gave the Iggys one more look. They were 100 percent identical. I was already out anyway.

"Good luck with that," I said. "Ready, set. Go!"

Epic barely had time to say, "Um . . ." before Elvis burst out with, "Cheek mole white spot on the butt three dark brown toes I win!"

"What'd you do, inspect them already?" Epic asked.

"Yes!" Elvis grinned.

"She could be bluffing. We should go look."

I said it mainly to give Elvis a chance to talk to Heaven Hsu, and she knew it. My sister beamed at me and raced to the back table. Heaven and Raúl were deep in conversation while Heaven took notes in her notebook. It occurred to me that they might not love being interrupted by a dog inspection, but Elvis was already on the floor petting Doughboy.

"If it isn't the Perro kids," Heaven said.

She looked happy enough to see us, or at least neutral, but I noticed that she closed her notebook and shoved it in her messenger bag.

"What are you working on? Is Raúl giving you acting tips?"

My sister said it in a voice that implied that Heaven might *need* acting tips, which was a) rude and b) wrong. Heaven didn't seem to care.

"Chatting about ideas," she said. "Elrond gave me a couple good ones yesterday."

I did? Epic and Elvis both swiveled their heads and gaped in my direction.

"You let her call you Elrond?" El whispered, but plenty loud for everyone to hear.

I bent down to pet Roo so they'd all stop looking at me. His ears perked up, and his tail went berserk. He glared at me, sneering with those awful teeth, but I could tell from his body language that he was glad I was there.

It was strange that Heaven, Raúl, and the dogs weren't on set. Filming officially started today, and according to the Boones' schedule, Pico had to be ready super early in the morning. Could they be on a break already? Or maybe the crew was filming other stuff—stuff that *didn't* involve the human star of the show and the dog trainer? That made no sense.

"Shouldn't you be on set?" I asked.

"Late start," Heaven said. "They're having some kind of electrical problem with the generator."

Raúl tapped the table, clearly waiting for us to leave, but Elvis chatted Heaven up long enough for me to play tug-rope with Roo and for Epic to confirm the white spot, cheek mole, and brown toes.

"You win, El," he said. "We can go."

"Pay up!" Elvis stuck out her palm while Epic and I each handed over two dollars and fifty cents. Even though we could easily have paid her later. She wanted someone else, preferably a celebrity, to see her win.

"Extortion?" Raúl raised an eyebrow at Heaven.

She shrugged a shoulder and nodded. "Maybe."

"No way!" Elvis put her cash-filled hands on her hips and shook her curly pigtails at him. "Extortion is obtaining something through force or threats, and it's illegal. I won this money fair and square!"

Her cutesy outrage got a smile out of Raúl. Which made Elvis so happy that she gave all three dogs several goodbye hugs each.

All morning, my brain wouldn't stop spinning. What kind of ideas would Heaven need to run by the *dog* trainer? It wasn't like Roo was launching an acting career. From what she'd told me, all it would take for the studio to shut down *Bentley Knows* was one small catastrophe. As far as I knew, there were exactly two people who would be better off if that happened.

Heaven, because she'd get out of her contract. And Raúl, who obviously did *not* like working with Mrs. Boone.

One person who *wouldn't* be better off? Me. I'd already rewatched *Bentley Knows* twice. I was bored of reruns. The way I saw it, if Hollywood was going to take over my house and ruin Restorative Week? I'd better get a new season out of the deal.

"Do you want to go back to the Perro and watch the filming?" I asked as we crossed the street to Paradiso Park. I wanted to snoop around. If sabotage was in the works, someone needed to stop it.

Epic thought I was joking. "Definitely," he said. "And maybe we can help the Boones set up some big publicity stunt for Pico. You could do his makeup."

He laughed so hard at his own joke that he snarfed.

"Normal day!" Elvis yelled, and threw herself into a cartwheel. It did feel good. Hanging out with El and Epic with nothing to do but live out our school motto: Follow Your Curiosity. The sleuthing could wait.

At the farmers' market, Epic found some tinkering supplies, and Elvis smelled every single one of the oils at Flo's Floral Essences. She even gave me one of my dollars back so I could get a half-broken pendulum from the Martinez Antiques dollar bin. It looked like a chipped crystal teardrop on a rusty chain.

"Is it jewelry?" Elvis asked.

"It's a dowsing crystal," I said. "For psychic location." It was ridiculous to think that a piece of rock could find anything, but it'd be helpful to have one. For research.

"Ew! Smell this eucalyptus." Elvis handed me a vial.

"What is that? It smells familiar." I passed it on to Epic, who took a whiff.

"Smells like El's feet."

"Ha! Exactly!"

"Give it!" El snatched the vial back and waved it under her nose a second time. "Oh! You're right," she said with a surprised grin. "That totally smells like my feet!"

It was starting to feel like old times. Which I guess should have been a warning. Like Heaven said, time doesn't move backward.

We finished our rounds at the farmers' market, checked out the action at Dog Run, and stopped to watch part of a soccer game outside Carmelito Middle School. Maybe it was the reminder that his middle school friends were away at soccer camp, but Epic suddenly went back to acting cranky and distracted. When Elvis started in about her latest postcard from Madeleine and Sir Bentley's Norwegian cruise, he inched away.

"Madeleine's going to invite me to visit the *penthouse* at the Moondoggie. Did you even know the Moondoggie *had* a penthouse? Epic, what are you doing? You're not even listening! Wait, what is *that*?"

El's hands went straight to her hips, and Epic quickly crumpled a piece of paper in his fist.

"Nothing," he said. "Trash." But his cheeks were red.

"Not that!" Elvis said. "You *know* what I saw. You put it in your bag!"

"Forget it, El."

My sister reached for his messenger bag, but Epic turned his body away from her, and they kept at it until they were basically spinning in circles.

"Leave him alone, El. Maybe it's a love note or something."

I was joking, but a blush spread to Epic's ears, and now I was interested. Who would he be getting love notes from? Miyon? No way. Besides, she was three hundred miles away in Malibu.

Elvis made one last lunge before looking my brother straight in the eye. "Did Mom and Dad get you a phone?"

Now I was *really* interested.

"It's not a big deal," Epic said.

"It's a *huge* deal!" I said. "They said no devices until . . ."

It hit me that high school for Epic was less than six months away. If he thought he was too grown up for us *now* . . . Heaven Hsu's "mind reading" session popped into my head. The close family, drifting apart. I wished she'd never said any of it.

"It's not fair!" Elvis said. "Unless . . ." She changed her tactics and gave her head a sweet-sister tilt. "You want to share? We could look at Pico's feed together! Mrs. Boone says it's *ah*-mazing!"

"It's not mine," Epic said. "I'm borrowing it from Dec while he and Carlos are at soccer camp. Don't tell Mom."

Elvis and I were stunned. Epic's chin looked normal, which meant he wasn't lying. To us. But he was totally lying to Mom and Dad. It was one of the most un-Epic things I'd seen him do. Besides taking the Boones' pet cam. And lying about that, too. In fact, my brother had been acting funny all week.

"Why'd you take the pet cam and the dog treats?" I asked.

I thought he wasn't going to answer, but then my brother made another confession. Or *half* of a confession.

"Don't ask me about the dog cam," he said. "I stole the treats from Mom."

"The ones *she* stole from Raúl?" Elvis asked. "Why?"

Epic groaned. "I heard her talking to herself. About blackmail. I thought—"

I laughed. "She was *joking*!"

"I know, but . . ." Epic's serious look made us both lean in. "Don't you get the feeling she's going to snap?"

"Mom? Not really," I said. "Heaven, though—"

"Never mind." Epic sighed. "Just be cool. I don't rat you out for watching TV."

"We're not going to tell Mom and Dad about the phone," Elvis said. "Or any of it. When we get to the Moondoggie, you can show us the apps."

"I need to stop at home first," Epic said. "To check on Pico."

"You said you didn't want to watch the filming!" El said.

"Just for a minute, El," I said. "I need to check something, too."

SUGAR

The thing I needed to check for, obviously, was sabotage. But nothing was happening on the *Bentley Knows* set. At least, not outside where they were filming. Heaven was standing around while the lighting crew set up her next shot, and since the scene didn't involve any Italian greyhounds, Raúl was in the kitchen whipping up another batch of his special dog treats.

Mom and Dad were skeptical when we told them we were on our way to the Moondoggie Inn to spend the afternoon with Denver.

"You're not mad that you're going to miss the filming?" Mom asked Elvis.

"Or that you have to hang out with a nine-year-old?" Dad was looking at me.

They didn't have to ask Epic anything because he never complains.

"Can we have money for the taco truck?" El asked.

Before Dad could hand it over, a loud crash and a high-pitched shriek came from the kitchen.

"*Un-believable!*" a voice bellowed.

We found Raúl and Mrs. Boone standing in what was apparently the aftermath of a sugar cyclone. At Mrs. Boone's feet, a giant bag of sugar had spilled out onto the floor, but somehow, it had exploded all over the kitchen before it landed. Tiny white grains covered every surface. The counter. The sink. Raúl's mustache. Mrs. Boone's hair. Dad rushed to his coffee station to brush sugar out of his espresso machine.

I nudged Epic. He'd been right that someone was going to snap. It wasn't Mom. Or Heaven.

"*He* did it!" Mrs. Boone pointed at Raúl. "He threw it on the floor. Like a *child*!"

"She does *not* respect my authority!" he shouted.

"I respect my *own* authority! Pico's our dog, not yours!"

"Hey! Let's calm down!" Mom did not look calm.

"Pico's exercise routine is *not* optional!" Raúl barked.

"Well, *Pico* told Mandee he needed a rest today, and Pico is in charge of his own body—"

"Who's Mandee?" Mom asked.

"The BarkAngel," I said. "Dog psychic."

I had to admit, Mom *did* look a little twitchy around the eyes. Luckily, the showrunner and three assistants showed up with clipboards, took one look at the situation, and whisked Mrs. Boone and Raúl out of the kitchen.

"Don't worry, Mr. and Mrs. McDade. We'll get this cleaned up." The showrunner gave an embarrassed shrug on her way out the door. "It's the price of working with Raúl. He's a genius."

"Hefty price for genius," Dad muttered.

Mom winced. "Could this count as a reason to shut it all down?"

"No!" I said at the same time that Elvis said, "You *can't* shut down the show!"

"I know, I know, settle down," Mom said. "I just miss the way things used to be. Don't you?"

For the first time in a long time, my entire family was on the same page.

The *Bentley Knows* showrunner must be some kind of magician, because within ten minutes, there was an entire crew cleaning our kitchen, and Raúl and Mrs. Boone were at a picnic table in the backyard politely sharing a box of donuts from Dogma Cafe.

"Didn't he eat donuts two hours ago?" Elvis asked as we passed through the backyard.

"Can you have too many donuts?" I asked.

"Where's Pico?" Epic scanned the backyard. "He's not inside, and he's not filming."

"Maybe he's taking that nap he told Mandee about."

Based on my brother's anxiety level, it probably wasn't the most sensitive joke I could have told. But as soon as we got to the gate, we saw Heaven Hsu and Mr. Boone walking down the alley with Pico and Roo. Pico spotted Epic and ran greyhound speed ahead on his leash. Epic barely had time to unlatch the gate before the little dog hurled himself at my brother, who immediately relaxed.

I almost didn't catch it because Elvis was talking so much baby talk to the dogs, but Raúl waved Heaven over and offered her a donut.

"I thought it over," I heard him say. "I'm on board."

MIRRORS

I tried every excuse in the book to stay and keep an eye on Heaven and Raúl. I even tried telling the truth. It was bad enough that my siblings thought my theory about Heaven and Raúl wasn't rational. It was worse that they thought it was hilarious. Epic had to wipe away tears, he was laughing so hard.

I rolled my eyes. "Glad I could cheer you up so much."

You'd think they'd care more. Pico and Sir Bentley were their favorite dogs on the planet, and they liked *Bentley Knows* as much as I did. But they didn't buy Heaven's motive, and Epic said Raúl had already sunk too much time and energy into training Pico. If he gave up now, all that effort would be wasted. At least if he stuck it out, he'd get paid and maybe have a hit show. It was a decent point. Raúl didn't seem like the quitting type.

"You should tell this to Denver," Elvis said, still giggling. "He'll believe you. He's such a Mini-Rondo."

"He is not!" I said.

But when Elvis announced that we'd shown up to help plan his Yips & Sips magic show, Denver Delgado-Doyle smirked.

"I knew you'd come around," he said.

Which, I had to admit, was a pretty Mini-Me thing to say.

We hadn't spent much time inside the Moondoggie Inn before, and it turns out, there were some interesting things I didn't know about the place. The rooms were decorated with a 1950s surf theme. There were cupboards built into walls and window seats with secret cabinets. And Brody Delgado hated to go in the penthouse, because he thought it was haunted.

At least it was a good distraction from uselessly running through the details of the sabotage theory in my brain. Maybe my siblings were right and I was drawing connections that weren't there. It's what I always gave the Boones a hard time about. Just because someone tilts their head and your dog does the same thing, it doesn't mean they're talking to each other in their minds. Besides, at Sunny Day Academy, they taught us that if you're stuck on a problem, one of the best ways to solve it is to focus on something else for a while. Your brain will keep working on it in the background, and in the meantime, you might learn something new.

"This bookcase is a *secret passageway*?" Elvis squealed.

There was a hidden door in the Moondoggie's lobby. It was legitimately cool.

"It's an emergency exit from the olden times," Denver

explained with a slightly embarrassed blush. "In case the police came when guests were drinking or gambling."

"We *have* to use that for Yips and Sips," Elvis said, which nobody argued with. A hidden doorway in a magic show was a no-brainer.

It wasn't that hard to put together ideas for the performance. Everyone agreed Bella should do her best tricks, including the happy birthday song. Denver and Elvis would ham it up with the French Drop and a card trick called the Whispering Queen. And the grand finale, obviously, would be a disappearing act. It was the details that gave us trouble.

"We've got to build a box with hidden mirrors, like Houdini," Denver said.

"I'm telling you, it was a double wall."

"Don't start that again!" El complained, and Epic came to the rescue by pointing out that big mirrors might be hard to find but that we could easily use some of Mom's building materials to build a container with a false back.

"Thank you!" I said. I'd *maybe* started to gloat, but Epic shut me down.

"It doesn't even matter until we decide what we're going to make disappear," he said. "The materials we use will be determined by the size of the subject."

"It's got to be something *spec-TAC-ular*! Something that'll go viral!"

"Viral, El?" Epic gave my sister a disappointed look.

"You're right, you're right. Not viral, but . . . *spec-TAC-ular*!"

Elvis did jazz hands in the air. Denver shook his hands, too, and showed her how to add an elaborate rainbow arc with her arms. The two of them came up with a slew of impossible ideas about what we should vanish. A tiger. A rocket ship. The entire hotel.

"Oooh ooh ooh, I've got it!" Elvis shouted. "Let's disappear Pico! He's tiny, so that makes it easy, and we could post it online so it'll get spread around and he'll get all the new followers he needs to be a mega-influencer and . . . *What?*"

Epic and I stared at her until she figured it out on her own.

"Oh yeah, not viral. Normal summer." She looked a little deflated, but perked up again and said, "We could use Doughboy! Nobody cares about Doughboy!"

That led to a whole string of ideas about disappearing dogs. We could make Bella vanish, or Roo, or choose a random dog from the audience. Denver was really into the audience-participation idea.

"It seems kind of cruel," Epic said. "To put a dog in a dark box when they have no idea what's going on."

"Rondo could tell the dog what's happening," Elvis said. "He could explain it with his mind."

"Let it go, El," I said. "I seriously can't do that."

"We'll see." She shrugged.

"What's that supposed to mean?"

Denver looked at us nervously, like he was afraid we were going to start another sibling fight and end up drawing lines in the sand again. He patted Bella and changed the subject back to the disappearing act.

"Epic has a point. It would take a while to train even a smart dog like Bella to be comfortable with a trick like that," he said. "Maybe a few weeks. We'd have to slowly acclimate her. I mean, there's no rush, right? We could save that part of the act for when I come back in the summer."

"Sooner is better," I said. El beamed at me, so I didn't say the rest of the sentence I was thinking: *So we can get it over with.*

"We *need* a dog, though," Elvis said. "If we're going to do a disappearing act, it'll be so much better if it's something adorable that the audience will love and care about. That way, when it vanishes, it *matters* to them."

She was right, actually. I'm pretty sure Epic, Denver, and I had the thought at the exact same time, because it was like we'd rehearsed it when all three of us pointed at El.

"Me?" Elvis squealed and pointed at herself, too. "Yes! Let's make *me* disappear!"

It was all she talked about while we ate dinner, while we did the dishes—in a surprisingly well-scrubbed, sugar-free kitchen—even while the film crew set up for the nighttime roof scene. It seemed like a rooftop stunt with three dogs, a crane outside, and a Hollywood film crew in our own house would take up all El's attention. But she was so excited about getting to be the star of her own show that she flitted around, announcing it to anyone who would listen. Mom. Dad. Mr. Boone. The lighting guy. The showrunner. Raúl. Roo.

"We're doing a magic show!"

"It's a disappearing act!"

"Wait'll you find out who vanishes!"

"It's someone you know and love!"

"It's going to be *ah*-mazing!"

"Did I tell you we're doing a disappearing act?"

It was the kind of thing that should have been fine. Normally. It was El being El. It didn't bother *me*. Most of the adults thought it was cute. Adorable, even.

But a couple hours later, when the lights went out and three Italian greyhounds disappeared into thin air?

It got pretty inconvenient.

DOGNAPPED!

"I'm telling you, I have no idea how the power went out," I said.

"And?" Mom stood in front of the family stairs and pushed her hair behind her ears.

"I don't know where the dogs are, I swear." I clenched my teeth before saying the next part. "It's unfair that you automatically assume—"

"*Rondo.*" Mom looked exhausted. "Help me out here."

"That's what I'm *trying* to do!" But no one in my family was helping *me*.

Dad and most of the film crew were outside searching for the missing Iggys. Epic had left in a huff, supposedly to get Luis on the case. The Boones were in the lobby waiting for Mom to finish giving me and El the third degree so that I could try to locate the Iggy. Telepathically. Using the dowsing crystal I'd picked up at the farmers' market. I had Elvis to thank for that one.

"Rondo can do more than talk to Pico!" she'd announced

when the Boones had asked me to find their dog with my mind. "He has a special pendulum he can swing over a map and find Pico's location in a snap! It's going to be *ah*-mazing!"

It was so annoying, I had to wonder if Revenge-Elvis had some reason to be back in the game.

"You have been talking about a disappearing act all night," Mom said. "And now three dogs are missing."

To be honest, I thought it was fair that Mom was suspicious about El. When my sister gets something in her head, she always finds a way to make it happen. She'd been dying for a mystery, and normally, I wouldn't have put it past her to create one so we could solve it. If I hadn't known what I knew about Heaven and Raúl, I'd have been suspicious, too.

"That's our *magic show*!" Elvis protested. "We're disappearing *me*, and thanks a lot, because now you made me ruin the surprise."

Mom looked pained. "Look, I feel guilty enough about all of this. I hope you're telling me the truth, but your dad and I agree: Past experience dictates that I'm going to have to search your room."

"*What?*" we said in unison.

I didn't have time for this. Despite El's weird behavior, I was 99 percent sure the power outage was all part of Heaven's plan. The first day we'd met her, I'd seen it in her notebook. *Step 1: Total darkness is key.* Now she could be gearing up for whatever *Step 2* might be. I needed to get my hands on that notebook. It also wouldn't hurt to check the guest wing windows for signs of an escape route. Stray dog hair, paw prints, nail marks—all of those could be helpful clues. But I couldn't discover them from my bedroom.

"Wait. Why do *you* feel guilty?" Elvis asked Mom.

It was a good question, but before she got an answer, Brody Delgado peeked into the stairwell with Denver close behind him. That kid always had an overly dramatic look on his face, and he outdid himself this time.

"Whoa!" Denver held his hands on his head like if he let go, his brains might explode out and ruin his perfect haircut. "Who could have seen *this* coming?"

Only the way he said it, it sounded sarcastic. Like everyone could have seen it coming. In fact, the way my sister was grinning and bouncing around and specifically *not* looking at Denver Delgado-Doyle? They were practically forcing me to rethink my theories.

"Hey, Elly, sorry, is it still cool . . . ?" Brody asked. "I kinda gotta get back to the Doggie?"

Elvis poked me in the ribs and grinned. "Denver's sleeping over!"

"Oh, Brody, of course. I forgot," Mom said with a fake-cheerful smile. "Sorry we can't take Bella, too, but Raúl insists she can't be here during the filming . . . *if* that's even still happening tonight. Come on upstairs, Denver."

Denver and Elvis high-fived like we were about to have birthday cake. Which we definitely were not.

As soon as Brody took off, Mom's smile disappeared. We

followed her up to the family wing, past my parents' bedroom, but she paused in the hall, her hand on the doorknob to our room. Like she almost didn't want to open it and see what she expected to see.

"No matter what we find—"

"You mean *nothing*?" I said, but Elvis didn't back me up. My jaw felt tense.

"I need you three to stay up here until we figure this out. No one leaves the bedroom."

I groaned. Everyone knows the quicker you get to a crime scene, the better. If Raúl and Heaven were in cahoots, one of them could be in the guest wing right now, burning the notebook and sweeping away the clues.

"Not even Denver?" El asked. "What if he has to go out and do something important?"

Like what, El? I tried to read her brain waves, but it wasn't working.

"No," Mom said. "He's your guest. He stays with you."

"A-*hem*." A cough from the bottom of the stairs made Mom wince. Guests, even the Boones, weren't allowed in the family wing, but Mrs. Boone jogged right up the stairs and put her hand on Mom's shoulder like she needed the support. Her glittery eyelashes blinked at us. The colors in her makeup had started to smear from all the crying.

"Elly, we need Rondo," she said in a hoarse voice.

"You need *Rondo*?"

Mr. Boone appeared at the bottom of the stairs. "As soon

as possible!" he snapped, and then quickly added in a softer tone, "*Please*. The Department of Lost Dogs only has *one* BarkAngel on duty! We don't have forty-five minutes to wait."

I wondered how long it would take for the network to hear about the missing-dog disaster and pull the plug on *Bentley Knows*. If it was after hours for the BarkAngels, it was probably after hours for TV executives, too. Which was a good thing. Maybe we had until morning to find the dogs and calm everyone down.

Elvis tugged Mom's hand away from the doorknob.

"Pleasepleaseplease Rondo *needs* to help them."

At the sound of El's begging, the Boones' patience evaporated, and they joined right in.

"Pico's been *dognapped*! Aren't you worried about him, Elly?"

"Every minute we're standing here is a minute my baby is lost! My *baby*! Tell her, Rondo! Tell her you can help."

It's not like I wanted to lie. Or fake-communicate with Pico. But how else was I going to get to the guest wing?

"I can help," I said to Mom. "And I promise, the dogs aren't in our room." Those facts were true. At least, as far as I knew.

"Okay, okay." Mom nodded. "Of *course* I'm worried about Pico. I didn't think a power failure would lead to—"

Elvis grabbed my arm with one hand and pulled Denver by the strap of his backpack with the other. We were down the stairs before Mom had a chance to finish her sentence.

"If you see Epic," El yelled over her shoulder, "tell him

we're in Pico's suite. Tell him we need him! Tell him things are about to get . . . *ah*-mazing!"

She whispered the last word in my ear, but I was pretty sure it was the exact opposite of how things were about to get.

PET DETECTIVES

Mr. Boone took the stairs two steps at a time, and in the rush, Mrs. Boone almost tripped on an extension cord that was taped to the top stair. I hadn't been up to the guest wing all day, and in less than twenty-four hours, it had turned into a complete disaster area. There was a folding table set up in the hall with half-eaten drinks and food. Bags and stacks of equipment were stashed in every available nook. A network of cords snaked from Room 4, where the filming was happening, into a couple of the other guest rooms and the laundry room.

"I thought they had a generator," I said. "Why are they plugging stuff into the guest rooms?"

What I *wanted* to know was why Raúl's and Heaven's doors were propped open to let extension cords through. Even with the cords taped to the floor, the whole setup didn't seem dog-safe enough for Raúl's standards. Was this mess part of Heaven's plan? I stepped over a cord in the hall and flipped through my notebook, looking for the list of reasons she'd said the show could get shut down.

If the execs didn't like the episode.

If they got an American Humane violation.

If someone got sick or went missing.

"Focus, Rondo," Mrs. Boone said.

She unlocked Room 1 and shooed us all inside. I didn't have a choice. The faster I could get through the "animal communication," the faster I could sneak into Heaven's room and find her notebook. I started to take my usual place on the floor, but Mrs. Boone took my arm and ushered me to the center cushion of the couch.

"Are you comfortable?" she asked, sitting on the cushion next to me.

"Do you need anything? Water? Snacks?" Mr. Boone sat down on the other side and handed me one of the Perro's tourist maps of downtown Carmelito.

"Where's the dowsing crystal?" Elvis asked.

Denver raised his eyebrows at me. I was pretty sure he was working up an entire I-told-you-so lecture about Houdini and the messes you get yourself into when you play around with the occult. I wasn't in the mood for smug nine-year-olds. I shoved my hand in my pocket and pulled out the pendulum. Even holding it made me feel like a liar. I set it down on the map and left it there.

Based on everything I knew about Mrs. Boone, I would

have thought she'd be more hyped up and excited by now. Like getting dognapped was proof that Pico was as mega-famous as she wanted him to be. That was how she'd been acting before. But now that Pico was gone, she looked terrified. They both did.

Mr. Boone moaned. "We only wanted him to have more followers—"

"And be a mega-influencer! But this is *too much*." Mrs. Boone wiped away another tear.

"It would help to know how he's doing," Mr. Boone said. "Ask him that first. Make sure he's okay. Please?"

I couldn't go through with this. It was one thing to pretend to talk to Roo as a magic trick, or to read Pico's mind to expose the BarkAngels. But to fake a conversation with a missing dog? Even if it made the Boones feel better, it didn't feel right. I should have been out in the hall, *actually* helping them.

"I'm sorry, I can't talk to Pico," I said. "It's a scam."

"I know it's a scam," Mrs. Boone said. "We're probably going to get a call any minute now asking for ransom money! That's what happened to Sharon Henderson."

"Seriously, I can't. But I *can* help you investigate."

"Right." Denver opened his observation notebook and scribbled in it. "How do the dognappers find people's phone numbers? For the ransom calls?"

"Great question, Detective D!" El said, but I wasn't impressed.

First of all, it *wasn't* a great question. If somebody had gone to all the trouble to figure out where you lived and if they'd worked out the optimum time to steal your dog and get away with it, finding a phone number wasn't going to be that hard. Second of all, what was Denver doing? Mocking me? Playing copycat? Or trying to solve the mystery before *I* could? I knew one thing: It was super annoying.

The Boones were annoying me, too. It was obvious Pico hadn't been dognapped. At least not like they thought he had. For one thing, *three* Italian greyhounds were missing. If dognappers were looking for celebrity-level ransom, they wouldn't bother to take the stuntdog and the understudy, too. Unless they had a different goal. Like sabotaging a TV show. I stared at the map on the coffee table and tried to figure out my next move.

Elvis moved over to look at Denver's notebook. They huddled together, whispering. Like conspirators. Laughing, too. They were taking this all pretty cheerfully. Which was a problem. Before I could gather evidence against Heaven and Raúl, I needed to rule out one more possibility. I needed to know if Denver and my sister were in cahoots.

I couldn't remember if Elvis had been in the lobby at the exact moment the power went out, but Epic had taught us all about how circuits worked. She *could* have tripped the circuit breaker and then raced to join in the screaming. Denver and Brody had been awfully quick to show up at the scene.

What if they'd snagged the dogs and hidden them some-where? I really hoped it wasn't our bedroom.

"Are you getting anything?"

Mr. and Mrs. Boone looked at me hopefully, and it hit me that while I'd been thinking, *they* thought I was talking to their dog.

"Um . . . just a minute," I said, holding up a finger to buy myself some time.

I wasn't interested in getting Elvis in trouble. If she and Denver hadn't done it? Fine. But if they had, I knew Mom and Dad would never believe they'd pull a stunt like this without me. I needed to know what I was in for. The next thing I said wasn't for the Boones. It was for me.

"He seems safe," I said. "I don't think he's hurt."

Elvis straightened up and stared at me. I watched every muscle of her face. I knew if I pretended to "see" something that hit close to the truth, I'd be able to tell. Elvis is a better liar than my brother, but I know when she's faking for show and when she's not.

"My *baby*!" Mrs. Boone said. "What else is he saying to you? How do we get him back? Find out where we should bring the ransom money!"

Mr. Boone was frozen, waiting for my next words. I didn't like lying to them, but if it proved that Elvis was the culprit, I'd help her find a way to sneak Pico back from wherever she and Denver were hiding him. If she didn't have anything to do with it, I knew exactly where to go next.

"I think he's on a bed," I said. "With some stuffed animals? I see an elephant, a giraffe, and a bunny."

Elvis didn't move. "Really?" she said quietly. "How'd he get *there*?"

She looked confused, and she wasn't trying to win any acting awards with her dramatics. El hadn't stashed the dogs in our room. Which was a good thing. It meant Mom wouldn't find anything.

"That's good information," Denver said. "It tells us the dognappers probably have a kid."

He wrote it down in his notebook, which made me suspicious again. Unlike Elvis, Denver didn't believe I could talk to animals. So why was he pretending to?

"No, no, I take it back," I said. "I think that was a memory Pico was having. Telling me where he *wishes* he could be right now. I'm getting a different image . . . It looks like a hotel room. First floor, no, second . . ." Mrs. Boone looked like she might start crying again, so I quickly added, "He says don't worry, he's under the bed hiding, and no one can hurt him right now because he's all the way back by the wall. He's totally safe. But"—I looked meaningfully at El—"he really, *really* wants to come home."

My sister wasn't taking the bait. And she didn't look cheerful anymore. She looked upset. Like this had suddenly gotten all too real. I didn't have to be a mind reader to know what was going on with El. It was all fun and games when there was an exciting mystery to be solved and she could pretend to be Detective McDade. But when she finally thought about Pico, the actual dog who was missing, huddling in a corner? My sister was scared. Not scared of getting caught. Or scared because she didn't have a plan. She believed 100 percent that Pico was being held by bloodthirsty criminals.

Elvis was not the mastermind here.

"How long has it been since the power went out?" Denver asked, scribbling in his notebook. "We could make a list of all the hotels that someone could get to in that amount of time. You don't think they're at the Moondoggie, do you? I mean, that would be the closest!"

His eyes were wide in that signature Denver Delgado-Doyle style. A little *too* excited about the whole thing. I'd still have to keep an eye on him.

"It's a good thing you've got the pet detectives on the case!" Denver held out his hand for a high five, but Elvis shook her head, dead serious.

"Use the crystal," she said.

"That doesn't work, El."

But Elvis put the chain in my hand and tapped the crystal so it swung back and forth over the map.

"Please?" she begged. "Don't move for ten seconds."

The Boones leaned forward to watch.

I decided to try logic. "See? It's not doing anything different from a regular pendulum. Plus, it can't be the celebrity dognappers. There hasn't even been a ransom call."

Denver checked his watch. Like he could figure out

precisely how much time should have elapsed before the criminals made their demands.

"It stopped!" Elvis stared at the pendulum. My hand must have dropped a bit, because the tip of the stone rested on the map. I let the chain fall to the table as Elvis breathed, "Pico's *here*. At the Perro!"

Milliseconds later?

Mr. Boone's cell phone rang.

THE DEPARTMENT OF LOST DOGS

"This is a callback from the BarkAngels' Department of Lost Dogs. I have Leif Skye available for you now." The voice on Mr. Boone's speakerphone was cheerful and motherly, and she sounded like she was reading off a script. "We're proud to offer Lost Dog services for our clients, and you should feel confident that we have a ninety-five percent success rate. May I send you a link for the video call?"

While the Boones frantically got the laptop set up, I watched Denver. He'd been lying on his back on the floor, staring at the ceiling with his pencil in his mouth. Every once in a while, he'd rub his head, flop over on his belly, scribble something in his notebook, then go back to his original position and stare at the ceiling again. Elvis had quit paying attention to any of us and sat quietly, legs crossed, eyes closed. She didn't even budge when the BarkAngel popped onto the screen.

"Oh man, you guys must be worried sick," Leif said. "I'm sorry it took awhile, I was working on a tough one. A Maltese got her hair stuck in a rosebush, but it's all right . . . We found her! Good thing, too, because she has her first audition at a modeling agency tomorrow."

Mrs. Boone puckered her lips. She clearly didn't care about that dog's audition.

"I also spent some time on Pico," Leif assured her. "I've already got a direct psychic line to him. He says, first of all, he wants you to know that he loves you."

"Oh! Pico!" Mrs. Boone leaned in, squashing me between her shoulders and Mr. Boone's.

"I can move," I offered. In fact, this was a perfect time to leave. But Mr. Boone shushed me and leaned forward, locking me in even more.

"How do we pay the ransom?" he asked.

Leif shook his head. "This isn't a dognapping. No offense, but Pico's not rich and famous enough. Yet."

Mrs. Boone sucked in her breath. "That's what *Rondo* said!"

"Based on what I'm seeing, I don't think he's gone far." Leif held up a pendulum that looked a lot more professional than mine. "I did some dowsing while we set up the call, and I'm pretty sure he's somewhere on your block."

Mrs. Boone sucked in her breath a second time. "Rondo found that, too!"

"Who's Rondo? The boy with you now? Clever kid."

Leif sounded like he was impressed, but he almost looked annoyed. Suspicious, like he thought *I* was the one duping the Boones.

I might not be able to help the Boones talk to Pico, but they were right about one thing. If they wanted their Iggy back, they needed *me* on the case, not the BarkAngels. I had to get out of Room 1.

"I should go," I breathed. "I mean, I can't right now, but I could if you move a little—"

"*Shhhhhhhh!*" the Boones hissed in unison. The BarkAngel had started to describe the images Pico was sending him. It was the usual generic stuff—someplace dark, someplace lonely.

On the other side of the coffee table, Denver was completely absorbed in his notes, but Elvis was acting strangely. She still had her eyes closed, but she'd started sniffing the air. I sniffed, too, but I didn't smell anything. Nothing burning or cookies baking. I almost chalked it up to El being her usual weird self, but then she tipped herself onto all fours and started crawling slowly toward the kitchenette. Her polka-dot skirt got caught under her knees, but she adjusted it, kept her eyes closed, and made her way toward the hallway door.

The Boones finally shifted enough that I was able to escape from between them. El crawled out into the hall, but as I started to follow her, Mr. Boone's phone buzzed.

Unknown number.

"It's happening, it's happening!" Mrs. Boone grabbed my arm and pulled me back down to the couch.

"Trace the number!" Denver said. As if any of us had the capability to do that.

Leif Skye looked surprised, but said, "Go ahead and answer it. I'll stay right here in case you need me."

It wasn't the dognappers. It was my brother.

"He says it's important. Keep it short. Real short." Mr. Boone handed me the phone and shooed me off the couch.

"Detective agency meeting." Epic was breathless. "Behind the Moondoggie if you can sneak out."

Was that a joke? We didn't have a great connection, but "sneak out" was such an off-brand thing for my brother to say that there was no way I'd heard him right. I took a few steps toward the hallway to try to get better service and to keep an eye on Elvis. I tried to ignore the fact that Denver was following so close I could feel his breath on my neck.

"Don't tell Mom and Dad," Epic said. "And *don't* tell the Boones."

"What? Why?" I asked, but Epic had already hung up.

I'd been watching Elvis inch down the hallway on her hands and knees. Every time she got to a guest room, she paused, listened at the door, and crawled on. When she got to Room 5, she paused a bit longer and rested her forehead on the door. Like at Raúl's room, Heaven Hsu's door wasn't shut all the way. A thick black extension cord kept it slightly ajar, and apparently El took that as an open invitation, because she nudged the door with her head and crawled right in.

"El," I called, and followed her down the hall. "Come back!"

"What's she doing?" Denver asked. I'd forgotten he was right behind me, and I flinched and spun around so hard that my elbow knocked into his face. I felt teeth and bone dig into my skin, and I dropped Mr. Boone's phone.

"Ow!" Denver yelled at the very same time that my sister shouted, "I did it! I found Pico!" Unfortunately, Denver's nose was already pouring blood.

It's not like I'm scared of blood. I don't even think it's that disgusting, but there's nothing I can do. If I see it, I have a gut reaction.

Literally.

As my sister ran into the hall to find us, eyes lit up like she'd done the world's greatest magic trick, I felt my stomach tighten and my chest heave. Before I could do anything about it, I'd puked on one of her pigtails.

Worse, the second Denver saw what I'd done, he leaned over with his bloody nose and puked, too. All over Mr. Boone's phone.

"Sorry," he mumbled. "I can't help it. Whenever I smell puke, I have to puke, too."

I'd thought everyone at the Perro had gone out to find the Italian greyhounds, but El's shrieking drew a small crowd. In addition to the Boones, there were two camera assistants, who had been hanging out in Raúl's room cleaning lenses, and a hairdresser and a makeup artist emerged from Room 4, where they'd been prepping for the touch-up work they'd have to do if the Iggys were found and the showrunner decided to restart the roof scene. Mom and a woman in a tool belt came out from testing some outlets in the laundry room. And Heaven Hsu walked up the stairs with Roo in her arms and a donut from the catering table half in her mouth.

Heaven's eyebrows lifted when she saw the commotion, the blood, and the puke, and she turned around and went right back down the stairs.

"El. Focus." I shook my sister's arm to get her to stop gagging and freaking out. "Did you really find Pico in *Heaven Hsu's* room?"

Elvis stood still for a second, and a smile burst onto her face. Like even though she had puke in her hair, she'd done something *ah*-mazing, and it was all coming back to her.

"I totally did!" She grinned.

I grinned back. "I totally called this."

SABOTAGE

Pico was tied with one of Raúl's training leashes to the leg of Heaven Hsu's bed, but the dog huddled in the back corner and wouldn't come out.

"It's happening like you said, Rondo." Mrs. Boone was on her hands and knees, head under the bed, trying to coax Pico out into the open. "He's under a bed in a hotel on the second floor! You *saw* it! You were even more accurate than the BarkAngel! Clive, tug at the leash again. But gently! Rondo, talk to him. Ask Pico why he doesn't want to come out."

"That won't work," I said. I stepped around her to get to the armchair where Heaven Hsu had left her messenger bag.

While someone cleaned up the carpet and a member of the camera crew put Mr. Boone's phone in a bag of rice to dry it out, Mom and the hairdresser brought Elvis to Room 4 to wash her hair in the sink. I knew my sister was going to milk her time with a celebrity hairdresser for all it was worth, but Mom could be back at any minute. I needed to find what I was looking for. Hard evidence.

"You've got to quit doubting yourself, son." Mr. Boone lowered himself down to his knees on the floor with a grunt. He stuck his head under the bed and added, "She's right. You've got a gift."

I'd only said the thing about Pico being under the bed to throw the Boones a bone. To make them feel like he was safe. Not because I'd seen or heard anything in my mind. The fact that he was under there now didn't have anything to do with me, it had to do with random chance and probability.

People always think that the odds of a coincidence happening are rare, but they're not doing the right calculations. In a regular situation, for instance, if Pico was on the second floor of the Perro when the lights went out, the probability that he *stayed* on the second floor is a lot higher than the chance that he somehow went out the window. And if you take into account how many pieces of furniture there were in the guest wing for a startled dog to hide under, and how many of those pieces were beds, the probability of my guess coming true gets even higher.

But that's in a regular situation. That's not even talking about the fact that Heaven Hsu was one of the two people looking for an opportunity to sabotage the film shoot. In that case, it wasn't only probable, but extremely likely, that Pico was under the bed in Room 5 of the Perro del Mar.

I glanced at the Boones to make sure they were both focused on the Iggy under the bed before I reached for Heaven's notebook and slipped it out of her bag. I'll admit,

I felt a tiny pang of doubt; I was stealing. But before I could think too hard about it, I shoved the notebook underneath my T-shirt.

That's when I felt Denver's hot whisper in my ear.

"I read the back of that Virginia Woolf book she was reading. It's a true crime story. About celebrity dognappings."

"For real?" I asked. Denver's breath smelled like vomit, and he really should have learned his lesson about sneaking up on people. But this was good information.

"Yep. Flush was a springer spaniel who was dognapped three times, and his owner was a famous poet, who paid the ransom every time. Do you think that actress was going to ask the Boones for ransom?"

I blinked at him. I'd believed Heaven would sabotage the show, but would she also dognap Pico? For cash? Why? I supposed if *Bentley Knows* got canceled like she hoped, she'd be out of a paycheck. If she was already going to the trouble of making a dog disappear, it wouldn't take much to copycat the crime. Still. I shook the thought out of my head. No one had asked the Boones for ransom. This was a straight-up sabotage job.

"Pico, baby, we know you're scared, but you're safe now, I promise."

Mrs. Boone's voice came from under the bed. "Talk to him, Rondo," she said. "Ask if he's mad at us."

Denver swiped at something on the dresser and handed it to me. It was one of Raúl's special barrel-shaped dog treats.

"Fine," I said.

I knelt down and stuck my head under the bed. Sure enough, Pico was huddled way in the back corner, exactly as I'd described him. He blinked his eyes at me, and tilted his head. He looked scared, and I suddenly thought about Heaven. Even if she wasn't planning to blackmail the Boones for ransom money, she was going to be in big trouble for pulling this stunt. What if they kicked her off the show? That would be good for her, but what if they got some boring actress to replace her? I almost thought about covering for her, like I'd planned to do with El. But as much as I liked Heaven Hsu, she wasn't my sister. I couldn't let her get away with it.

"Come on, buddy," I said, and reached out my hand, the treat tucked into my palm. "You can come out now. Everything's okay."

We stayed like that for a minute, my arm stretched out and the Iggy staring at me. It honestly looked like he was thinking it over. Then he sniffed, took a couple steps forward, and paused. I pulled my hand back a couple inches, and Pico stepped forward again.

"He's moving!" Mrs. Boone said. She got so excited that she clocked her head on the side of the bed and while Mr. Boone rushed to make sure she was okay, Pico made his way out into the open. His tongue was rough on my skin as he licked every last crumb of the treat out of my palm.

"You did it! Rondo, you're amazing!" Mrs. Boone reached for Pico, but he flinched and wiggled out of the way.

When Mr. Boone moved toward him, the Iggy whined.

"I knew it." Mr. Boone looked at me. "He's mad, isn't he?"

It *was* strange, the way Pico was stepping backward and dropping his nose to the side. Like he didn't want to see them.

"He's probably in shock," Denver said. "Wouldn't you be?"

"That's not the problem." The chemical smell of fake fruit and flowers filled the room as my sister burst in with blow-dried, poufy, TV-show hair all done up in glittering barrettes. She stood in the doorway for a second to let us soak in her new look before she raced toward me and knelt down on the ground to pet Pico.

"Not bad for my first try, right?" Elvis beamed at me.

"First try at what?"

"Talking to animals!" she said. "I mean, I didn't get it totally right, but I *did* it! I knew I could! I closed my eyes and concentrated on thinking like an Italian greyhound. I didn't hear any words or see any pictures or anything, but I *felt* like I should go out in the hall and I did and then I was *drawn* straight here. Telepathically!"

"No you weren't," I said. "I saw you peeking in the rooms. That's not telepathy. It's deductive reasoning."

Elvis stuck her tongue out at me. "You're not the only one who can do it, you know."

"I can't talk to animals!" I said.

"You just did!" Mrs. Boone chimed in.

The whole animal communication thing needed to stop. It wasn't even fun anymore.

"I faked it. Didn't I, Denver?"

Denver looked from me to El like he wasn't sure whose side to take.

"Seriously?" Maybe it was the bad taste in my mouth or the nauseating smell of Elvis's hair spray, but I was done. "It's not real. It's *bunk*! They're doing it to *cheat* people out of their money!"

Mr. Boone frowned. "That's a little harsh, Rondo."

"That's *very* harsh, Rondo." My sister glared at me. "You don't always have to act like you're the smartest. Do you even know how telepathy works? I do, because I researched it, and we're all made out of the same subatomic particles and waves. And those waves are connected with an invisible energy field—"

"That's not real science, El," I said.

"You don't know that because *you* didn't do the research." Elvis stuck her tongue out at me. "What do you have in your shirt?"

"Nothing."

"You said you'd *stop* being so secretive."

"I didn't say that. I'm not even that secretive."

"Fine, if it's nothing, let me see it!" El lunged for my T-shirt collar, but surprisingly, Denver held her back.

"Don't worry about it, Elvis." He tugged at her arm.

Something about the look on his face told me he'd decided to pick a side. The wrong side.

Mom and the *Bentley Knows* showrunner were standing in the doorway now. The hairdresser and the camera assistants were behind them.

"It's evidence," Denver said in a stage whisper that was way too loud. "For the detective agency. Rondo took it from Heaven Hsu's bag."

In fact, it was so loud, it didn't even sound like a whisper.

It sounded like sabotage.

DOUGHBOY

Mom had her hands on her hips exactly like Elvis does when she's mad.

"Are you serious right now?" I hissed at Denver. I knew there was a reason I didn't want him around.

"Do you have something that belongs to our *guest*, Rondo?" Mom asked, but she didn't wait for an answer. She didn't even look surprised. Instead, she turned straight to the Boones and started to apologize. "I'm sorry you've had to go through all of this tonight. Rondo should know better. And Elvis is not off the hook, either."

The Boones looked confused. "But the dognappers . . ."

Mom stared me down with fire in her eyes.

"I've got a hunch there aren't any dognappers," she said. "Are there, Rondo?"

I let my hair fall in front of my face. They were *not* going to pin this on me. As much as I hated to get Heaven Hsu in trouble, this was her fault, not mine.

"No. There aren't any dognappers." Technically, it was

true. Even if Heaven *had* been reading about dog ransoms, she hadn't stolen any money. But she did take Pico. I couldn't keep that a secret, no matter how cool she was. I pulled the notebook out from under my shirt. "Heaven Hsu stole Pico because she and Raúl are trying to sabotage the show. They want the *Bentley Knows* reboot to get canceled."

Mrs. Boone gasped, but Mom's jaw tightened.

"Rondo, we have *talked* about this."

"About Heaven Hsu stealing Pico? I don't remember talking about that." I knew it wasn't what she meant and that talking back was only going to get me in more trouble, but I was mad that she wouldn't believe me.

"*Rondo.*" Mom's voice was stern.

"I have proof!" I said. "Heaven wrote down all the details about how to make the power go out and steal Pico."

"Heaven didn't steal Pico," Elvis said.

"Right. He turned out the lights and leashed himself to her bed?" I asked.

Elvis didn't dignify my sarcasm with a response. She reached for the Iggy, rubbed the tip of his tail, and held up her fingers, covered in white chalk.

"See? I told you. I didn't get it perfectly right. I thought I was talking to Pico, but this is Doughboy."

"Doughboy?" Mr. Boone squinted at the dog. "Then where's Pico?"

"Shouldn't that be obvious?" Heaven Hsu's voice came from somewhere in the hallway. Dripping with professional-level sarcasm. "The little sleuth sleuthed it out. Can I get into my room, please?"

The crowd in the hallway had gotten bigger as members of the search party returned. People moved out of the way to let Heaven and Roo through the door to Room 5, and the second an opening cleared, an Italian greyhound who looked identical to the one next to me wriggled past her and practically flew into Mr. Boone's arms.

"Pico!" Tears streamed down Mrs. Boone's face while Mr. Boone smothered the dog in kisses. "No one *stole* you, Pico! Did you hear that? No one is *ever* going to steal you. We promise!"

Doughboy went in the opposite direction. He yipped and hopped over my knees, his tail flopping like a windshield wiper as he raced to reunite with Raúl and Cheddar, who were right behind Heaven.

"Good boy, Doughie. That's a good boy." Raúl smiled as he knelt down to rub Doughboy's head. He looked so relieved to have both of his Iggys in his arms, I instantly had to second-guess my theory. If he'd been involved in the sabotage scheme, would he be that surprised and happy to see his dogs? I needed to recalculate. If Raúl didn't have anything to do with it, it didn't mean I was wrong. It just meant Heaven had been a lone operator. Maybe she'd been using the dog trainer to get information.

"If he wasn't stolen," Mr. Boone said, "what happened?"

"They got spooked when the circuit blew," Raúl said.

"Heaven caught Doughboy on the stairs, and we found Pico and Cheddar over by the Moondoggie."

Raúl looked directly at the showrunner, who flinched, probably bracing herself for another sugar situation.

"I'm *so* sorry, Raúl," she said. "The Perro doesn't have the security systems we're used to. If you want me to hire a night guard—"

But Raúl played it cool. "I think we learned a lot tonight. And you had a good point today: My plans are *too big* to let small annoyances slow me down. No need to call for security."

Call. I'd completely forgotten that Epic had called and asked us to sneak out and meet him at the Moondoggie. He was going to be so mad that we'd bailed on his detective agency meeting. I tried to think of an exit plan, but with Mom blocking the door, there was no way we could get over there now. Besides, the chances that Epic was still waiting for us were slim.

"All right, everyone!" the showrunner hollered, relieved that Raúl was being so reasonable. "Crisis averted. Let's get this thing back on track. Where are we at on the electrical? Are we stable?"

"We're good." A woman in the tool belt held up a laptop. "Someone jacked into the laundry room without telling me. Blew the circuit."

"That's mine." Heaven reached for the laptop. The showrunner shot her a look that I recognized. *Screwing things up. As usual.*

"What?" Heaven threw up her hands like she was caught. Which she was. Sort of. "I needed a charge, and the lighting crew used up the outlets in here. Elly showed me the one in the laundry room. I didn't think it was a big deal."

The showrunner turned to Mom, who blushed like giving directions to an outlet was on her Most Embarrassing Moments List.

"It's not *her* fault," Heaven said. "If the studio had sent us a *functioning* generator, we wouldn't be plugging all this stuff in. That was a bad idea in the first place."

Mom bit her lip and blushed harder. "Who could have known?" she said.

"Right." The showrunner put on a chipper voice. "All's well that ends well. Let's roll it again!"

People kicked into gear, picking up cords and camera bags. My hands were sweaty, still holding Heaven's notebook. All the pieces had fit together so perfectly. How could I have been wrong?

"Can I have my notes, please?" Heaven snatched the notebook, and Roo locked his rat-killer eyes on me. "Good sleuthing, though. Really top-notch."

The way she said stuff like that, with her deadpan voice and barely a smile, you seriously couldn't tell if Heaven Hsu thought everything that was happening was hilarious or if she was plotting to take me down with some kind of diabolical revenge.

She brushed past me and shoved the notebook back

into the bag where I'd found it. Something still didn't seem right. *Maybe* Heaven accidentally tripped the circuit by plugging her laptop into the laundry room. *Maybe* the dogs got spooked and ran, like Mom and everyone else believed. But I had questions.

What if there was a reason Heaven was on-the-ready to catch Doughboy? And a reason Raúl *didn't* go ballistic about the lack of security? What if they had bigger plans?

Roo sneered at me as a new theory formed in my brain.

What if this whole night was a trial run?

As if she could read my mind, Heaven pushed a stray hair behind her ear and winked at me.

"I already told you," she said quietly. "They won't care unless someone *important* goes missing. And there's still plenty of time for that."

HASHTAGS

"I think they're on to you." Denver snuck a look behind him to see if anyone was eavesdropping as we walked through the lobby toward the family wing. Where, according to Mom, my dad and Epic were waiting for us.

"Obviously," I said. "Heaven knows I tried to snoop in her notebook. Thanks to *you*."

"No, the BarkAngels." Denver explained impatiently. "Did you see Leif's face when he called you 'clever'? I *told* you to be careful."

Leif's expression had definitely had a keep-an-eye-on-this-kid vibe, but I wasn't about to give Denver the satisfaction of agreeing with him. I was annoyed that he'd ratted me out.

"I didn't see Leif's face." Elvis shot me a smug look. "I was too busy *communicating* with Doughboy."

"You were not," I said.

Elvis poked me in the side. "I was *so*."

"You don't have a clue about—"

"Ha! Clue?" El said. "*Your* clues were all wrong . . . *Elrond!*"

Denver paused at the top of the family stairs. He stood there and stared at our bedroom door, like he wasn't sure he wanted to go in. Let alone stay overnight. This probably wasn't the friendly sleepover he'd imagined.

"What's wrong?" Elvis paused, too.

"You three aren't . . ." Denver rubbed his hand over his head. "I guess you're different than I thought you'd be."

What was that supposed to mean?

"Like?" Elvis asked.

"You fight a lot."

"We do not," I said at the same time that El said, "It's his fault. He's so *myopic*."

"I don't even know what that is," I said. "Quit showing off."

"*Myopic* means you only care about yourself—"

"See? Fighting?" Denver said. Which shut us up for a minute. He looked at Elvis and added, "You *are* kind of a show-off."

"*What?*" El's hand dropped from the doorknob.

Denver shrugged and ticked a few things off on his fingers. "The trivia, the singing, those postcards from Sir Bentley?"

I glared at Denver. Even if it was true, *he* didn't get to say it.

"It's not *her* fault that she's smart," I said. "And so what if she has famous friends? You show off plenty."

Denver narrowed his dark eyes in my direction. "*You* act like the world revolves around you." He didn't look like he was angry, exactly, just disappointed. "You only like your own ideas, and . . ." He took a breath like he was deciding if he wanted to say it or not. "You do what you want even if it makes other people feel bad. It's not very nice."

He mumbled the last bit, but El put her hands on her hips.

"Are you going to say something about Epic, too?" She asked it like a threat. Like she wasn't going to stand there and let some new kid bad-mouth her family.

Denver sighed. "Not really," he said. "He's quiet. And a little weird."

"*Weird?* You want to talk about *weird*? I'll show you *weird*!" Elvis blurted.

With her hands on her hips and her fluffy Hollywood hairstyle bouncing around her raged-out face.

I couldn't help it. I laughed. "Yeah, you will," I said.

El's mouth twitched, and she laughed, too.

Denver stared at the two of us like "weird" wasn't even the half of it. We all flinched as the door to our bedroom opened from the inside.

"Hey!" Epic stood in the doorway, eyes wild, his hair sticking up in all directions, like it gets when he's been thinking hard and running his fingers through it distractedly. "Come in here. Dad's looking at the hashtags I found all over town."

Denver's jaw dropped, and Elvis and I laughed even harder.

It was such an undeniably weird thing to say.

At least Denver Delgado-Doyle wasn't afraid to tell the truth. You had to respect the kid for that.

We stopped laughing when we saw Dad sitting at Epic's project desk. He frowned at several half-crumpled pieces of paper with all-caps handwriting that looked a whole lot like Epic's perfect block letters. Every single note was written on notepaper with the Perro del Mar Bed & Breakfast logo in the top corner.

"Don't get mad, but there's some stuff I haven't been telling you," my brother said.

No joke.

"You've been writing ransom notes?" Elvis looked super confused. For good reason.

I picked up one of the notes. It had pinholes in the corners like it had been posted on a bulletin board.

WARNING CARMELITO, CA! DOGNAPPERS ON THE LOOSE!!!!!!!!!!
RANSOM FOR PICO BOONE = 1 MILLION DOLLARS!!!!!!!!!!!!!!!!!!!!!
#BENTLEYKNOWS #SAVEPICOBOONE #CELEBRITYDOGNAPPED

Even though the notes were written neatly, it was obvious whoever wrote them wasn't my brother. He would never use that many exclamation points, and he barely knew what a hashtag was.

"It wasn't me," I said, in case Dad was jumping to conclusions.

Which, surprisingly, he wasn't. He and Epic were staring at Elvis instead. But I knew it wasn't her, either.

"I don't get it," El said. "Nobody asked for a million dollars. Nobody even took Pico. Is this about that whole Raúl mix-up on Sunday? Why would somebody—what? Why are you looking at me like that?"

"What happened to your hair?" Epic stared at her poufy glamor-do. "It looks so . . ."

"Beautiful?" Elvis said. "Elegant? Adorable?"

Dad and Epic looked to me for help.

"*Ah*-mazing?" I offered. El's current favorite word seemed like the safest way to go. Enthusiastic without having to commit to liking the new look.

"It is!" she said, puffing the bottom of her hair a little with her hand. "It's *ah*-mazing!"

Denver Delgado-Doyle was studying the notes. "When did you find these?"

It was a smart question. Pico had only gone missing an hour ago. Which was technically enough time to start posting notes about it, if that was the sort of thing you wanted to do. But the notes didn't look that fresh, and like El said, they weren't even accurate. Maybe someone *had* posted them after we'd accused Raúl of stealing Pico. The first time.

"I found that one tonight at the Moondoggie," Epic said. "But the ones Mom saw in my drawer are from bulletin boards all over town this week. The farmers' market, the dog park, the—"

"Middle school?" I asked, remembering the paper he'd crumpled while we were watching the soccer game.

"Exactly. Every time I take them down, more show up."

Dad rubbed his beard and laughed. "Could you ever have guessed there'd be all this fuss about Pico Boone? You'd expect it with Sir Bentley, but I remember when Pico first came to Carmelito for the Puppy Picnic. He was this nervous little thing . . ."

None of us were listening to Dad's trip down memory lane.

"That's why you stole the pet cam," I said to Epic. "For surveillance."

"I wasn't *stealing it*, but yeah. I was going to plant the Peek-a-Boo at the dog park and try to find out who—"

"Why wouldn't you *tell* us?" Elvis looked stunned. "We could have helped you!"

I agreed with her. El and I should have been the *first* people he came to. This was insulting.

Dad raised his eyebrows at the stolen pet cam reference, but he let it go. He stacked up the notes, rubbed his eyes, and yawned.

"I think we're good here. You should have come to me and your mom first," he said. "But it doesn't sound like that big of a deal. I bet someone put them up as a joke. I'd say forget about it and get some sleep. I'll run it by Luis in the morning."

"Don't bother," Epic said.

"Don't *bother*?"

Epic grimaced and avoided my eyes. He wouldn't look at Elvis, either. Whatever he was about to say, he knew we weren't going to like it.

"Luis thinks El and Rondo did it."

COPYCAT

"I don't get why you're both mad at *me*," Epic said after Dad left. "I told Luis it wasn't you. Plus, I spent half the week taking them all down so he wouldn't think you were doing it again! To help *you*!"

He grabbed his pajamas and his toothbrush and headed for the bathroom. El stomped around our room in her bare feet for a while, then collapsed onto the sleeping bag Mom had set out for Denver and flopped her feet on the pillow with a huff.

"Gross, El," I said. "Your feet are disgusting. He's got to sleep on that!"

El stuck out her tongue, but sat up, tucking her stinky feet under her skirt. "I can't believe Epic told Luis about a mystery before he told us!"

"Yeah. You said that," Denver mumbled. He'd been mostly quiet since we'd come upstairs, and after Dad left, he'd parked himself in a corner of the room, eyes glued to his notebook. I got the impression he wanted to stay as far away from the sibling drama as possible.

I was mad, too. Half at Luis, and half at Epic for leaving us out. Sure, it was nice that he'd tried to help. And that he didn't assume we were posting weird signs about Pico. But Elvis was right. When we were younger, we would have been the first people he told. We would have figured it out together. Was that how it was going to be now? Epic not trusting us? Leaving us in the dust?

Elvis sighed. "Do you think my hairdo's still going to look this good in the morning? I wish I could sleep without sleeping *on* it, you know?"

"*That's* your problem right now?" I asked.

"Why don't you sleep standing up? Like a horse," Epic joked, coming back from the bathroom. As if we'd all have one big laugh, and my brother's betrayal would blow right over. Elvis didn't crack a smile. She hopped to her feet, swiped her own toothbrush from her dresser, and stomped past him without a look.

"*I* thought it was funny," Epic tried.

I ignored him, and Denver focused on rummaging through his backpack. Finally, my brother shrugged and climbed into bed.

Instead of pulling out pajamas, Denver took a coin from his backpack and rubbed it between his fingers. I wondered if he wished he was home. The only sleepover I'd ever been to, if you don't count grandparents, was last year for this kid Eugene's birthday. It was fine, except that I had to call Dad in the middle of the night to come pick me up. It's not like there was anything wrong with the party. I just didn't want to be in a sleeping bag in some strange house. The problem for Denver was, he didn't have anyone to call. His parents were in San Diego. His uncle was busy at the Moondoggie. Even his dog, Bella, was off-limits, banned from the Perro. Which was my fault.

"You can sleep in my bunk," I said to Denver. "I'll take the sleeping bag. Elvis had her feet all over it."

He shook his head, still rubbing the coin. "It's all right."

"I could hang out down here for a while. If you want."

"Sure. If *you* want."

So after Elvis climbed into her bottom bunk and the lights went out, Denver zipped himself up into the sleeping bag and I handed over my best flashlight.

"I have another one," I said, and settled into my beanbag with my book.

After a while, we heard El snoring, and Epic's slow, quiet breaths. Denver was still fiddling with the coin, rubbing it between his fingers as he stared into space. It reminded me of the coin trick Dad had taught me to perform for the guests. I bet Denver could do it perfectly.

"I'm sorry I haven't been very nice," I said quietly. "It's nothing against you."

"What's it against, then?" Denver looked up, his face dimly lit by the flashlight.

"I don't know." I had to think about it. "I guess it's fine that you want to be like me. It's just, you've got the facts wrong."

Denver looked confused. "What?"

"I'm not a magician."

"I figured that out."

"Fine, but it was annoying. That you got into magic because of me. And now you want to copy me with all the detective stuff. I like to do my own thing."

Denver sat up in his sleeping bag and let out a serious Mini-Me laugh.

"You think I got into magic because of *you*?"

This was awkward. "Didn't you?"

He shook his head. "I got into magic because my grandpa Doyle taught me how to do a French Drop. And because Alex Ramon did a magic show at our library when I was five. You know who he is?"

"Nope. Should I?"

"Yes! He was National Stage Magic Champion by the time he was eighteen," Denver said. "He told us he was going to be the first big-time Latino magician in the US, and he totally did it. I mean, David Blaine is part Puerto Rican, but the point is . . . Alex Ramon became the 'Magical Zingmaster.'"

"Is that a thing?"

"Yeah. And you know what he did? He made an elephant disappear every night for two years straight."

"Seriously?" I asked. "Don't tell me he did it with mirrors."

Denver sat up on his knees. "I don't know how Alex did it, but check out what my dad sent me. It came in the mail today."

He rummaged in his backpack and pulled out a book called *Hiding the Elephant*.

"You've probably already read it," he said, and when I shook my head, he handed it over. It actually looked interesting.

"*How Magicians Invented the Impossible and Learned to Disappear*," I read.

"Maybe we can find out the true story of how Houdini did it," Denver said. "Do you know Dorothy Dietrich? I've been thinking about her. She performs lots of Houdini's original escapes, but she's also a debunker."

"Really?"

"Yeah. She exposes fake mediums like Houdini did." He paused. "They use a lot of the same tricks that those BarkAngels do."

"*Right?* That's what I've been trying to tell everybody!"

Denver leaned forward. "I bet my mom wouldn't mind the psychic stuff so much if we were trying to *stop* it. We could look up Dorothy Dietrich and see if we could get some tips."

"You do your research," I said. "I respect that."

Denver was smiling now, and looked way more relaxed.

I was smiling, too. Instead of rubbing the coin, he'd started doing some amazing one-handed flippy thing with it, moving it in and out of his fingers without even trying.

"What's that coin?" I asked. "Is it for one of your magic tricks?"

"It's not a coin, it's a medal."

"That you won?"

"No, my mom gave it to me."

He handed it over so I could look at it with my flashlight. It was the size of a nickel, but it had a guy in a robe engraved on the front.

"It's Saint Christopher, the patron saint of travelers. He keeps you safe when you're away from home and stuff."

"And you said your mom doesn't believe in magic?" I joked.

"Ha. Ha." Denver held his flashlight up to his face so I could see his eye roll before he swiped the medal out of my hand. "I like having it around. It reminds me my mom is thinking of me." He shrugged. "And maybe Saint Christopher's looking out for me, too. That would be a bonus, right?"

"For sure." I'd been kidding about the magic, but it sounded a little like the Boones. They liked that the BarkAngels watched over Pico. Like they had a whole team of Saint Christophers looking out for him.

"Maybe you could teach me how to do a French Drop," I said. "I've tried, but I was terrible at it, so I gave up."

"Sure." He started to grin, but the smiled faded. Even in

the dim light, Denver had a look on his face that I recognized. A spaced-out, putting-the-pieces-together look.

Something about it made pieces start to click in my own brain.

"Did you hear what Heaven said before she left the room tonight?" I asked.

Denver nodded. "*They won't care unless someone important goes missing.*"

"Exactly." Pico wasn't going to make or break the show. That was why he was only part of the trial run.

"When does Sir Bentley come to town?" Denver asked. "Tomorrow?"

"Yes!"

A shoe, launched from the other side of the room, smacked into my shin.

"Can you please go to sleep? Or be quiet?" Epic grumbled.

Denver and I mouthed, *Tomorrow*, at each other. Quietly, we each scribbled in our own notebooks for a while, and I had to admit, it wasn't horrible. Being on the same page.

When I woke up, it was ten in the morning and I was sprawled out on the floor next to my beanbag. My thumb was still stuck in Denver's *Hiding the Elephant* book, holding the place where I'd left off. Denver's sleeping bag was spread out on the floor in front of me, but he wasn't in it. In fact, he, Elvis, and Epic had been up for hours. They were all dressed and gathered around, poking at me.

"See?" Elvis said, shaking my shoulder. "He—*hic*—never wakes up. It's impossible to—*hic*— Oh, look, I think I saw his—*hic*—eyes flutter."

I rolled over and rubbed sleep out of my eyes.

"El?" I asked. "Why do you have Idea Hiccups?"

My sister used to be convinced that all her best ideas came with hiccups, but she didn't answer. Instead, she handed me Epic's borrowed phone and pushed a pair of earbuds into my ears.

"Listen," she said. "You'll see. Denver's a genius."

WEDNESDAY

TRANSCRIPT: DAILY DOG DISH PODCAST
Wednesday Wonderful Woofers

(Daily Dog Dish intro music.)

Del: A wonderful woofy hello to all the doggos and dog lovers out there. Thanks for joining us at the *Daily Dog Dish*—

Mel: Your five-minute furbaby fix!

Del: Hey! That's *my* line!

Mel: *(Giggles.)* I'm your host Melissa Dubois, joined, as always, by the doggone delightful Delphi Jones. Say hello, Del.

(Del and Mel laugh.)

Del: Fine. I'll bite. Hello, Del.

Mel: Wait. How do you play the sound effect? I guess I should have figured it out before I took control of the intro!

Del: No worries. I got you.

(Sound effect of groans and laughter.)

Mel: There it is! You're a great partner, Del.

Del: That's the point, right? Good partners help each other out, strengthen each other's weak spots, encourage each other to grow into the best versions of themselves . . .

Mel: Sounds like today's Wonderful Woofers!

Del: As always, our Wonderful Woofer segment is sponsored by American Humane.

Mel: Thanks to American Humane, film and television productions provide a comfortable working environment for every animal actor.

Del: You know the whole "No animals were harmed in the making of this film" line? That's guaranteed by our Wonderful Woofer sponsor!

(American Humane jingle plays.)

Mel: Today, we're excited to interview THREE Wonderful Woofers who are also excellent partners. Leif, Mandee, and Tara Skye founded the BarkAngels, a pet psychic collective designed to help dogs and their people communicate better.

Del: Let's see if we can get the BarkAngels on the line.

(Wonderful Woofers jingle plays over a telephone ringing.)

Tara: Hi, Mel and Del! Thanks for having us!

Del: We've seen mentions of the BarkAngels now and then in our DMs, but it wasn't until yesterday's interview with Newt and Sharon Henderson that I realized we *had* to meet you. I heard the BarkAngels started as a small family

business. Now you're landing superstar clients? How'd you do it?

Tara: We're still a small family business. It's me, Leif, and Mandee. Our mom answers the phones. I think that's why we've been successful. Clients feel the family vibe.

Del: That's a talented family! Are you all telepaths?

Leif: All three! When we were little, Mandee was always the most in tune, though. People thought she was kooky at first, but eventually, all our friends wanted her to talk with their animal companions.

Tara: Some even offered to pay her! That's when Leif and I were like, Hey, do you think the Universe is telling us to make this a business?

Mel: Mandee, how'd that feel? To have your "kooky" skill suddenly be in demand?

Mandee: *I* never thought it was kooky. But . . . now that you say it . . . yeah, it felt good not to be the odd one out.

Del: Sometimes I swear our bulldog, Morrissey, is communicating with me, but Mel says I'm only projecting my own thoughts onto him.

Mel: Or letting your imagination run away with you?

Del: Totally! You say that one a lot!

Mel: I'm a science girl. No offense to the BarkAngels, but I don't go in for the woo-woo stuff.

Leif: Trust me, your dog understands you.

Tara: Dogs are *so* intuitive, anyone can learn to communicate with them. Mandee taught me that dogs communicate with images not words. Don't *tell* your pup you'll be home later this evening—imagine the sun going down, then picture yourself walking through the door. They'll understand.

Del: I'm totally trying that!

Mel: Follow your curiosity, Del! Here's what *I'm* curious about: sibling dynamics. What's it like for you three?

Del: Oooh, good question! Leif, are you the typical protective older brother?

Leif: Definitely. I'd do anything for my sisters, but . . . they also know how to push my buttons.

Tara: *(Laughs.)* Mandee especially.

Del: True? Mandee, dish the dirt!

Mandee: *(Pauses.)* Maybe. I don't always agree with my siblings, that's true.

Tara: She's a *classic* middle child.

Mel: The rebel?

Leif: Kinda rogue. But she always comes around. *Eventually.* Don't you, Mandee?

(No response.)

Del: *(Laughs.)* Silence speaks! Last question: Tell us about your Department of Lost Dogs. The BarkAngels helped Newt, Baby BombBomb, Trixie, *and* Chippy Chihuahua after they were dognapped? Talk about an A-list celebrity clientele! Can you spill the deets?

Tara: Wow. You did your research!

Leif: We like to protect our clients' privacy. I'll just say we're glad we can use our empathic abilities for a good cause.

Mandee: *(Coughs.)* That's my brother. Always in it for a good cause.

Mel: Okay, but tell us this. All those stolen dogs? Their owners paid the ransom right away. Doesn't that encourage the thieves to move on to the next victim and do it again?

Mandee: Yes.

Leif: Helping bring the dogs home is our number one priority. Trust me, these dognappers are scary dudes. Paying the ransom as quickly as possible is the only sure bet.

Tara: You can't put a price on your furbaby's safety!

Del: Thank you for your service, BarkAngels! It's been

an enlightening journey. I'm going straight home to ask Morrissey which one of us he loves better. How do you think I can communicate that in images?

Mel: *(Giggles.)* Easy! Show him a picture of me!

Del and Mel: Hug ALL the dogs!

(Daily Dog Dish outro music.)

HUNCHES

"I know things got kind of exciting last night, but we need you to cool it today," Dad said.

He and Mom eyed me as I sat on a stool in the kitchen and scarfed down a bowl of cereal as fast as I could. Everyone else had already eaten breakfast and was waiting for me out by the chicken coop.

"I talked to Luis, and he says those notes Epic found were a prank," Dad said. "So . . . can you forget about all that?"

"Sure."

"Good. I think we *all* agree that last night was out of hand."

Dad gave Mom the same stern look he'd given me, and she winced. She looked like she hadn't slept.

"I already said I'm sorry. It was *one* momentary lapse of sanity . . ." She paused and unplugged the toaster, avoiding Dad's gaze.

"Wait," I said. "You *knew* the circuit would blow if Heaven plugged into the laundry room!"

I should have realized it earlier. Mom was the one who'd

taught Epic everything he knew about circuit boards and electricity. She knew exactly how many kitchen gadgets Dad could plug in before blowing a fuse. Still, I was stunned. How many people in this house were trying to sabotage *Bentley Knows*?

"I knew it was a possibility. Fifty percent." Mom bit her lip. "I was annoyed with Raúl and only thinking about myself. I screwed up. Could you . . . not tell your siblings?"

"I get it," I said, thinking about Denver. Everything he'd said about me had been right. I'd wrecked his French Drop trick, gotten his dog banned from the Perro, and ignored all his ideas just because I wanted to have Restorative Week to myself. In my case, the damage was done. I couldn't undo any of those things. Mom, on the other hand, had lucked out. The power outage was a blip. No one was hurt, everyone had moved on. She had a second chance to do things right.

"Next time, try the Path of Least Resistance," I said. "Be nice, give Raúl something he wants, make him feel good, then walk away."

Dad tried to keep a straight face, but he burst out laughing. "You *do* listen!"

Dad was even *more* excited that we planned to spend the day with Denver, out of everyone's hair. He didn't know all the action was at the Moondoggie. Sir Bentley was checking in today. And the Masterful McDade and D-Cubed Detective Agency was open for business.

Of course, there were a few kinks to work out.

No one liked El's new name for the agency.

My brother was still a traitor for keeping us in the dark about the whole hashtag thing.

And then there was the issue of *which* mystery we were trying to solve.

Luis was right. The notes Epic had found *did* look more like a joke than a mystery. Elvis had searched for the hashtags on Epic's borrowed phone, and only one person had posted #SavePicoBoone. El showed us the one-liner from @glittergirl: "Pico Boone dognapped? Oh no!!!"

"*No one* commented," El said. "Sad, right?"

Even though they looked fake, Epic thought the responsible thing was to find out who created the notes and make sure Pico wasn't in danger. Denver thought we had bigger fish to fry. The only thing we could all agree on was Sir Bentley. Sort of. We actually argued about it while we walked to the Moondoggie to pick up Bella.

"Denver was a genius to think of Sir Bentley," El said, gazing at herself in the window of Digger's Dentistry & Doggy Clinic. Her fancy hairdo was still mostly styled and poufy on one side, but the side she'd slept on had gone right back to the old-school Elvis tangle. She looked like a living before-and-after shot.

"Technically, it was my idea first," I said.

"No it wasn't." Denver shook his head.

"Fine, we figured out the Sir Bentley thing at the same

time, but *I'm* the one who uncovered the sabotage scheme in the first place."

"You're not listening, Rondo." Epic tapped his ear like I needed a visual. "Denver's not talking about Heaven Hsu. He's talking about the BarkAngels."

"If they hurt ONE hair on Sir Bentley's head—" Elvis set her jaw, ready to single-handedly take on the fake psychics herself, but Epic was still talking.

"It makes a lot of sense," he said. "They've got a direct line to super-rich clients who would do anything for their dogs. It would be easy to extort them for ransom money."

Ransom money? I had to wonder if being a teenager really was turning my brother into a different person. How else could the same guy who'd dragged his feet about every perfectly reasonable idea I'd ever had—including my hunch about Heaven Hsu—jump right on board with Denver Delgado-Doyle's completely off-the-charts theory about the celebrity dognappers? The BarkAngels were fakers, for sure. Were they charging the Boones too much money for questionable services? Yes. But other than that, they mostly seemed like they wanted to help.

"The brilliant part is . . ." Denver gave a flourish with his hand, like he was practicing swirling his cape. "When you call the Department of Lost Dogs, they can claim to 'see' the dog's in danger and tell you to pay the ransom right away—"

"For safety!" Epic gave the kid a high five.

As mad as I was that Epic trusted the new kid more than he

trusted his own brother, it wasn't an uninteresting argument. If El's podcast was correct, the BarkAngels had worked with *all* of the missing celebrity dogs. Which was maybe more than an odd coincidence. And the dog psychics had advised clients to pay the ransom. Immediately. For their pups' safety.

But the Department of Lost Dogs had tried to help *find* Pico. They hadn't asked for ransom money. They didn't even charge for lost dog services. Mandee Skye had said it herself: It'd be pretty low to cash in on someone else's suffering.

I got out my notebook and flipped to my notes about Sunday's video call. It was a little weird that Leif had told Mrs. Boone that Pico wasn't famous enough to be dognapped—*yet*. The dog he'd helped before Pico's call was a Maltese starting her modeling career. I knew it was completely bonkers, but what if the BarkAngels were choosing to work with up-and-coming dogs so they'd have a new batch of celebrities to ransom once they became famous? That would be some serious, diabolical long-term planning. Or maybe those dogs were simply the most likely to be in close contact with superstar dogs. Like Pico and Sir Bentley. Because of Pico, the BarkAngels knew every detail about Sir Bentley's arrival and when she was going to be on set.

I wrote it down: *Are the BarkAngels running a long con? Or using B-list dogs to get to A-listers?*

"Sir Bentley *has* to be next!" Denver was excited. "If you were going to hold a dog for ransom, wouldn't you go for the highest-paid canine actor in Hollywood?"

Yes. Yes, I would.

Just because I knew my hunch about Heaven Hsu was solid, it didn't necessarily mean Denver was wrong. I couldn't help wondering if there was a way to do two things at once. Save a great television show from sabotage *and* uncover a criminal dognapping ring?

Why not?

"What makes you think they're going to come to Carmelito?" I asked. "They could snag Bentley anytime."

"True," Epic said. "Why not next week when the film crew goes back to LA?"

Denver laughed like it was a silly question. "What would *you* do? A heist in Los Angeles at a major television studio with security and cameras and the LA Police Department everywhere? Or . . ."

He waved his hand at the scene around us. For all the Hollywood commotion up at the Perro del Mar, Main Street was not a bustling place. We passed a lady scrolling on her phone while her corgi used a mobility scooter to zip ahead to the canine fountain. Up on the Moondoggie patio, dogs sniffed at bushes or slept under tables while their humans sipped lattes. Across Ocean Drive, all kinds of large and small canines chased seagulls on the leash-free beach.

If I were a dognapper, I could nab four or five pups right now without breaking a sweat.

The gears in my brain were spinning. Thanks to Tara's "emotional forecasts," the BarkAngels knew Sir Bentley was flying in from Norway today and leaving again on Friday. If they were planning something, it was going to happen in the next forty-eight hours. Maybe even sooner.

Sure, the whole theory *could* be a bunch of bunk. Circumstantial evidence that seemed like it was connected but wasn't. No different from Mrs. Boone believing that Pico licked his lips because Epic made him nervous. If I was honest, though, Denver could say the same about *my* hunch about Heaven and Raúl.

As far as I knew, the only way to tell the difference between bunk and reality was to study the connections.

Then find a way to test them.

PUPCAKE PARADISE

The way Bella was acting—jumping and yipping and lick-ing everybody, including me—I'm pretty sure she'd thought Denver had disappeared forever. Now that he was back, it was the greatest day of her life.

"It's gonna get even better, you wittle sweetie cutie!" Elvis let Bella give her a full, slobbery kiss on the lips. "We're tak-ing you for PUPCAKES!"

Denver was relieved to be back with Bella, too. It reminded me that in Carmelito, if you didn't count us, Bella was Denver's only friend. He kept smiling, rubbing her head, and asking her to do tricks to make us laugh. Outside Pupcake Paradise, he had her stand on her hind legs, tilt her head, and let her tongue loll out like she was drooling over the window display of HOMEMADE PUPCAKES: DELICIOUS FOR PEOPLE AND PUPS!

"Does Saint Christopher watch over Bella, too?" I pointed to the medal on her collar as we followed my siblings into the shop. The smell was enough to make all of us drool, not just Bella.

Denver shook his head. "This one is Saint Francis. Patron Saint of Animals. He's the best saint."

"Who's the worst saint?" I asked.

Epic cleared his throat and coughed several times, which I assumed meant that my question was inappropriate and I shouldn't be asking people to rank their religious icons.

Elvis was quicker on the uptake. She poked my arm until I noticed what Epic was coughing about.

In the back of the shop, sitting at a table with a massive pile of pupcakes between them, were Mrs. Boone, Heaven Hsu, and Roo. Roo let out a yip when he saw me, and Heaven waved us over.

"What are *they* doing together?" Epic whispered. "How come Heaven's never on set?"

They were good questions, and I had a few more. The last time I'd seen Heaven Hsu, I was in her room outing her sabotage scheme to the entire crew. How mad was she? And what was she going to do about it?

"Nicole went overboard on the pupcakes." Heaven stood up and pulled her messenger bag over her shoulder. "Knock yourselves out."

I hesitated, but it wouldn't make sense to say no to free pupcakes. We pulled up chairs, and Heaven actually smiled at me. Not mad. Relieved. Like we were her ticket out of an awkward conversation.

"I wouldn't say *overboard*." Mrs. Boone pulled on Heaven's arm, making her sit back down. "Stay. *Enjoy.* I want to properly apologize, and one Pupcake Platter is hardly enough. We shouldn't have barged into your room. We feel so—"

"It's *fine*," Heaven said. "It's not like you accused me of sabotage or anything."

I choked a little. There was no way to tell if that was a joke.

They'd clearly been through it already, but Mrs. Boone kept her hand on Heaven's arm and droned on about the stress everyone had been under and how poor Pico got the brunt of it all and she couldn't help but feel responsible for the pressure they'd put on their sweet, talented Iggy, who was acting his heart out right this very moment and was probably well on his way to winning a Pawscar. Not that she expected awards.

I reached for a pupcake with orange frosting, but Heaven made a gagging motion and steered me toward a green one instead.

"Elvis, how about that *fascinating* magic show you were plugging yesterday?" Heaven didn't look interested in anything but changing the subject. "Please. Tell us more."

"It's tomorrow, and our big finale is a vanishing act! Me! Oops, that's a spoiler." Elvis fed half a rainbow-confetti pupcake to Bella and the other half to Roo before choosing one for herself.

"We're still doing that?" I asked, but Denver, El, and Epic all said "Yes" in unison. I don't know. I thought maybe we had more important things to do? Like stopping crime.

"Uck, ew, blech!" Spit-covered pieces of an orange pup-cake exploded into the air. El had shoved the whole thing into her mouth before anyone could warn her. "What *is* that?"

"Fish flavor," Heaven said. "Roo liked it. I didn't."

Bella and Roo immediately went to work cleaning up, and Mrs. Boone, who'd been in the direct line of fire, stood up to brush fish-cake shrapnel off her arms and lap. Cleaning out her purse wasn't so easy. Whole chunks of fishy cake and frosting had fallen inside. Mrs. Boone emptied the contents on the table, and everyone but Heaven froze.

Mixed in with tubes of glittery makeup and chew toys was a small stack of Perro del Mar notepaper that read

WARNING CARMELITO, CA! DOGNAPPERS ON THE LOOSE!!!!!!!!!!
RANSOM FOR PICO BOONE = 1 MILLION DOLLARS!!!!!!!!!!!!!!!!!!!!!
#BENTLEYKNOWS #SAVEPICOBOONE #CELEBRITYDOGNAPPED

"You made those?" Epic had cupcake in his mouth, but he'd stopped chewing.

We all had.

Heaven *was* interested now. She picked up one of the notes and studied it with a small smirk on her face.

"Nonononono!" Mrs. Boone started talking extra fast. "It's not what you think. I mean it is, but not like that. We had so much trouble getting followers for Pico, and after Raúl's dognapping mix-up went so *well* for us . . . we thought people were interested in that sort of thing."

"'That sort of thing' being . . . Pico getting dognapped?" Heaven asked.

"We posted the hashtags to boost his numbers . . . but never again. Never! I'll *never* let fame come before my baby's safety!"

She looked so miserable that Elvis patted her arm like she was an upset toddler or a pup. Heaven, though, was enjoying every minute.

"Wait. So you . . . *posted* these? With actual thumbtacks? Do you know how social media works?"

"Apparently not." Mrs. Boone put her head in her hands. "We thought people would see the posters and use the hashtags. It didn't work very well."

"Yeah, only one person used #SavePicoBoone. It was—wait!" Elvis slapped her forehead like she couldn't believe we'd missed it.

"You're @glittergirl," I said.

Mrs. Boone took a breath and pulled herself together. "Well. It was a terrible plan. Who wants their dog to be so famous that someone would *steal* him?"

"No one." Denver put a protective hand on Bella's back.

"Right. No one." Mrs. Boone took the notes and started to rip them, one by one, into tiny little pieces. I saw Epic sneak a look at the Pupcake Paradise owner, like he felt the need to apologize for our mess.

"Next time, ask *me*," Elvis said. "I could have helped you with an *ah*-mazing publicity stunt!"

"I bet you could," Heaven said. "You're a natural."

Elvis grinned like it was a compliment, which I'm pretty sure it wasn't.

"We could video Pico vanishing in our magic act!" she said. "If we make it super cute, it'll go viral!"

Heaven shrugged, unimpressed. "Cute doesn't cut it anymore," she said. "You need another hook."

"Like if Pico vanished and Bella showed up in her place?" Denver asked, getting so into the game that on the word *vanished*, he made a *poof!* sound and waved an invisible magic wand in the air. I almost expected him to add ABRACADABRA! But he didn't.

"Cuter, but still not enough."

Elvis started to hiccup. "If Sir Bentley—*hic*—vanished, and tiny—*hic*—Pico showed up in her place! That's hilarious, cute, *and* Bentley's 4.7 million—*hic*—followers would watch it and follow Pico!"

"There it is." Heaven gave El a slow clap. "Miniature publicist in the making."

But something else was going on with Heaven. I could see

it happening as she rubbed Roo's ear. Exactly like she'd done at Yappy Hour, she looked thoughtful for a second, then got a cartoon-light-bulb look on her face.

"Where would Sir Bentley go?" she asked. "If you vanished him?"

"Most magicians use a trick box or a cabinet," Denver said. "You put an angled mirror inside, and when you close the box, Sir Bentley 'disappears' by hiding behind the mirror. Then when you open the box back up, the audience sees the sides of the box reflected in the mirror, so it looks like it's empty. It's an optical illusion."

He did the exact same *poof!* routine, and El grinned like it was just as entertaining the second time. It wasn't.

"Nope," I said. "Pico's waiting in the same box, right? Hidden behind the mirror until the big reveal?"

"Sure."

"See? That can't work. Where are you going to put the dog who's *not* hidden? In front of the mirror? You'd see a reflection behind them!"

"If you get the *angle* right—" Denver started to protest, but Epic interrupted.

"I think we should use the secret exit," he said.

I'd thought this was all hypothetical, but my brother was seriously ready to swap two famous dogs during our cheesy Yips & Sips magic show.

"Remember the bookcase?" he asked. As if we could possibly forget a secret exit.

Heaven raised her eyebrows.

"It's the easiest method," Epic said. "There's no box. You have Sir Bentley stand in front of the wall of bookshelves, and the whole audience can see there's no place for her to go. Meanwhile, Pico's waiting *behind* the bookcase, outside the secret door. Then we put up a 'vanishing' curtain to hide Sir Bentley, and while Denver says the magic words, we secretly open the door behind the curtain, swap the dogs, let the curtain fall down, and—"

"Abracadabra!" Denver shouted. Which seemed inevitable.

"So then . . ." Heaven squinted, thinking it through. "While everyone's distracted and focused on Pico, Sir Bentley's waiting outside in a secret location behind the inn?"

"Yes! Let's do that!" Elvis said, still hiccuping.

"You should totally do that," Heaven said.

Mrs. Boone had been quietly ripping the tiny pieces of paper into even tinier pieces, and now she let out an Elvis-worthy dramatic sigh.

"Thanks but no thanks," she said. "It's not about the fame anymore. Clive and I have turned over a new leaf. We're focused on Pico's talent. In fact, I should leave. Pico has a BarkAngel session during his next break."

Heaven Hsu gave Mrs. Boone a strangely kind and helpful look.

"I've been in the business a long time," she said. "If you want Pico's talent to be recognized, he *needs* viewers. He can't be an actor without fans. No one will give him roles."

"True . . ." Mrs. Boone considered it.

"And if he wants viewers," Heaven said, "they need to know about him. Even then, it's not a guarantee. Talented actors flop all the time. So you might as well use the connections you've got to give Pico the shot he deserves."

It was a decent pitch. Mrs. Boone squeezed one of the tiny bits of paper into a miniature pebble.

"Clive won't like it," she said.

"You'll convince him," Epic said. He wasn't wrong. If Mrs. Boone could talk her husband into eating chia seeds for maximum crossword-puzzle performance, she could talk him into anything.

"I can't ask Madeleine for a favor like that. You know how busy Sir Bentley is—"

Elvis interrupted. "She'll do it for *me*!"

"But Raúl." Mrs. Boone lowered her voice, like Raúl Flores was the biggest obstacle of all. "He'll say it'll make the dogs too nervous and affect their performance."

"*I'll* take care of Raúl," Heaven said. "Trust me. He'll want to do this."

She was so earnest, you almost believed she suddenly cared about Pico's career. Like all she wanted was to help Pico earn the fans he deserved. But I saw the part of our plan that had gotten her attention. The secret door. Sir Bentley, waiting outside while everyone else was focused on Pico. It was the perfect opportunity to nab the Saint Bernard, and she knew it.

I'd always thought Heaven Hsu was one of the best actors on television, but now? I was convinced. She deserved *all* the Pawscars.

Except for the one reserved for the Masterful McDade and D-Cubed Detective Agency—*not* that I was agreeing to that name. Because as we sat there shoveling pupcakes into our mouths, I finally figured out the value of the Yips & Sips magic show.

If we planned it right, it was going to be a performance Carmelito would never forget.

THE PRICE OF JUSTICE

"We need to use the vanishing act to set a trap," I said. "We'll catch them in the act!"

I looked behind us to make sure no one was close enough to hear as we hurried toward Ocean Avenue.

"Who? Raúl and Heaven Hsu?" Epic asked. "Or the BarkAngels?"

I shrugged. "Either? Both? If we use Sir Bentley to lure them in, we'll find out pretty fast."

"I read about the sting operation that caught the jewel thief at the Perro del Mar," Denver said. "Do you think it'll work?"

"Of course it'll work!" I said.

"What if the BarkAngels don't come to Carmelito?" Epic asked.

"Then we only catch *one* pair of criminals? I'm okay with that," I said. "What's the problem? You seemed like you wanted to do it."

"The publicity stunt for Pico," Epic said. "I wanted to do *that*. To help his career."

My brother couldn't let anything be easy. I could practically see him running risk calculations in his head. To be fair, the look on his face reminded me there'd be downsides. If we captured celebrity dognappers, my family would be in the news again, reporters would get their facts wrong, and the Perro would be more famous than ever. Which wouldn't be great. It'd be the opposite of great. But maybe that was the price of justice.

"I mean . . . I *like* it, but . . ." Elvis had stopped skipping and was walking in front of us now. Backward, so she could see our expressions. "Won't the BarkAngels *see* it's a trap? With their minds?"

"Elvis. I swear," I said. "Telepathy isn't a thing."

"It looked real when *you* did it."

"I was pretending."

We were almost back at the Moondoggie, and I could see people milling around in front of the inn. A whole crowd. Maybe Brody was having another event.

"What if you thought you were pretending but you were actually communicating?" Elvis asked me. "Like the stuff you said *seemed* like you were making it up in your own brain but really it's because the dog was talking to you the whole time?"

"Is that what happened when you talked to Doughboy?"

I put the word *talked* in air quotes. "It seemed like you were pretending?"

Elvis nodded sadly. "Kinda."

"That's because you were," I said.

"What about the dowsing? Your crystal stopped at the Perro!"

"That was an accident," I said.

"Plus," Epic said, taking my side for once, "Pico wasn't *at* the Perro, that was Doughboy. They found Pico at the Moondoggie, remember?"

My sister went silent. She put her hands on her hips, and her expression went dark. Real dark. Temper-tantrum dark.

"Those BarkAngels," El said, "had better keep their fake, fakety-fake hands *Off. My. Bentley.*"

"Is she okay?" Denver asked.

Epic looked nervous, but I grinned. If we were going to catch a bunch of dog-stealing criminals, Revenge-Elvis was exactly who we needed.

"You know who we need?" Epic pointed ahead toward Ocean Drive.

The crowd at the Moondoggie was even bigger up close. A couple police cars were parked diagonally in the middle of the street to let pedestrians walk where they wanted. I followed Epic's gaze to the bald cop who was rerouting traffic.

"*Luis?* Right. Great idea," I said. "Take it to the guy who tells you to keep secrets from your siblings."

"Rondo, I wasn't trying to leave you out of it," Epic said. "I mean, I *was*, but only because I knew you were going to make a whole thing out of it. I was trying to keep you out of trouble!"

"I'm not a two-year-old. I don't need you to take care of me," I said.

But I could tell he felt horrible.

"Fine," I said. "Tell Luis."

It's not like we weren't going to need him eventually. We could set the trap and catch the culprits in the act, but if Denver was right and the BarkAngels had stolen millions of dollars from celebrity dogs? We were going to need the police to put them behind bars.

"I think your sister's got it covered," Denver said.

Elvis had already raced ahead, waving at Luis. By the time we caught up to her, she was laying into him.

"I can't believe you thought *we* wrote those silly notes! Who do you think we *are*? Do you know us at *all*?"

Luis stifled a laugh and put his hands up like he'd been caught. "You're right, El. That was my bad," he said. "Epic set me straight. He said you're both too smart to do something that amateur."

"He's right!" Elvis said. "If we'd done it, we would have done it *professional*!"

"That was Epic's argument." Luis held up a hand to an oncoming car and motioned them to turn onto the detour street.

I looked at my brother. He seemed kind of embarrassed, but he shrugged.

"You're both smarter than me," he said. Which wasn't exactly true, but not horrible to hear. "I should have told you. I like it better when we're a team."

"Yeah. Me too," I said.

Satisfied with the apology, El threw her hands in the air and launched into the next topic. "Luis, we're on to something huge! Gigantic! And we need your help!"

It had the exact opposite effect El was hoping for. Luis held back an eye roll, and his mouth tightened into a line that told me this conversation was not going to be worth our time.

"Technically, we don't need *help*," I said.

"We don't?" My siblings and Denver stared at me.

"We want you to come see our magic show at Yips and Sips tomorrow night," I said. "We're working on a disappearing act."

"We are!" Elvis gave an excited hop. "It's *ah*-mazing!"

"I heard about the McDade magic show." Luis was obviously relieved we weren't trying to rope him into some big scheme. "I wouldn't miss it!"

"Denver's the magician, not us," I said. My brother's apology had made me feel generous. "He's really good."

"I'm only okay," Denver said, but his grin said otherwise.

"Promise, Luis?" Elvis asked. "*Promise* you'll be there."

"I promise." Luis bumped each of our fists. "Relax. You

know I'm your biggest fan. Plus, I'm off early tomorrow. My work friends and I were gonna go to Yips and Sips anyway."

Epic nodded at me. Work friends meant extra backup. That was all we needed to hear.

A black car flashed its lights at Luis, and he waved it slowly forward.

"Here we go. Showtime," he said.

"Sir Bentley's here? Already?" Elvis touched her funky hair and looked panicked, like she was about to see her hero and she'd suddenly remembered she looked like a science experiment.

"*They* think so." Luis shook his head. The crowd cheered as the car slowly moved forward, revealing the droopy jowls of a Saint Bernard in the back window. "Keep it on the down-low, but that's Bentley's stunt double. Wild week, huh?"

I tugged Epic's arm.

"It's about to get wilder," I said.

My brother and I watched a woman with messy reddish-brown hair and a face full of freckles stand on her tiptoes to watch the Saint Bernard in the car pass by.

Then Mandee Skye pulled her small rolling suitcase straight through the front door of the Moondoggie Inn.

MOONDOGGIE INN

There were so many people crowding the Moondoggie Inn that by the time we made it inside, Mandee Skye had disappeared into thin air.

Denver and Epic examined the guestbook Brody had left open on the desk.

"No Skye," Epic said.

"Of course not," I said. "What kind of criminal checks into a hotel and uses their real name? Besides, we don't need to find her."

"We only need to make sure she knows about the magic show. And the secret door," Denver said.

"Exactly."

Catching a dognapper in the act was no different from catching a jewel thief. You had to make it clear *where* you planted the jewels and *when* they were going to be unguarded. Heaven already knew the details about Sir Bentley's "vulnerable" location. Now we needed to tip off Mandee Skye.

El flopped into a lounge chair and stared at the wall of

books. "It'd be so much easier if she *could* read my mind. I'd walk through the secret door, and she'd *see* me do it."

"That's not a bad idea," I said. "Epic, hand me Declan's phone."

He already had two texts from Mrs. Boone:

Clive agrees to the plan!

Send us the details!

We'd had to swear Mrs. Boone to secrecy about the borrowed phone, but in the service of Pico's career, she'd exchanged numbers with Epic and agreed to keep quiet.

I used the phone to take a video of Elvis, Denver, and Epic walking through the hidden door, which felt like something straight out of a detective novel. The secret component was a wooden block painted to look like a copy of Sir Arthur Conan Doyle's book, *The Hound of the Baskervilles*. It looked real, but when you pulled on the block, it unhooked a latch and a small section of the bookcase opened out to an overgrown path behind the Moondoggie.

"Where *are* we?" El peered around a juniper bush. I'm pretty sure she was hoping we'd walked through a magic portal to another universe.

"There's Carmelito Beach." Epic pointed down the path.

"And there's Main Street," Denver said.

"Okay, let's redo the video," El said. "I'm going to say, 'Oh! Carmelito Beach!' and point over there. So they know exactly where we are. Take two!"

It was a good idea, but Elvis made us sit around while she

practiced six different ways of saying "Oh!" When she had it perfect, we texted the video to Mrs. Boone.

Will Pico/Bentley feel ok alone out here?

Ask the BarkAngels!!

Do an emotional forecast for the magic show!!!!!

"We aren't going to leave them alone on this creepy path, are we?" Epic looked alarmed. "Pico will freak."

"Relax," I said. "It's what we want them to think. It's not what we're going to do."

"What *are* we going to do?"

I pulled out my notebook. "Get some snacks and figure it out? We'll start by making a list of our assets."

Denver nodded. "Frozen pizzas?"

"Definitely an asset."

Our list wasn't that impressive, but it would do the trick: *two celebrity dogs, a secret doorway, one pair of walkie-talkies, a borrowed cell phone, and the Carmelito Police Department in the audience.*

"We'll get Mom to help us build the vanishing curtain," I said.

"I could get the pet cam from the Boones again," Epic said. "Legitimately this time."

"Smart," I said.

If we planted the pet cam on the bookshelf, Epic and I could stand outside with Pico and watch the whole magic show using the Peek-a-Boo-Peek-at-You app on Declan's phone. We'd be able to see when Elvis and Denver pulled the curtain in front of Sir Bentley, and we'd be ready to swap the dogs. Once we had the Saint Bernard outside, Epic and I would hide in the bushes so it looked like she was alone, and when sabotagers and dognappers showed up, we'd record everything.

It was so easy to plan, we got bored. Epic checked Dec's cell phone for the zillionth time and showed it to Elvis.

"Did you send it right? What if it didn't go through? What if—"

Elvis confiscated the phone. "We need to listen to the *Daily Dog Dish* again."

She'd said it to distract him, but it was a good investigative strategy. Once you've gathered evidence, it's important to study it multiple times. Even the best detectives can accidentally skip over an important clue. In the case of the *Dog Dish*? We'd definitely missed something. The Skye siblings were fighting.

"Mandee's the odd one out!" Elvis said. "Like me!"

"Like *you*?" It was ridiculous. The odd one out was obviously me.

"*I'm* the one you two are always mad at," Epic said.

We all stared at one another, stunned, and then burst out laughing.

Denver looked confused.

"I don't get it," he said. "Mandee's siblings said nice things about her. She's the whole reason they have the business. What makes you think they're fighting?"

Denver clearly didn't have a sister.

"She pushes his buttons," Elvis said. "Like I do with Rondo."

"And they called her the rebel who has to 'come around,'" I added.

"When she said Leif's in it for a *good cause*," Epic said, "she was annoyed. Or sarcastic. Maybe both."

"Or maybe she meant what she said?" Denver offered.

All three of us shook our heads.

"So . . . ," Denver said. "Does that mean Mandee's working alone?"

"Or the opposite," I said. "Maybe Mandee's innocent, and she's mad at *them*?"

"Then why's she here," Epic said, "and they aren't?"

"I think they're *all three* guilty," Revenge-Elvis growled. "And they are *not* going to get away with this."

Epic's lap buzzed, and he jumped, sending the phone flying. All four of us dove for it.

Leif talked to Pico AND Bentley!

Both doggos feel GREAT about the magic trick!!!!!

L says it's a COSMIC opportunity!!!!! ☺ ☺ ☺

I grinned. "Looks like Leif will show up."

Elvis grabbed the phone and started typing.

Bentley?????? Bentley's at the Perro???? Now????

She didn't even wait for an answer. She threw the phone back at Epic and started running.

"I'm going home!" she yelled over her shoulder. As if we hadn't figured that out.

OLD FRIENDS

If any of us were worried that our plan wasn't going to come together, that Madeleine Devine wouldn't let us use Sir Bentley, that the vanishing curtain wouldn't work, or that Luis wouldn't show up, my sister took care of all that. Which was a good reminder: Never underestimate Elvis McDade.

In the time it took me, Denver, and Epic to clean up our pizza mess, sort out the magic show props, and walk back to the Perro with a short stopover at the dog park to throw a Frisbee for Bella, the film crew was setting up for their final scene of the day and El had been busy making her own kind of magic.

She'd talked Mom into setting aside time the next morning to help us build a portable structure for the vanishing curtain. She'd talked Dad into making her favorite Woofy Waffles for breakfast—to "set us up for success." Somehow, she'd even managed to convince Raúl to un-ban Bella from the Perro del Mar. Mrs. Boone had texted us before we'd even left the Moondoggie: *Bring Bella-wella!!!!! She can sleep over!!!!!!*

Raúl's in a GREAT mood!!!!!! Which, in retrospect, was probably a message typed by El.

On top of it all, she'd gotten the Boones and Madeleine Devine extra hyped about the publicity stunt. Maybe too hyped. Mr. Boone had ordered fifteen hundred custom T-shirts that said PICO + BENTLEY = MAGIC. And Madeleine had posted about tomorrow night's Yips & Sips Magic Show all over social media.

"It's a cute idea, Rondo." Madeleine ruffled my hair. Which I hate. "No haircut yet, huh? You're getting tall. Anyway, if Heaven thinks it'll go viral, it probably will. She knows what the kids like these days."

"I *do* know what the kids like these days," Heaven said without cracking a smile.

I didn't expect Madeleine and Heaven to be so chummy, but I'd sort of forgotten that they went *way* back. The first episodes of *Bentley Knows* came out when Elvis was still a baby. Back then, Sir Bentley was a fresh young pup solving crimes, and "his" partner, Lulu, was a kid. Which meant Heaven had known Bentley as long as I'd known my own sister.

It was a weird feeling, standing in your own house with actors you'd watched on television while a crew ran lighting cues with the body doubles. They moved around cameras, lights, and giant fuzzy microphones. A guy with a clipboard adjusted the stand-in Sir Bentley's chin until a woman at a monitor told him the angle was right. I knew from the script, this was going to be the big emotional scene. The one where Sir Bentley learned "he" was finally getting a canine partner. I almost wished things had gone a different way. It probably wouldn't have been so bad to spend Restorative Week watching them film *Bentley Knows* instead of catching criminals.

While my siblings and Denver chatted up Madeleine and the Boones, Heaven and Roo had moved off to a quiet corner with the Saint Bernard. Heaven's head rested on Sir Bentley's massive, fluffy back while she wrote in her notebook. Cuddled up like that, concentrating and biting her lip, she looked a lot like young Lulu from the old episodes. Lonely, smart, brave, even a little sad.

That's when I knew I had to rethink my evidence. There was a key piece I'd been missing. Bentley was like family to Heaven. Maybe she wasn't happy about her contract, but this show was her whole life. She wouldn't sabotage her oldest friend, would she? No way. I had to admit, I'd gotten so caught up in being right. But I'd totally gotten it wrong.

I took a few steps toward them, wondering if I needed to apologize. But as I got closer, Heaven closed her notebook, sat up on her knees, and whispered to the Saint Bernard. She looked nervous. Again, more like ten-year-old Lulu than the cool, tough Heaven Hsu I knew. I couldn't hear everything she was saying, but I heard enough. *It's the only thing I could think of . . . nothing against you . . . I feel so stuck . . . sick of acting . . . just . . . help me out, and we'll still be friends, okay?*

It wasn't rehearsal for the scene. I'd read the script. It was a confession.

Someone called out, "Five minutes!" and Heaven hugged Bentley, then did her good-luck ritual—touched her thumb to her lips, her chin, then her forehead—before she turned around and caught me staring at her. I could have sworn she wiped at her eye, but before I could be sure, she'd already transformed from Lulu back to Heaven Hsu.

"Guh, forget you saw that." She winced and changed the subject. "I left your Houdini book at the front desk for you. It was helpful. Thanks."

Helpful? How?

Bella chose that moment to scurry toward Sir Bentley, with Denver and Epic close behind.

"Why does it smell so good in here?" Denver asked.

Suddenly, I realized the Perro did smell extra good. Even better than Pupcake Paradise.

"Raúl's in the kitchen," Heaven said. "He's teaching some dog psychic his secret recipe."

"What?"

"Yep. I never thought I'd see it. Maybe she's a hypnotist, too."

Epic, of all people, was the one who said, "We should find Elvis and go get a snack."

Raúl *was* in a good mood. Not only did he not bite our heads off for walking into our own kitchen, he smiled, brushed some flour off his mustache, and introduced us to a woman with red-brown hair and a freckled face.

"Oh, we know each other!" Mandee Skye said. "Rando, right? Isn't this exciting? I've always wanted to visit a film set!"

"What are you doing here?" I blurted before I could stop myself. Was she scouting the scene? Stalking Sir Bentley? Shouldn't she be hiding out and plotting at the Moondoggie? And how did she know Raúl?

Elvis already knew all the answers. Her eyes were shooting daggers at the BarkAngel.

"Mandee *says* she's here to learn about canine acting," she said, fake-grinning and gritting her teeth. "She *says* she's here to help Pico give his best performance. And Raúl is letting her shadow him. To learn the ropes. Isn't that . . . *nice*?"

"Mrs. Boone put in a good word." Mandee dropped to her knees and held out a hand for Bella to sniff.

Epic elbowed me. I knew what he was thinking. We were supposed to believe that Raúl was doing something because *Mrs. Boone* suggested it? In what universe?

"You're beautiful, aren't you?" Mandee said while Bella licked her hand like it was a pupsicle. "Look at those blue eyes! How old is she? It looks like she has some Alaskan or Siberian husky in her?"

"Can't you *tell*?" Elvis was full-on glaring now. "Why don't you *ask* her?"

El had her hands on her hips, and the look on her face told me if we didn't get her out of here, she was going to blow our cover for sure. As far as Mandee knew, we were just a bunch of clueless kids. For our plan to work, we needed to keep it that way.

"Come on, El." I tugged her arm.

But El's expression had already changed. I followed her gaze toward the Perro del Mar's back door. Mom and Dad were outside greeting two women with suitcases in the back-yard. One of the women was tall and thin, in a long, flowy skirt. The other was short and had tattoos all over her arms. At their feet was an old, wheezing bulldog.

El's lips curved into a smile. "Morrissey!"

I spent most of the night reading through my notes. Epic tossed and turned, Elvis snored, and Denver slept with his arm around Bella and his Saint Christopher medal in his hand, but I went over everything we knew until my brain hurt.

Things weren't adding up like I'd thought they were going to. If Mandee and Raúl knew each other, had I under-estimated the dog trainer? I'd thought Heaven had pulled him into *her* sabotage plan, but maybe it was the other way around. Or maybe Raúl wasn't in it for sabotage at all. I knew he'd worked with lots of famous dogs. What if he had some-thing to do with the celebrity dognappings? What if he was working with the BarkAngels? Or with one of them? Was that why Leif and Tara were fighting with Mandee?

I had all questions and no answers. Eventually, I heard another flashlight click on, then footsteps. Someone was climbing up the bunk bed ladder.

Denver's head appeared, and he handed over a coin.

"Saint Francis," he whispered. "Bella won't mind if you borrow it."

The metal felt warm from the heat of his hand.

"Thanks," I said. "Do you think we figured it out right? What if we got it all wrong?"

Denver shrugged. "That's why we made the trap. To find out."

"True."

He grinned and pointed at the saint in my hand. "Besides, Saint Francis takes care of the animals. He'll help us out."

I didn't really believe an old dead saint was going to show up to save the day, but there was something calming about holding the coin. Whether it was Francis or magic or battery technology, eventually my flashlight dimmed and went out, and finally, I fell asleep.

THURSDAY

TRANSCRIPT: DAILY DOG DISH PODCAST
On Location: Carmelito, California

(Daily Dog Dish intro music.)

Del: Good morning, everybody! I'm Delphi Jones with the *Daily Dog Dish*, and I am so tail-wagging *excited* for this episode! Say hi to all our pup-tastic listeners, Mel.

Mel: Hi to all our pup-tastic listeners, Mel.

Del: It never gets old.

Mel: *(Giggles.)* Maybe for other people. Not for me.

Del: Do you want to tell everyone where we are today?

Mel: Naw, you do it. I know you're dying to spill the beans.

Del: I kind of want to do it like a newscaster at the Pawscars.

Mel: *(Laughs.)* Here. I'll set you up.

(Sound effect of a drumroll.)

Del: *(Serious newscaster voice.)* Folks, we're coming to you from the once-sleepy town of Carmelito, California, recording on location at the Perro del Mar, where right this very minute, Pico Boone and Sir Bentley are in hair and makeup for episode one of the *Bentley Knows* reboot. How does it feel to be back at the Perro, Ms. Dubois?

Mel: *(Claps.)* Nice newscaster voice! It's definitely . . . *different.* We were here two years ago, but . . . holy Hollywood! Times have changed! The room we're staying in is literally a social media staging site for Pico Boone. They're letting us crash there, but . . .

Del: I feel like I'm sleeping inside a commercial for canine swag.

Mel: Seems like a decent lead-in to today's sponsor?

Del: Yes! Watch Pico Boone's Yips and Sips Moondoggie Magic Extravaganza Featuring Sir Bentley World-Famous Canine Star of Mega Television Hit *Bentley Knows* Rebooting This Fall Look for It on Pico's Feed Tonight at 7:00 P.M. or Anytime After That It Will Be Online.

Mel: That's a mouthful.

Del: It's what they asked me to say. Let me translate to human-speak: Tonight, Pico and Bentley are teaming up for a publicity stunt to promote the *Bentley Knows* reboot. And we're here to get you pumped about it. I'm pumped because: a) magic, b) dogs.

Mel: What else could you ever want to watch?

Del: Okay, we've done what they paid us to do, let's sniff around and give our listeners a sneak peek behind the scenes of *Bentley Knows*.

Mel: *(Lowers voice.)* We're walking across the hall to Hair and Makeup. I see Heaven Hsu, Bentley, and Pico . . .

awww, Heaven's mini schnauzer is cuddled up with the Saint Bernard. I'm in love.

Del: Excuse me, Heaven, we're with the *Daily Dog Dish*, and we'd love to ask you—

Heaven Hsu: No thanks.

(Sound of footsteps and a door latching closed.)

Del: She's friendly.

Mel: Definitely not a morning person. Let's go downstairs and check out Pico's body doubles. Did you know Raúl Flores trained Chippy Chihuahua for that new film with the talking Ferrari?

Del: That movie was dog food.

Mel: The stunts were impressive, though. Hey, there he is!

Del: Hi, Mr. Flores, I'm Delphi Jones with the *Daily Dog Dish*. Do you have a moment to say hello to our listeners?

Raúl: No media, please—

Mel: We were recently talking about your groundbreaking work in *Fur Fur Ferrari*.

Raúl: *(Clears throat.)* Oh, really? Thank you. That was a challenging film.

Mel: I saw you recently got called in for emergency scene work in *Dogs of War III* when they were having trouble with one of Trixie's big moments? What's your secret? How do you get such moving canine performances?

Raúl: Dogs are like people. Even an unbearable job seems worth doing if the reward's good enough.

Del: I've been there.

Mel: Were you on set when Trixie got dognapped? That must have been traumatic . . . Oh—

(Sound of a scuffle, dogs barking, then silence.)

Mel: Sorry!

Raúl: We're done here.

Del: *(Whispers.)* Oh-kay, so Morrissey got a little too friendly with one of the stuntdogs, and now we're getting escorted to the back door by a very strong assistant. The rumors are true: Raúl is intense.

(Sound of a squeaky screen door opening and slamming closed.)

Del: I wanted some fresh air anyway.

Mel: Hmph. I wasn't going to dish this, but now I will. Marc McDade told me Raúl cooks up special dog treats every day.

Del: Um . . . that's dish?

Mel: He also told me he's gone through three pounds of sugar this week. Sugar! Do you know how unhealthy that is?

Del: Mel! Are you spreading . . . *ingredient* gossip?

Mel: It's actually scandalous. Hey, is that . . .

Del: Mandee Skye, BarkAngel extraordinaire! We just saw your brother and sister at Dogma Cafe. I think it's super sweet that the whole fam is here to support Pico.

Mandee: Leif and Tara are *here*?

(Silence.)

(More silence.)

Del: Just so we're clear . . . The BarkAngel ditched us, right?

Mel: We should probably edit some of this out.

Del: No way. Weirdest. Episode. Ever. We're keeping everything. Don't miss the magic show tonight, folks. We'll be there in person, and tomorrow we'll give you our hot, hot take. Don't forget . . .

Mel and Del: Hug ALL the dogs!

(Daily Dog Dish outro music.)

SIBLINGS

The mood had changed completely on the *Bentley Knows* film set since Madeleine and Sir Bentley arrived. Last night had felt like a big, friendly reunion with everyone hugging and swapping old stories. Even Delphi and Melissa, who we hadn't seen since Carmelito was named America's #1 Dog-Friendly Town, seemed to already know everyone involved in the show.

But today, everything was all business. Instead of hanging out at the snack table like they'd done earlier in the week, assistants were speed-walking with their clipboards. Everyone was in a rush, like every minute was costing buckets of cash. Which, if El was right about Sir Bentley's fees, it was.

We weren't exactly banned from the Perro, but there were whole areas of the house that were off-limits, which was fine. We needed to focus. We spent the morning putting together the materials we'd need for the magic show. Mom was acting funny. Shooting sly smiles and telling us she had a couple of her own magic tricks up her sleeve, which I guessed were the supplies she'd found in the shed—two rolling carts and a stash of PVC pipe.

It turned out converting carts and pipe into a movable curtain rod wasn't a five-person job, so while Mom, Denver, and my siblings built the vanishing curtain, I decided to head for my tree stump behind the chicken coop and finish reading the book Heaven had finally returned. A few *Bentley Knows* crew members carried crates into the Perro, and before I got to the henhouse, two of them veered off, set their boxes on the ground, and headed straight for my spot.

I don't know what made them look more suspicious—the fact that they were hurrying away from the Perro and toward a chicken coop, or the way their *Bentley Knows* caps were pulled down tight, intentionally hiding their eyes.

"I told you not to follow me here," a woman's voice came from behind the coop. "What are you wearing? If you're pretending to be part of the film crew, that's ridiculous. This isn't a detective show. I mean, it *is* inside, but . . . ugh . . . you know what I mean."

The chickens were still on "Hollywood vacation," so I let myself in through the wire gate, tiptoed to the henhouse, slipped inside, and leaned against the roosting perch, breathing in the warmed-over coop dust as quietly as possible. Getting my notebook and pencil out of my pocket without making a sound was tricky, but I pulled it off.

"We're *not* a team anymore, remember? You made your choice."

The voice was definitely Mandee Skye's. And the two "crew members" she was talking to weren't hard to ID.

"Come on, Dee. Don't be so heavy. The Universe is telling us something, and I think we should listen."

"Save your breath, Leif. I thought we could talk sense into her, but she's too stubborn."

"Please?" Mandee asked. "Don't ruin this for me. It's my whole future on the line."

"Kinda seems like you're ruining your future for yourself? No shade. Just being honest."

"You're making a bad choice," Tara said. "Trust me, you're going to regret it."

"Yeah, well, we agreed to go our own ways, right? You should both go home."

I was writing as fast as I could. *Bad choice? Like stealing dogs? L & T trying to stop M???* I needed to show this conversation to Epic and Elvis. It wouldn't hurt to hear what Denver thought, either. But the thing about warmed-over chicken coop dust is that it's a combo of wood shavings, feathers, dead chicken skin, dander, and poop. And you can try everything—wiggling your nose, holding your breath, biting your lip—but eventually it's got to come out.

"A*choo!*"

My book and notebook fell to the ground. I froze, but it was too late. Footsteps hurried toward the coop's wooden door. I jumped off the roost and looked for an exit plan. If

I dove, maybe I could fit through the chicken-sized window and slide down the ramp, but then what?

The door creaked open.

"Jeez, kid, you scared the heck out of me. Are you all right?" Leif had his hair pulled back in a ponytail under his *Bentley Knows* cap, but his freckled face was unmistakable.

Mandee and Tara peered in, too. Tara wore a matching *Bentley Knows* hat, but Mandee was in her regular clothes. I followed their eyes to the spot on the ground where I'd dropped my stuff.

"It's Rando!" Mandee said.

Tara jutted her chin toward my Houdini book. "The Boones' friend, right? The kid magician?"

Leif's face burst into a smile. "I love magic!" he said. "We can't wait for the show. It's going to be a mega-boost for Pico."

"What are you doing in here?" Tara asked.

Mandee's eyes were still on my stuff. I took a step forward to block her view of my notebook. Had she seen anything? I should have been writing in code.

"Rehearsing," I said. It was the first thing I could think of. I stuck my hand in my pocket and pulled out Bella's Saint Francis coin, holding it up like I was about to practice a trick.

Tara looked skeptical. "In a chicken coop?"

I let my hair fall in front of my eyes and tried to sound confident. "It's quieter here." I shrugged. "My siblings were bugging me."

Leif nodded like that made perfect sense.

"What coin tricks can you do?" he asked. "Show us one."

"Show you a coin trick?" I gritted my teeth and held up the coin. I stared at it like I was deciding which of my incredible, jaw-dropping coin tricks I should show him. Then I put Saint Francis back in my pocket.

"I don't want to jinx it," I said. "Performing in front of an audience before the show is . . ."

"Bad luck?" Leif asked.

"Very," I said.

"Hey!" someone yelled from the porch of the Perro. "You two! Can you bring those crates in?"

Leif turned and gave the shouter a thumbs-up. Tara took one last glance at me and the chicken coop and pulled her *Bentley Knows* cap down over her eyes. "Good luck tonight," she said, and turned to go, but Mandee touched her arm.

"Tara." Her voice was quiet, but it had an edge to it. "If you leave this alone, I'll leave you alone."

"And if not?" Tara asked.

Mandee's face went dark. Revenge-Elvis dark. "No promises."

I bent down to pick up my notebook. *A Magician Among the Spirits* was covered in coop dust, and I brushed it off, waiting for Mandee Skye to leave. Or at least to stop blocking the door.

"I saw you writing in that notebook on some of our calls," she said. "You seem pretty observant."

I didn't like the way she was studying me. Like she was trying to read my mind. Or worse, like she didn't have to try because she already knew what I was thinking. I should have checked to see what page my notebook had fallen open to. I had no idea what she'd seen, but she'd seen *something*.

"People and dogs are easy to read if you understand how to pay attention, aren't they?" she asked. "You could be an animal communicator. You're like me. You've got the right mind for it."

That made me laugh. I was nothing like her. "I'm going to be an *investigator*," I said. If she took it as a threat, fine. I meant it that way. The next question came out before I could stop it. "Don't you feel guilty ripping off the Boones?"

"Ripping them off?" Mandee laughed. "You tell me. Do they feel better or worse after a BarkAngel call?"

It wasn't what I expected her to say, and it stopped me for a second. Sure, the Boones usually seemed happier and less anxious after "talking" to Pico. But I didn't think that made it okay to lie. Or take money for it. It especially didn't make it okay to pump people for information and then use that intel to hold dogs for ransom.

Mandee pointed at a sticker on the front of my notebook. "Where'd you get that?" she asked.

"*Follow Your Curiosity*? It's our school motto."

"I heard it on a podcast this week." Mandee sighed. "For a minute, it made me think I could have been a great Hollywood trainer. Even better than Raúl."

"Can't you still? Why not just . . . change careers?" It seemed like a quality move. Giving Mandee one last chance to change her mind and do the right thing. Exactly the kind of generous twist our detective agency would probably become famous for.

But Mandee looked toward the house where her siblings had disappeared, and I realized that was silly. If her own family couldn't change her mind, some kid in a chicken coop wasn't going to do it.

"Not really," she said. "I'd have to do something drastic."

Fine, I thought. *But you won't get away with it.* Suddenly, we both jumped at the sound of feet scrambling up a chicken ramp.

Elvis stuck her head through the small side window, a couple wood chips stuck to her curls.

"What's happening?" she asked, looking from me to Mandee Skye and back again. "Are you being held hostage?"

Mandee rolled her eyes and opened the door of the coop wide, waving her hand to show that I was free to go. But as I walked past her, she winked.

"Keep paying attention, Rando," she said. "I predict you'll be an ace detective . . . very soon."

It would have been a nice compliment. If it didn't sound so much like a dare.

THE TRAP

The pipes-on-wheels curtain rod was massive. We rolled it down to the Moondoggie where Brody Delgado gave us a stack of old shower curtains that we stapled together until we got the right height and width to hide the bookcase door. Then we practiced rolling the "vanishing curtain" into the perfect location for the swap. Elvis and I stood in for Pico and Sir Bentley.

"Now I know what Doughboy feels like!" Elvis said. "We're the understudies!"

I could tell it was killing Denver that his magic show looked so kiddish, but he tried to be a good sport about it.

"Maybe we could redo the show in the summer," he said. "Then we'll have time to do it right, and plus my parents could come." For a second, I could see how much he missed his family. "If we use something smaller than a Saint Bernard, we could try a mirror trick."

"Good idea," I said, and I actually meant it. In his *Hiding the Elephant* book, there were whole chapters and diagrams showing how one magician had spent years trying to re-create Houdini's elephant trick with a donkey. I was pretty sure we could figure out how to vanish a chicken in less time than that. Plus, if we had all summer, we could try the trick with mirrors *and* a false back. Then we'd know once and for all who was right.

Epic had brought all the tech—the Boones' pet cam, Declan's phone, and his souped-up walkie-talkies. We'd checked the equipment a thousand times, tested the pet cam app on the phone, and made sure the battery was at 100 percent. Our magic trick might *look* shabby, but we had everything else under control.

Even though it was all falling into place, I couldn't shake the bad feeling I'd had last night. That we'd missed something. Or we were doing it wrong. I kept imagining Luis putting Heaven Hsu into handcuffs, and it made me wish I'd given *her* a chance to change her mind instead of Mandee. It would have been a better move.

It was a lot of prep work for a fifteen-minute sting operation, and the last two hours seemed to drag on for a whole day. Then, all of a sudden, it was 6:45 and Elvis was putting on her stage makeup, Denver was running Bella through last-minute tricks, and the Boones were straightening the collar of Pico's LuxLux Luxury Sparkle Suit and blowing him good luck kisses so they didn't mess up his perfectly combed hair.

Seconds later, Epic and I were standing outside the

secret door at the Moondoggie Inn trying to keep an overly dressed-up Italian greyhound from freaking out.

Pico didn't love the fact that we were hanging around on an unfamiliar, creepy path overgrown with juniper bushes. The sun was starting to go down, and the shadows did kind of make it feel like the setup for a bad horror movie. The Iggy shivered and whined.

"Where's Luis?" I asked. For Pico's sake, obviously. Not because the shadows were making my skin crawl.

Convincing Luis to meet us *outside* behind the Moondoggie had been a little awkward.

"I thought you wanted me to see the show," he'd said, but Elvis told him that Epic and I were scared to be on that path alone. So we needed his help. To keep us from screaming in fear and ruining the show.

"Thanks a *lot*, El," Epic had fumed, but now he looked totally freaked out. I didn't blame him. The faster we could get this over with, the better.

We checked the Peek-a-Boo app on Dec's phone. Our view of the lobby was decent. Brody had set up a spotlight, a microphone, and a whole bunch of folding chairs in front of the bookcases. Denver, Elvis, and Bella were greeting guests and helping them find seats. Madeleine was in the front row with Sir Bentley at the ready. The Boones sat in the second row next to Delphi and Melissa.

Unsurprisingly, Heaven, Mandee, and Raúl were nowhere in sight.

Which pretty much meant one thing. All of them were taking the bait. I was surprised Leif and Tara weren't in the audience, after all their excitement about the magic show. Maybe they were making one last-ditch effort to talk their sister out of a life of crime. Or maybe they'd decided to do what she'd asked: go home and let Mandee do her thing.

I slipped the walkie-talkie from my back pocket and pressed the button to broadcast. "Any sign of Luis?" I said into the microphone.

"Not yet." Denver's voice came through the speaker, scratchy but clear.

I kept staring at the phone in Epic's hand, waiting for a glimpse of *anyone* from the Carmelito Police Department in the crowded room, but Mom and Dad walked in instead, looking conspiratorial. Elvis threw her arms in the air when she saw who was with them.

"Miyon!" I said.

I almost forgot to keep an eye on Pico because Epic and I were so busy grinning at each other.

"I thought she was in Malibu!"

We couldn't leave our post, so we had to be content with watching Elvis race toward the front door and throw her arms around our friend. Seconds later, El's voice came through the walkie-talkie.

"Miyon's here! I repeat: Miyon's here! Say hi, Miyon!"

"Hello? This is Miyon. Who am I talking to?"

Epic tried to respond, but in her excitement, El hadn't let

go of the TALK button. She couldn't hear a word Epic said, because she was still pressing it down, broadcasting to us.

"You have to sit in the front!" we heard Elvis say. "Did you bring Layne?"

"Of course!" Miyon said. "My dad has her. The waves were terrible in Malibu, so we decided to come here for the rest of the week!" She waved her hand toward the entrance, where we could see Jay Kim with a white, brown, and black speckled dog.

"Lucky us!" Elvis said. "Yay for terrible waves!"

That's when our view of the lobby got blocked by the other couple who had walked in with Mom and Dad. Denver's parents hurried toward the pet cam and stood right in front of it while they smothered the kid magician and his dog in hugs.

"They came up for the show," Epic said. "That's nice for Denver."

It wasn't nice for *us*, because they were blocking everything. Which meant we couldn't see what was happening when my sister asked, "Wait. Where's Bentley?"

And suddenly, we couldn't *hear* anything, either. Elvis had either remembered to let go of the TALK button or her walkietalkie went dead.

As if on cue, quick footsteps pounded on the path.

Someone was coming toward us. Fast.

Epic sucked in his breath, and my heart started to race. This wasn't happening at the right time. We didn't even have

Bentley yet. Pico looked up at Epic, and his propeller ears flopped back. He was stressing out. Me too.

"*Record record record,*" I whispered while Epic fumbled to switch from the Peek-a-Boo-Peek-at-You app to the camera.

"I'm trying," he said.

"It's *that* button! On the bottom!" I reached for the phone, but instead of helping, my shaky fingers knocked it out of Epic's hand. Pico yelped as it fell in the dirt next to him.

Epic and I both dove for the phone, but we were too late.

A man's hand reached it first.

MAGIC SHOW

"Wow, Elvis wasn't kidding. You guys really *are* freaked out back here. I thought she was being dramatic."

Luis brushed some dirt off Declan's phone and handed it back to Epic. My brother's hand shook as he took it.

"Look at that, you can watch the whole show on the phone? Cool setup. When's the switcheroo? The big magic moment? Don't be nervous. It'll be great."

Epic's face was pale and I thought I might puke right then and there, but our Peek-a-Boo view was clear again and Elvis, Denver, and Bella were taking their places in the spotlight. I knew their cheesy jokes by heart. They'd practiced them so much that even with their backs to us, I knew what they were saying.

"Ladies and gentlemen . . ."

"And *ah*-mazing canine companions!"

"As you can see, I have nothing up my sleeves."

"Yes you do! What about your arms?"

Standing outside the Moondoggie, staring at the phone screen and trying to act normal after I'd been scared out of my mind, it seemed like it took an hour for Denver and Elvis to get through their opening card tricks. But by the time Bella was doing her hind-leg dance, I felt like I could breathe again. We were on track. Luis was here. When the real criminals showed up, we wouldn't be sitting ducks.

Inside, Madeleine Devine brought Sir Bentley up on stage, and after some more rehearsed banter, Denver pulled the vanishing curtain in front of the Saint Bernard. This was our moment. Behind the curtain, we watched Elvis take Bentley's leash and lead her toward us. Her head got huge as she peered into the pet cam and then the secret door creaked open.

It was working. At least the disappearing act was working.

Epic and Elvis swapped leashes.

"There's a big problem. Sir Bentley isn't Sir Bentley . . ." Elvis started, but Pico didn't want to go inside with her. He wanted to stay with Epic.

"I might have to come inside with him," Epic said as Pico whimpered and kicked his feet.

Denver's head popped out the door. "You can't come in," he said. "You'll ruin the effect. Hurry, hand him to me."

Somehow, Epic managed to sweet-talk Pico into Denver's hands while I held on to Sir Bentley's leash. The Saint Bernard was so well-trained, she didn't make a peep. She came right over to me, sat her giant body down on the path, and didn't move. Perfect. I pulled Luis back farther into the bushes.

"We don't want the audience to see us," I explained.

Luis looked at me like I was losing it. There was no way the audience could see us out here, no matter where we were standing, but he humored me.

After Elvis shut the door, Epic closed the pet cam app, switched over to the camera, and started recording the pathway like we'd planned. Inside, the vanishing curtain must have opened, revealing a tiny Italian greyhound in place of the Saint Bernard, because we could hear the audience *ooh* and applaud.

"Cool trick," Luis said. "All set?"

"Not yet," I said. "Here's the thing. We need you to be ready, okay?"

Luis gave me a wary look. "Ready for *what*, Rondo?"

Exactly as I'd predicted, a woman's unmistakable voice drifted down the path. Epic sucked in his breath, but he kept filming.

"I promise I can pull this off," we heard Heaven say. "You *have* to trust me."

I couldn't tell what I felt more. Bummed that Heaven actually came for Bentley, or satisfied that I'd been right. I gripped Sir Bentley's leash and took another step backward into the shadows.

"Hey, that's Heaven Hsu!" Luis waved his hand as she came into sight, and I shushed him.

"Okay. *What* are you up to?" Luis frowned. "Tell me now."

But Heaven was getting closer, and we could hear everything she said. It was like she didn't even care if anyone heard. Like she wasn't even trying for the element of surprise.

The reason for that? She wasn't.

"I envision it as a two-part episode. But we'd have to come back here, on location. I wanted you to see it in action."

"I don't know," the person behind her said.

Epic looked at me. It wasn't Raúl. Or any of the BarkAngels. It was the *Bentley Knows* showrunner. And Heaven was giving her the hard sell.

"My idea is so much better than the season finale we have right now. I'm almost done writing the script, and Raúl agrees, it's good enough to save the show." She took a breath like she needed extra courage before plowing forward. "I won't give it to you without a producer credit, though. And I want a guarantee that I can write for upcoming seasons, too. I've got a new agent, she'll talk to you about . . . Hey, Elrond. How's the magic show going?"

Heaven waved at me like standing in the bushes with a police officer while your brother records video of a Hollywood star, a showrunner, and a mini schnauzer walking down a secret pathway was a perfectly normal thing to do.

But she stopped in front of Bentley and frowned. Roo sniffed at the Saint Bernard and sneered.

"You used the *body double*?" Heaven asked. "That's *not* going to go viral. Not in a good way. Fans notice everything."

Epic stopped recording.

"This isn't Sir Bentley?" I asked.

"Definitely not."

Which is pretty much the moment when I realized our plan *had* worked perfectly. We'd created the perfect distraction. The optimal setup for stealing Sir Bentley. And the celebrity dognappers had taken the bait.

Only they were smarter than us. And "they" weren't Heaven Hsu.

I would have felt relieved about that last part except someone inside the Moondoggie started screaming. Elvis opened the secret door. She had tears in her eyes.

"Madeleine got a ransom call," she said.

"What?" Heaven Hsu looked horrified. Like someone had stolen her best friend. Or her family. Which they kind of had.

Luis grabbed his radio. "Where'd she leave Bentley?" he asked. "The hotel room?"

"No." Elvis couldn't even get the words out. Denver had to push her aside and say them for her.

"She left Bentley at the Perro," he said. "To shoot one last scene. With Raúl."

VANISHED

"You three have a knack for this, that's for sure." Luis shook his head and radioed for backup. "One of these days, my boss is going to fire me and hire you."

It would have been a better compliment if it actually meant anything. Because after we'd thought up the ideas, tipped him off, and set the trap, Luis wouldn't let even us come with him to the Perro to look for clues and witnesses.

"Everyone stay here," he said. "Go inside, find your parents. I'll secure the Perro, and I'll call when I have new information."

What else could we do? Heaven, Roo, Bentley's body double, and the showrunner filed through the secret door into the lobby. Epic and I had to follow. Two of Luis's friends from the police department were doing crowd control, while Mom, Dad, and the Boones tried to calm Madeleine.

I was glad I'd been wrong about Heaven. She hadn't teamed up with Raúl. *He'd* teamed up with Mandee. It was a genius duo. A one-two punch. The psychic who has access to all the clients' daily routines, and the dog trainer who has access to the dogs. But as stressed as she was about Bentley, Heaven didn't buy my theory.

"Raúl didn't do anything," she said. "I can guarantee it."

"*Can* you, though?" I asked, and Heaven's nervous frown turned up at the corners.

She nudged the showrunner. "This is the kid," she said. "The one I based the new character on. The show needs some comic relief."

"I can see it." The showrunner nodded and looked me over like I was a pair of dog booties she was considering buying.

I looked to El and Epic for help, but my sister was glued to Madeleine's side, and Miyon had thrown her arms around Epic's neck.

"Oh my gosh," she said. "Elvis told me everything. Are you okay?"

And Epic, who had literally been green with anxiety three minutes before, looked like he was . . . okay. Better than okay.

Even Denver was off sitting with his parents, petting Bella and looking relieved.

Our entire sting operation had just begun, and after all that work—all the hours of scheming and arguing—one word from Luis, and everyone seemed fine with letting it go. I got the eerie feeling that I was living out the scene Heaven had invented at Yappy Hour. *A close family . . . but one person is*

standing farther from the others . . . He's about to make some deci-
sions . . . about how far away to drift?

I wanted to light into them. We didn't have time to stand around and chat. We needed to look for clues. Figure out *where* Raúl might have taken Bentley. But like the cherry on a fish-flavored pupcake, the door to the Moondoggie opened, and Raúl Flores burst into the lobby, Cheddar and Doughboy tucked all snug into the dog sling on his chest.

"Madeleine!" he yelled. "I need Madeleine Devine!"

What was he doing here? If Luis was on his way to the Perro, wouldn't they have passed each other? Why didn't Luis arrest him? Or at least keep him for questioning? Raúl looked wrecked, like he'd been crying, and he sat next to Madeleine and held her hand while everyone gathered around.

"There was a power outage," he said. "Thirty seconds at the most. I'm so sorry. You know I never would have let her out of my sight."

My first thought was that he was faking, but the way his mustache was twitching . . . it was pure panic.

Heaven almost looked like she felt bad for me. "It was a good theory," she said. "If I didn't know Raúl, I would have bought it. Give him five minutes, though, and—oh, yep, there it is."

Raúl jumped up from his seat and started to pace, hugging his Iggy sling to his chest. His fingers scratched Doughboy's ear, or maybe Cheddar's, as he ranted. "I've *had* it with these *hooligans* interrupting my process! We are going to launch a world-class investigation . . . no . . . a *documentary*. We'll use my contacts at the CIA . . . we'll cross-promote it with the *Bentley Knows* release in time for awards season. Is anyone here filming right now? *You!* Podcasters. I need some media attention, stat!"

Melissa Dubois and Delphi Jones hurried to his side with their bulldog and a backpack full of audio equipment.

"I think I figured out his ulterior motive," Heaven said. "He wants everything he touches to be gold. Cash or quality, ideally both."

She put her hands in her sweatshirt pockets but then immediately drew them out, like she'd remembered something. "Oh yeah. This is for you."

It was a folded-up note, addressed to *The Kid Detective*.

I crunched it in my hand. I didn't feel like being teased by Heaven right now. I was starting to feel out of breath. Maybe I was a terrible investigator. I'd had so many theories that I'd thought were right, but it was like a series of Denver's mirror tricks. Every time I thought I was looking straight at the answer, it turned out to be nothing. A reflection of something else. A vanishing act.

I took a breath and tried to shake it off. So what? So I was wrong. About *two* suspects. There was still one left. Mandee's siblings had tried to talk her out of the ransom scheme, but she went ahead with it anyway. All we had to do was find her. But my team had ditched me. They'd either given up or forgotten that we had a mystery to solve. Obviously, the detective agency had vanished, too.

Fine. I didn't need them. I could do this myself.

I turned to walk away, but Elvis called my name.

"Rondo, come on! We're moving to the kitchen. Madeleine's going to call the Department of Lost Dogs!"

I stared at her, and Epic waved at me, exasperated.

"Don't just stand there," he said. "We've got a mystery to solve!"

Turns out, while I'd been standing around feeling sorry for myself, Elvis had been explaining our BarkAngel theories to Madeleine.

Epic and Miyon had texted Luis everything we knew.

Denver had gotten all our parents up to speed and ready to help.

Not everything had vanished. I'd thought my siblings and Denver had given up, but instead, they'd been busy.

Getting backup.

FOLLOW YOUR CURIOSITY

"Department of Lost Dogs, could you please hold?"

Elvis bounced around the Moondoggie's kitchen while Madeleine waited on speakerphone. Epic was fidgeting, too. We knew from the past celebrity dognappings that once the ransom money was wired, the thieves always returned the dogs right away. Which meant Sir Bentley had to be close by. If she was at the Perro, Luis would find her. But my hunch was that she was here. At the Moondoggie. We'd seen Mandee wheel her suitcase into the lobby less than twenty-four hours ago. And with all the focus on the magic show, it would have been easy to sneak in through the side door unnoticed. Even with a Saint Bernard. That's how "good" our distraction was.

The McDades+Denver+Miyon Detective Agency had worked it all out. We knew that the Department of Lost Dogs only had one BarkAngel on duty after hours. If Mandee answered the call, we'd be able to keep her in a fixed location for as long as the call lasted, and maybe get some clues about where she was. If we got Tara or Leif, they might have information about their sister, and given how much they disapproved of Mandee's life choices, they might be willing to help.

"What do these 'communicators' have to do with anything?" Raúl grumbled. "It's a sham operation. They *undermine* the hard work that . . ."

"You're right," I said without listening to the rest of his lecture. Madeleine had a video link now, and while we waited for her to connect, I crumpled and uncrumpled the piece of paper in my hand. Not that I was nervous. I just really needed this to work.

I wasn't close enough to see the freckled face or the fuzzy Milky Way background on the screen, but I recognized Tara Skye's voice. And her words. They were the same words Leif had said to the Boones two nights ago.

"I understand how worried you must be," Tara said. "I've got a direct psychic line to Sir Bentley, and he says first of all he wants you to know that he loves you."

"*Liar,*" Elvis whispered. "If she had a direct line, she'd know that Bentley's a girl!"

"Shh," I said.

What is that? she mouthed and pointed to the paper in my hand.

I looked down at Heaven's note. I'd been crumpling it without thinking, but I hadn't opened it. Why would she write me a note, anyway? If she had something she wanted to say, I was standing right here.

I shrugged at El, so she grabbed it and unfolded the paper.

Rando—

Follow your curiosity.

Cluck cluck.

"*Ran*-do?" El asked. "Whoever wrote this doesn't know how to spell."

"I've dealt with a couple of these celebrity dognappings before," Tara said to Madeleine. "I don't want to scare you, but they mean business. We need to get Sir Bentley to safety as quickly as possible, and paying the ransom immediately is your best bet. You can't put a price on your furbaby's safety!"

I snatched the note back from El and turned to Heaven Hsu.

"Where did you get this?" I waved the note, and Roo's eyes tracked it like it was a mouse he wanted to snap up.

I motioned for Heaven to follow me out to the hall and rephrased the question.

"When did Mandee give you this note?"

"Right before I came over here. She said she was leaving and had a message for the kid detective. Obviously, that had to be you— Wait . . ." Heaven shifted Roo in her arms so she could grab her notebook from her messenger bag. "What's happening? Why do you have that look?"

I handed her the note.

"Follow your curiosity? Cluck cluck?" Heaven wrote it down before she asked, "Do you know what it means?"

"I hope so."

I'd been wrong so many times, I was starting to doubt I knew anything. I had to stop looking at what *seemed* to be in front of me. From the conversation I'd heard this morning, the Skye siblings were definitely fighting, but I'd thought Tara and Leif were trying to talk Mandee out of stealing Sir Bentley. *I think you're making a bad choice*, Tara had said. *You're going to regret it.* But what if that was nothing but another set of mirrors?

I looked at the note again. *Follow your curiosity.*

Mandee told me she wanted to work with canine actors. That was her excuse for coming to the set. To meet Raúl. *Don't ruin this for me. It's my whole future on the line.* Could she have been talking about a future . . . in Hollywood? I thought about her Revenge-Elvis look. The one she'd nailed Tara with. *If you leave this alone, I'll leave you alone.* And if not? *No promises.*

"She said she was leaving?" I asked Heaven, who was writing furiously in her notebook. "Leaving where?"

Heaven shrugged. "She had her suitcase. That's all I know."

"I think she's tipping me off," I said. "We were talking about my school motto, and she said she couldn't follow her curiosity unless she did something drastic."

"Like?"

"I don't know. Turn her siblings in?"

"Wouldn't she go to the police?" Heaven asked.

"Maybe she didn't want to get herself in trouble. Maybe she . . ."

Wanted to give *me* a chance? She'd told me to keep paying attention. *I predict you'll be an ace detective . . . very soon.* What if "soon" meant *today*?

She'd only left me one clue, but it was all I needed.

Cluck cluck.

Denver stuck his head into the hall. "Tara's definitely here at the Moondoggie," he said. "You know that virtual Milky Way background she uses? She waved her hands too much and the background failed and we recognized the bedspread pattern behind her! My uncle and the police are going to sweep the hotel."

"Good work," I said. "Now *we* need to get to the Perro and help Luis."

Heaven touched her thumb to her lips, her chin, then her forehead, and just in case it worked, I did it, too. We needed all the magic we could get.

CHICKENS

By now, it was dark and streetlamps lit our way up Main Street. Denver, Bella, Elvis, Epic, Miyon, and I took the lead. Behind us were Mom and Dad, Heaven, Roo, and Raúl with his Iggys. A whole crew. Much bigger than our original trio of detectives. But I didn't mind. It felt pretty good to know we weren't in it alone.

"Simple plans are always the best," I said as we ran toward home. "If Leif swiped Bentley at the Perro, he'd need some-place nearby to hide out until Tara convinced Madeleine to pay the ransom. I saw them checking it out earlier today, but I didn't know why until now."

The windows of the Perro del Mar looked bright and cheery. Every light in the house was on. Luis stood on the back porch with his flashlight. Dad turned on the Yappy Hour lanterns that zigzag from the tiki bar to the tree above the chicken coop. It made it feel like we were about to have a party. Which we weren't.

"I got your text about meeting in the backyard," Luis said.

"I don't see anything. Didn't find any fingerprints inside, either. We've got two officers searching the town, and two more sweeping the Moondoggie. That's everyone we've got on duty tonight."

"It's okay." I nodded toward the chicken coop.

Elvis was less subtle.

"Cluck cluck!" she yelled. "Come out with your hands up!"

Luis was skeptical.

"The coop?" he asked. "You sure?"

"I'm sure." This time it was real, not an illusion. It had to be. What else could Mandee Skye have meant by her clue?

Luis shrugged and put on a loud, official voice. "This is Officer Sánchez with the Carmelito Police Department. We have you surrounded."

We waited.

Nothing happened. Not even one tiny rustle of movement from the henhouse.

But then we heard it.

"A*choo!*"

Luis looked at me, eyes wide, and I grinned.

"Would you like to come out?" Luis asked in his loud police voice. "Otherwise, I'm going to have to come inspect the coop."

As Luis slowly and deliberately approached the wire fence, Elvis couldn't hold it in. She bolted past everyone, yelling, "Bentley! Bentley! We're here to *save* you!"

It probably wasn't the smartest move, but you had to

be impressed by El's fearlessness. She ran right past Luis, straight through the gate, and flung open the coop door.

"Stand back!" Luis yelled, but the rest of us were already running to her side. Leif Skye didn't *seem* capable of hurting anyone, but Madeleine said the person who'd called about the ransom had threatened horrible things.

But the only one who lumbered out when El opened the coop was Sir Bentley. She took a few steps toward Elvis and then sat her massive body down in the middle of the doorway.

Elvis showered the Saint Bernard with kisses. Luis had to maneuver around them to shine his flashlight into the doorway of the chicken coop.

"It's empty," Luis said.

"*Somebody* sneezed," Epic said.

"Bentley?"

The adults started to crowd around Luis, peppering him with questions. Heaven called Madeleine. Raúl called the podcasters. I wished they'd all be quiet. I was trying to think. *Maybe* Leif had left Sir Bentley in the coop alone, but I didn't buy it. If you were holding America's highest-paid canine actor hostage, you'd want to have an eye on that dog at all times. The stakes were too high.

Behind the chatter, I heard a soft scraping sound. I'd been caught in that same chicken coop earlier in the day, and I knew there were *two* ways out. The main door for people, and the chicken-sized window that led to the ramp for the hens. I stepped around to the other side of the coop and heard the sound again. A tree blocked the lantern light, but even in the shadows, I could see my hunch was right. The scraping was the sound of someone trying to slowly, quietly ease himself down a wooden chicken ramp without being seen.

It was Leif Skye for sure. He wore dark clothes and a black cap, but even in the weird light, his beard was unmistakable. He gripped something in his hand. A rock? I tried to yell out for Luis, but my throat was stuck. Leif was so focused on moving one silent inch at a time that it took a beat for him to see me.

When he did, he leaped into action. Something about seeing a large man vault himself off a chicken ramp in the middle of my shadowy, lantern-lit backyard unstuck my throat. I screamed loud enough for the whole neighborhood to hear.

SCAFFOLDING

My scream kicked off a panic in all the dogs and humans in the backyard. Luis was the first one to my side, but Leif chucked his rock with incredible aim and took out Luis's knee, sending him sprawling to the ground. Someone else screamed, which you could barely hear over all the barking, and Leif Skye took off running.

The guy was way faster than you'd think. Bella and Epic led the chase, with Sir Bentley and Luis hobbling in the rear. Even with all of us running after him, Leif made it to the front yard without getting caught.

But that was where he ran into another problem: the rest of our backup.

Madeleine and Sir Bentley's stunt double, the Boones, Melissa, Delphi, and Morrissey, Denver's parents, and one of Luis's cop friends were crossing Main Street toward the Perro. My heart raced. This was it. We'd caught him. He couldn't go backward, and he couldn't go forward. Our trap had worked.

Leif obviously disagreed. He made a quick side-pivot and ran straight toward the front of Perro where the scaffolding and safety equipment for the roof stunt was set up. He grabbed a metal bar and started climbing. Almost all the dogs were at his feet, barking like they had a squirrel up a tree. What did Leif think he was going to do? Climb up to the roof and wait?

Within a few seconds, Leif had disappeared into the shadows.

"Can we get some lights?" Luis asked. Heaven, Epic, Mom, and Dad raced toward the tent that held the outdoor film equipment.

"There he is!" Elvis yelled when the floodlights kicked on.

My sister has an eagle eye. The scaffolding was a tower made out of plywood and metal pipes, but up by the second-floor windows, there were large blocks of safety padding set up on the platforms. That's where she saw it. Peeking over one of the gray foam blocks. The brim of Leif's black cap.

"We can see you," Luis shouted. "Come on down!"

Everyone but the dogs waited silently. Leif didn't move. Not one inch. He was probably crouching behind that big block of foam, frozen with fear. Regretting his bad choices. Wondering how they'd led him to be stuck on a movie-set scaffolding with a mob of dogs howling at him and a mob of people waiting to throw him in jail.

Denver and Elvis stood in the bushes in front of the Perro trying to calm the dogs. A breeze kicked up and fluttered

Denver's magician's cape. Up on the scaffolding, the brim of Leif's cap wobbled. It tilted in the breeze, slid forward on the foam block, and plummeted to the ground. Which is when it hit me. Leif wasn't moving because Leif wasn't there. He'd pulled a reverse French Drop. Instead of making us think an object had disappeared when it was in the same place all along, he'd done the opposite. He'd planted his hat on top of the safety padding so we'd stare at it. But it was an illusion. Leif Skye had vanished.

I scanned the front of the Perro for any irregular shadows. Below the window of Room 4, another of the gray foam blocks moved. Like it had accidentally been kicked. I felt a hand on my arm.

"Come with me," Raúl whispered. "This is how we go global."

Before I could argue, Raúl had my arm in a grip as tight as Mom's. He walked just fast enough that no one noticed us disappear into the Perro, except one crew member who was leaving our house with a camera in his hand.

"Got your text," the camera guy said to Raúl. "I'll stay out of sight."

Raúl still had his Iggys snug in their sling, and he hugged them while he took the stairs two at a time toward the guest wing.

"What are we doing?" I asked. "I saw Leif. I know where he is!"

"Behind the padding. Under Room 4."

He *knew*? "We have to tell Luis!"

Raúl pulled me into Room 4, and with a wild look in his eye, he took off the pup sling and looked carefully at each of his Iggys. He concentrated and did the soul-searching gaze that Mandee Skye used to "communicate" with Pico.

"All right," he said quietly. "This is *your* time to shine."

Then, fast and efficient, he lifted one of the pups out of the sling, fed the other a treat and said, "Stay," then typed something into his phone. It took him about six seconds. The man was a professional. But I was getting mad.

"We need to arrest Leif," I said.

"We will." Raúl patted my head. "But this way, we'll get a bigger boost for the show and have a promo for the new documentary. Doughie and I are going out the bathroom window now. I need you to get that thief's attention. He has to stay where he is for fourteen and a half seconds. Keep him looking toward *you* so we'll be behind his field of vision. Got it?"

I gaped at him.

"What?"

"This is important," I said. "It's not all about *you*. You act like the world revolves around . . ."

I stopped talking for two reasons. One: It was the exact same sentence that Denver had said about me. And two: Raúl and the Iggy were already gone. From the open second-floor window in Room 4, I had a perfect bird's-eye view of the scaffolding. I could see Leif on one of the wooden platforms, hiding in the shadows behind the safety padding. He slowly inched his way toward the side of the house.

On the ground, the guy Raúl had texted stood in the shadows with a camera on his shoulder. Next to him, the podcasters were pulling out recording equipment and Heaven was manning the spotlight. Luis had four cops with him now, and my family had gotten all the dogs safely leashed and calm. Everyone else was on the ready to help at a moment's notice. Leif had no moves left. He was trapped.

I made a decision. I didn't like the way Raúl acted, and I wasn't going to *be* like him. But we were going to catch the dognappers, no matter what. If Raúl's plan would help Heaven and Pico make an amazing television show? And expose a criminal dognapping ring to the *entire* world? I could get on board with that.

"Hey! BarkAngel!" I yelled, and Leif almost rolled off the scaffolding in surprise. "Want to see a magic trick?"

Everyone below, including Leif Skye, looked up toward the second floor and stared at me. Leif didn't move a muscle. I held up Denver's Saint Francis coin and wondered how many words I needed to keep him frozen in place for fourteen and a half seconds.

"What you are about to see . . ."

I curled the fingers of my right hand and placed the coin on my middle and ring fingers, gripping the edge with my bent knuckles—a classic Finger Palm. My hands were sweaty, and I tried not to look toward the bathroom, where I knew exactly what was happening. Above Leif's head, a small Italian greyhound understudy was walking courageously along the roof's edge, like he'd been practicing all week. I wondered if he'd *wanted* a moment in the spotlight, or if he was happier hanging back, letting the big scenes go to Cheddar and Pico. Either way, here he was, putting it all on the line for the team.

I leaned farther out the window and started again.

"What you are about to see," I shouted, "is a magic trick beyond your wildest dreams!"

I held out my hands and rotated them to show I had nothing in my palms, though my sweaty knuckles were still gripping the coin, hidden in plain sight.

"Nothing to see here!" I shouted, still rotating my wrists.

Even in the shadows, the spotlight was strong enough that I could see the look on Leif's face. He hadn't thought he was going to get caught. Especially not by a bunch of kids. I watched his expression go from surprise to anger to complete astonishment.

Because now, the Iggy had made his way to the ledge. He knew his cues perfectly. So did I. This was the moment where I was *supposed* to make the coin appear out of nowhere by producing it out of my "empty" palm. The problem was, I could never get it to work.

As I fumbled with the coin, the Iggy leaped from the roof to the scaffolding, bright, shining eyes lit perfectly by the spotlight as he fell. St. Francis slipped from my palm and fell, too, tumbling in the night alongside Doughboy. Watching over him? Keeping him safe? The moonlight bounced off the image of the patron saint of animals. Almost like Francis was winking at me.

All at once, the coin hit a metal pipe with a *ping* and Doughboy landed safely on top of the padding next to Leif, growling and barking like his best friend's life depended on it.

It was, as my sister would say, *ah*-mazing.

M²D²

"Pico Boone saved the day!"

Even though my magic trick was a bust, I nailed my final cue. Raúl Flores had snuck back inside and whispered it to me so I could yell it at the top of my lungs.

I almost couldn't get it out without laughing. Because of course Pico Boone, still in his Sparkle Suit, was down in the front yard, cuddled up in Mr. Boone's arms while his understudy did all the work.

I ran downstairs to see Leif climb off the last rung of the scaffolding.

"Where's my sister?" he asked.

Luis held up his radio. "Officer Yuan has Tara in custody at the Moondoggie."

"No, Mandee. If she ratted on us, you should know she helped us with the first job. If we're going down, she'd *better* be coming with us."

"We'll worry about Mandee," Luis said. "For now, you have the right to remain silent."

Leif looked like he might try to run again, but Bella blocked his way.

"Shake hands, Bella," Denver said, and Leif had no choice. You'd have to be a real jerk not to shake hands with a dog. As the BarkAngel lifted his palm to meet Bella's paw, Luis slapped a cuff around his wrist.

I couldn't help myself. "It's hard to tell," I said. "But I think I'm seeing something in your future. It's dark and cold. Maybe there are some black poles? Or bars? Do you have any idea what that might be?"

Luis shook his head, and Epic dragged me toward El and Heaven, who were showering Sir Bentley with kisses and hugs. I took Roo out of Heaven's arms so he didn't get smooshed, and he snuggled right in.

"I don't know, El," I said as I scratched his ear. "Maybe you should get a mini schnauzer."

Epic nodded. "They're kind of cute."

"What's this?" Dad showed up behind us and squashed me and Epic in a hug. "We're getting a dog?"

"Yes!" Elvis hopped up and threw her arms around the three of us.

Mom joined the group squeeze. "It's probably about time," she said. "You three clearly need another project."

"You're smothering Roo!" I grunted, and wiggled out of the McDade sandwich, but it reminded me: No matter how much you mess up or annoy them or make their lives miserable, when it matters—when it really matters—my family always comes through.

"So," Miyon said. "What are we doing now? Family Game Night?"

"Nope. We haven't done that in *forever*," Elvis said. "We don't do anything anymore. We haven't surfed Dawn Patrol in *months*. Maybe a whole year!"

"You haven't?" Miyon looked at me and Epic. In case El was exaggerating.

"Nope," I said, and Epic shook his head.

"But that's your *thing*." This time Miyon shot my parents a wide-eyed look. "You're the best family I know. You can't just . . . *not* do the stuff you love together. Right?"

Mom looked at Dad for so long that he got his schmoopy-eyed look and had to wipe at his eyes.

"You're right, Miyon," Dad said. "Family Game Night. That's exactly what we're doing now."

"Yes!" Elvis fist-pumped the air.

"Denver can come, too, right?" I turned to the kid magician, who was practicing his cape flourish in the middle of a crime scene. "If you *want* to," I said.

"Sure. I'm in," Denver said. "I know summer's still a few months away, but maybe we can start making some plans. To get ahead of the game."

I nodded. "I like having you on this team, D-cubed."

"Thanks. But call me Denver."

Fair.

Elvis sighed a satisfied sigh. My siblings and I looked around at the Perro's yard. Filled with all the people who'd had our backs.

"Now, *this* is the kind of Restorative Week I wanted to have."

"Me too, El," I said. And suddenly, I had a brain spark. "I know what to call our detective agency. M^2D^2!"

El caught on immediately. "M-Squared, D-Squared! <u>M</u>iyon, <u>McD</u>ades, and <u>D</u>enver. It's perfect!"

Epic grinned at me. "So you do coin tricks now?" he teased.

I rolled my eyes and let my hair fall in front of my face, but I was grinning, too.

"If you want a show," I said to my brother, "go to the circus!"

JUNE

DAWN PATROL

"Rise and shine, the surf is fine!"

I flipped on the light in Mom and Dad's room, while Elvis ripped the comforter off their bed and Epic opened drawers.

"What's happening?" Dad's voice was grumpy through his pillow.

"Let me sleep." Mom squeezed her eyes shut so the light couldn't get in.

"Nope." I tugged at her feet until her legs dangled off the bed. "If *I* got up, so can you."

"Let me hear an okay," Epic said, dropping rash guards on each of their heads.

"Dawn Patrol," Elvis announced at top volume, "is nonnegotiable!"

We walked downstairs, the whole family together. Miyon was in the lobby, all ready to go.

"Do you hear that?" Mom asked.

"What?"

She took a breath. "The quiet."

It felt great. No film crew. No lighting equipment. No scaffolding or cranes or faulty generators outside. Not one single celebrity dog. Unless you counted Pico, but he was barely a celebrity. And he was upstairs sleeping.

"We've got to stop and pick up Denver on the way," I reminded Dad. "He's never surfed before. I'm going to teach him. In exchange for magic lessons."

Elvis walked next to me on the sidewalk, balancing her surfboard on her head. She was walking normally, not trying to skip or flamingo or balance-beam her way down the street. It was killing her to pretend that nobody noticed that Epic and Miyon were holding hands.

"It's not that big of a deal, El," I whispered.

"Yes it is!" she said. "Epic's going to be in high school now, and everything's going to change."

"Yeah, but we've got the whole summer. And things can change in a good way, you know. It's all about the choices we make."

I nudged her, throwing her surfboard off balance, and she nudged me back.

"What if he *chooses* not to hang out with us anymore?"

"Don't worry, El," I said. "We get to choose, too."

Which was when Epic turned around and grinned at us.

"Hey, Elvis," he said. "Miyon thinks you should sing a song during the new magic show. We're going to work on that later, right?"

Elvis looked at me, and I nodded.

"Absolutely," I said.

I *almost* added, *See, El? You don't have to worry. We'll choose each other every time.*

But I decided that would be too cheesy. So I just smiled and watched my sister add a small, happy skip to her step.

TRANSCRIPT: DAILY DOG DISH PODCAST
Hollywood Hounds News Roundup

(Daily Dog Dish intro music.)

Del: Thanks for joining us for another wag-tastic episode of the *Daily Dog Dish*! We're your hosts, Delphi and Melissa! Say hello . . . Mel, are you and Morrissey seriously eating pupcakes in the studio right now?

Mel: *(Mouth full.)* Hello . . . Mel, are you and Morrissey seriously eating pupcak— *(Bursts out laughing.)*

Del: Ewwww! That spit-take got frosting on the microphone!

(Muffled sound of laughter and microphone being cleaned.)

Del: Okay, we've got to pull it together, Mel. Think of our listeners.

Mel: Sorry, everybody. We're goofy today. Must be the sugar.

Del: You're right. I feel extra zippy. Want to skip straight to the Lightning Round?

Mel: Probably a good idea. Ready, set . . .

(Lightning Round bell rings.)

Del and Mel: DISH!

(Sound of a clock ticking.)

Del: First off, authorities are still trying to track down the third BarkAngel who was involved in the celebrity dognapping ring. She seems to have disappeared into thin air!

Mel: Well, nothing can completely disappear, Del. Even when water evaporates, it's still there in a new form. Water vapor is a gas—

Del: Yeah, yeah, science. I'm just glad the whole thing's over, and I can't wait to see the exposé! Raúl Flores is already in postproduction on his documentary, *Dognapped! Fighting Furbaby Fraud.*

Mel: I've heard it's a tearjerker.

Del: Pawscar *and* Oscar bait, for sure! Speaking of Raúl, we're still months away from the delayed release of *Bentley Knows*, but the buzz about the reboot has been off . . . the . . . charts! Especially after the studio announced that they officially fired the show's head writer and gave the job to Heaven Hsu.

Mel: Such a risky move . . . It's basically like starting over from scratch!

Del: Totally worth it, if you ask me! I think Heaven Hsu is going to take that tired old show and send it into the stratosphere. Did you see who they got to play the new villain she invented?

Mel: *Kendra Kwong!*

Del: Kendra signed on for three seasons . . . on the condition that her sister writes all her scenes.

Mel: Aw! Siblings are the best.

Del: Speaking of *siblings*, this summer, the Pendleton Triplets will travel to Bollywood for a guest appearance in a new romantic action flick. Rumor has it there's a new canine trainer on the scene who is getting some re-bark-able performances from India's rising doggo star, Casper Reddy.

Mel: *Re-bark-able*? Oof. Del, that's awful punny.

Del: It had to be done.

Mel: I've seen photos, and there's something familiar about that trainer, don't you think? I feel like I've seen those freckles before.

Del: It's hard to tell with freckles, Mel. But don't distract me. I have one more piece of news, and you're going to love it. Did you see Pico Boone's feed? The Perro del Mar crew live-streamed their . . . *puppy adoption*!

Mel: Puppy adoption! These are things you need to tell me *immediately*, Del! What kind of pup did they choose?

Del: We might have to go on location again to find out.

Mel: Good! Can we visit today's sponsor? These treats they sent us are super yummy.

Del: *(Gasps.)* Today's sponsor! Mel, we almost forgot to do the advertisement!

Mel: Hold on . . .

(Sound of shuffling paper.)

Del: This episode is sponsored by Pupcake Paradise, Carmelito, California's dogalicious pupcake shop with handcrafted treats for you *and* your doggo.

Mel: I've been told you should definitely eat the orange ones. Or was it the opposite? Definitely *don't* eat the orange ones?

Del: *(Laughs.)* I guess you're gonna have to follow your curiosity.

Mel: I'll use the scientific method. Tune in tomorrow and we'll share the results!

Del: Thanks for listening, furever friends! Don't forget to take some time to . . .

Mel and Del: Hug ALL the dogs!

(Daily Dog Dish outro music.)